Green *for* Love

By E.V. Bancroft

2023

Butterworth Books is a different breed of publishing house. It's a home for Indies, for independent authors who take great pride in their work and produce top quality books for readers who deserve the best. Professional editing, professional cover design, professional proof reading, professional book production—you get the idea. As Individual as the Indie authors we're proud to work with, we're Butterworths and we're *different*.

Authors currently publishing with us:

E.V. Bancroft
Valden Bush
Addison M Conley
Jo Fletcher
Helena Harte
Lee Haven
Karen Klyne
AJ Mason
Ally McGuire
James Merrick
Robyn Nyx
Simon Smalley
Brey Willows

For more information visit www.butterworthbooks.co.uk

GREEN FOR LOVE © 2023 by E.V. Bancroft
All rights reserved.

This trade paperback is published by Butterworth Books, UK

This is a work of fiction: names, characters, and incidents are the product of the author's imagination or are used fictitiously. Any resemblance to actual persons, living or dead, business establishments, events, or locales is entirely coincidental.

This book, or parts thereof, may not be reproduced in any form without express permission.

CATALOGING INFORMATION
ISBN: 978-1-915009-38-8
CREDITS
Editor: Victoria Villaseñor & Nicci Robinson
Cover Design: Lucia Morgan & Nicci Robinson
Production Design: Global Wordsmiths

Acknowledgements

I am so grateful to everyone who has given their time and expertise to bring *Green for Love* to fruition.

Thank you to Nicci Robinson and Victoria Villaseñor from Global Wordsmiths and Butterworth Books for putting up with the—at times—painful editing and for leading me through the whole process through to publication. Like Lia's geese, you helped me fly.

I'd like to thank Steve for driving me all over Northumberland, explaining about the geology and natural environment. And thank you to Margaret Gray, who donned her professional psychological astrologer's hat and gave me not just the details but also the charts of both Jay and Lia and honed down when their birth dates would be.

I'm lucky I have some awesome beta readers in the Swallows critique group: Joey Bass, Valden Bush, Jane Fletcher, Lee Haven, A J Mason, and Maggie Macintyre. I know the book is so much stronger because of all your input. Thanks also to Annmarie and Sue Llewellyn, and to Dave and Kev for their encouragement throughout.

I love the drawing of Jay and Lia; thank you, Lucia Morgan. Also, thanks to Nicci Robinson for coping with umpteen vacillations of different fonts and producing the book cover.

Thanks to Em, who has been insightful and supportive in her unique way, and Jerry, who has not been supportive in the slightest, demanding attention and frequently treading on the keyboard as I tried to work.

Finally, I'd like to thank you, the reader, for taking a chance on me and giving me such wonderful feedback. It's such an honour. Thanks.

Dedication

To everyone who cares about the planet,
I trust we'll prevail before it's too late.
And to Em, thank you for being here.

Chapter One

JAY TANNER INHALED THE peaty smoke of her Islay whisky and took a small sip. The burn coursed down her throat and settled in her stomach. She opened her eyes and smiled at Alice, the bartender. "You can't beat that first taste."

Alice grinned. "If you say so. Personally, I'm a vodka person, but yeah, a lot of our patrons seem to love the whiskies. But only you have the Ardbeg. It's too peaty for most."

Surprise flickered in Jay's consciousness, followed by a warmth as intense as the alcohol she'd swallowed. "You keep it in just for me?"

"Of course. We like to satisfy our members."

That's what Jay loved about this private women's club. They were always discreet and catered to every need. Alice would never let on how many married women had invited Jay up to their rooms when they were up in London for a few days. It was always understood it would go no further, and it was an easy way to scratch an itch. No drama, no complications, nothing more than a night. Just as Jay liked it.

She pulled out her trade journals from her briefcase. She wasn't in the mood for *Petroleum Engineering* this evening, so she retrieved the latest *New Scientist* and opened the cover to settle down and enjoy a restful hour before making her way home. She needed a distraction from the meeting tomorrow and wanted to wind down.

"No work tonight?" Alice asked as she polished the glasses until they reflected the lights from the chandeliers.

"I thought I'd relax and catch up with the wider scientific

community," Jay said then sipped from her crystal tumbler.

"Of course. I'll leave you to it." Alice moved to the other end of the bar and busied herself with another task.

After a few minutes, the doors opened and closed with a muffled whisper. Jay continued reading without looking up and was annoyed when the puff of the leather being displaced indicated the stool next to hers became occupied. What was wrong with the rest of the bar stools and easy chairs in the lounge? She wouldn't give the intruder the satisfaction of acknowledgement. If she was a previous lover wanting a repeat, Jay would remind them of her ground rules. No action replays. After nearly three years at the club, she still hadn't run out of unique opportunities.

"Are you actually engrossed in that, or are you trying to avoid talking to me?"

Hers was a cultured voice, a voice that belonged in a place like this and was probably born to it, with an accent so sharp it could cut ribbons at a hundred village fairs. Jay looked up, not wishing to be blatantly rude. She was surprised to see a younger woman, probably late-thirties, staring at her with big blue eyes. She had strawberry-blond hair, a pale face, and a flock of freckles on her nose that advertised some Celtic blood.

The woman's smile and confidence was appealing, and Jay felt a buzz below her belly. *Interesting.* She wore neither the standard business suit nor the comfortable tweeds and pearls favoured by the country set. Rather, she wore big hoop earrings and what looked like a hand-crocheted shawl over a flowing violet dress. On her slender wrists, half a dozen bangles clattered against each other when she moved her hands. She was making a bold statement, completely misplaced in this exclusive club, and yet, her confidence and accent asserted a familiarity with it all.

Jay shook her head as if to clear the judgement beginning to form. She hated it when people judged her because of where she came from. She relaxed her fingers from around her glass. "I haven't seen you here before," she said, although she seemed

GREEN *for* LOVE

vaguely familiar.

"I normally stay with friends when I'm in London, but they've been seconded to New York. My mother has been a member for many years and insists on a membership for me too."

She sneered as if she despised the thought. It should have been ugly but somehow, her disdain made her seem more remote and intriguing.

A membership wasn't cheap, so obviously the family were wealthy. A shiver of guilt passed down Jay's spine; she hoped she didn't know the woman's mother in the biblical sense. That could be a little embarrassing. "Who's your mother? I might know her."

"Catherine Armstrong-Forde, but honestly, she didn't really come down from the wilds of Northumberland that often, and she and my father recently emigrated to France."

Jay breathed a sigh of relief. She certainly didn't remember an encounter with this woman's mother. "So, Ms. Armstrong-Forde, do you have a first name?"

The woman leaned forward as though she was about to impart a secret, giving Jay a rather delicious sight of her cleavage.

"How do you know I'm not married with half a dozen screaming children?"

"You look too relaxed," Jay said. *And hot.*

"Hmm. You're right. I'm not married—I'm free. My name is Lia, short for Cordelia, but I hate that."

She smiled, and her whole face brightened in a way that made Jay's toes curl. There was a definite flirtatious edge to her smile, wide eyes, and batting eyelids. "I'm Jay. I notice you didn't say you were single. Free doesn't necessarily mean the same thing."

Lia raised her eyebrow and gave a small coquettish smile. "You're a sharp one. My friends say I'm too picky, that I have too many conditions to find true love, and that the perfect person doesn't exist, but I don't intend to settle for second best. So, I'm playing the field until the right person, my true soulmate, appears."

Jay placed her glass on the leather coaster. Somehow Lia

didn't seem to suit her, it was too ordinary to contain those upper-class clipped tones. And unlike Jay's own learned vowels, tutored to within an inch of her life to eradicate her natural West London Council Flat twang. Not that she was ashamed; it's just that people judged, and she wanted to present where she was now, not where she originated. Jay realised she hadn't responded. A recent article in the *New Scientist* drifted into her mind, and she pointed to her open magazine.

"So not monogamous? Scientific studies show monogamy encourages co-parenting of children."

Lia shrugged. "I'm a lesbian and don't intend to have any children, so it isn't relevant to me."

Well, that resolved one question. It would be easy to fall into bed with her, but something held her back from responding as she normally would. There was this niggling feeling they had met before, but that was ridiculous.

"How do you know there's one true love for you? Statistically, that's impossible," Jay said and caught Lia's flinch at her tone. She smiled to offset the vehemence of her statement.

Lia blinked. "It's all about energies. There are a group of people who resonate at the same frequency as we do. When we encounter them, our soul recognises them. Hence, soulmates."

Jay stared at her to see if she was being serious, though there was no tell-tale smirk on Lia's face. "How would the souls recognise each other's energy? Do they have an inbuilt oscilloscope?"

Lia's smile slipped a little, but Jay hated non-scientific explanations, and she wasn't going to let Lia get away with bullshit even if she was hot.

"I take it you're one of those doubters who will only believe something if they can measure it? You can't measure love. We can't even define it properly, but we feel it, like heat from a radiator."

Lia received a bottled mineral water from Alice, and it provided a welcome distraction from the unintentionally contentious conversation. Jay could never understand why anyone would

GREEN *for* LOVE

bother with mineral water when they could have tap water for free, but that might prove controversial too.

Lia fixed her with that knowing smile again. "Also, my psychic said I'll meet my soulmate this year, so who knows? She could be sitting beside me now."

Jay snorted her whisky and started to cough, caught between the forwardness of the statement and the utter nonsense behind it. "You don't really believe all that crap, do you?"

Lia sighed. "Okay, you're a non-believer. I told you, it's all energy. Rub your hands together and what do you feel?"

Jay wasn't going to fall for this ludicrous pseudo-experiment. "My hands will feel warm because of friction."

"And friction is energy," Lia said as if she had proved some great theorem.

"Which can be measured using the coefficient of friction multiplied by the normal force..." She trailed off as Lia gave her an arch look. "Science. Not woo woo mysticism." Okay, so maybe nerd speak wasn't a good idea, especially when it came to someone who believed in cosmic love. She was better at having sex with women than talking to them. Perhaps she spent too much time amongst technical people. It was little wonder she was alone.

Lia also seemed to be shifting topic as she slipped her index finger up the condensation on the outside of the glass and placed it between her lips, holding Jay's gaze. Jay swallowed, her nerve endings buzzing. She squeezed her legs together to stop the throbbing between her thighs. Lia was definitely doing things to her libido, and she was still gazing at her lips. *Oh, lord.*

She needed to steer the conversation back to where they started, to common ground. She didn't have to agree with someone's life outlook to enjoy their company for a minute or two. "I'm queer too, though I'm not sure about children as I might be getting too old for them."

Lia placed her hand onto the bar, as though calculating her next chess move. "You look like you're in your prime, and I'm glad we're on the same page. I was hoping you played for my team. Where might the evening take us?"

Lia placed her hand on Jay's forearm and left it there. Jay's skin tingled from where Lia touched her, and she enjoyed being admired, touched, and flirted with.

Jay gripped her glass in an attempt to focus. Once she was approached, she was normally the one controlling the dance of give and take, but this woman was bold, intriguing, and incredibly sexy. "Play, yes, but nothing more. I don't believe in romance or soulmates, and I'm too busy with work to commit to anything else."

"Play sounds perfect. Life is so much more than work, and until I come across my soulmate, I won't do commitment either. But that doesn't mean we can't have fun in the meantime, does it?" Lia wrapped her neatly manicured fingers around Jay's. "I'm in room five. We could take this conversation up there."

Normally, Jay would have been more than happy to do that, whether the talking was with mouths or tongues on skin and intimate body parts, but something held her back. Lia was different. She wasn't the usual married woman seeking a brief sapphic dalliance. There was something about her, something that suggested depth. Sure, the usual flirtation was in place, but her totally different approach to life made Jay want to have a real conversation with her, as frustrating as it might be, and she really didn't want the evening to end just yet. Maybe it had more to do with that nagging sense of loneliness that had been bothering her lately. One she'd been doing her best to ignore.

"We could, but I'm enjoying *actually* talking. You don't seem the usual club type, yet your accent indicates you clearly belong here."

Lia raised her eyebrow and didn't seem at all affected by the rebuff. "Those are a whole stack of assumptions and stereotypes."

Jay shrugged. "We all judge by first impressions. But you're a conundrum. Your bright colours, bohemian style, and designer shawl are at odds with a club where wealthy women come to relax."

Lia traced her index finger along Jay's jacket. "Whereas you fit

GREEN *for* LOVE

right in with your sharp business suit. What do you do that gives you all these little luxuries in life? No, don't tell me. Let me guess." She checked Jay out, slowly, from the top of her head to her high heels.

She wouldn't be seen dead with makeup or heels at home—it wasn't who she was—but fitting into the norm was all part of the expectations of her role, and that had been as carefully crafted as her accent.

"Definitely an executive of some sort, otherwise you wouldn't be here. Clearly an office job, and yet..."

Lia's tapping of her fingertips on Jay's arm echoed the racing of her pulse. She was almost reconsidering her decision not to go up to Lia's room. But that would just be sex; this was much more interesting. She hadn't really talked to someone in a long time.

"Ah. A scientist."

Jay gestured to the magazine next to her glass. "The open journal and me blurting out a formula earlier gave me away. That's cheating."

"Not at all. Didn't Sherlock Holmes say to Watson that he sees but doesn't observe? I merely deduced it from my observations. That's logic. I'm sure it would appeal to you as a scientist."

Her smile was one of triumph, and Jay melted a little. There was just something about a confident woman.

Lia sat back on her stool and Jay leaned towards her, even though she recognised the move as a power play. Lia had a little furrow between her eyes that Jay wanted to brush away with her finger.

"Why don't you believe in romance and relationships?" Lia asked.

"Relationships are complicated and require compromise," Jay said, pausing her flirtation. "I've fought too hard to establish myself, to be myself, independent and powerful, thriving despite working in a misogynistic macho culture—"

Lia tapped her nails against the glass. "It's interesting you go to work first, as though that defines you."

"It does. It's what I've devoted my life to. That and caring for my mum." Jay was unsure why she was offering up so much information. She didn't ordinarily give details about herself. Odd, but she'd go with it.

"Noble but rather mundane, don't you think? Safe and predictable."

Jay put her glass on the bar top a little too hard. "I may be boring to you, but I'm not interested in the highs and lows of emotions. I don't trust them. I don't trust the drama of being ruled by what you feel at any given moment."

Lia caressed Jay's forearm. "You're not boring at all. I never said that. I said that your life is safe and predictable."

Jay stifled a huff of exasperation. Lia was confident almost to the level of arrogance. Maybe they should have slept together and not had this talk. Jay didn't want to appear defensive so adopted her mediating business tone. "To you, maybe, but I'm happy as I am."

"Happy? Really? Don't you get lonely with your one-night stands? I know I do."

Lia had prised open her thoughts and peered inside, and it was disturbing. Jay opened her mouth to respond, but the moment was gone.

"Don't you want to kiss in the rain? Or be so sated with multiple orgasms you can't walk? Or experience the unfettered joy of being alive? Or watch a sunrise over the sea and revel in the glory of nature?" Lia asked.

In theory, those sounded nice. "I'm a city girl. I don't do nature unless it's in a park. And I can do all those things without a soulmate."

Lia threw her head back and laughed, causing her hair to bob as her shoulders shook. Was Lia mocking her? She was certainly challenging her very existence, and it was uncomfortable. Jay took another sip of her whisky.

Still with a twinkle in her eye, Lia leaned forward again, and Jay caught a whiff of her scent, something exotic and expensive. Ylang

ylang maybe?

"So, Jay the Scientist who doesn't believe in soulmates or romance, what sun sign are you?"

Jay was about to assert that she could make romantic gestures if she really wanted to, but that wasn't true. She hadn't had something that passed for a romantic relationship in a long time. It would be easy to blame her driving ambition, but the raw wound from her childhood constantly whispered that she wasn't quite good enough. Despite the money, the status, and being able to afford these luxuries now, she simply didn't think there was someone for her. She sipped at her drink, and the burn trickled down her throat.

"Come on, surely you know when you were born?" Lia asked her eyebrow raised.

"Twenty second of April," Jay said.

"Ah, a Taurus. That makes sense." Lia rattled her bangles, as if Jay had revealed the code to a magic kingdom.

"With your sun in Taurus, you love the finer things in life, like money and status." Lia spread her arms to indicate their surroundings. "And you're sensual. I bet you have a regular pampering in that beauty salon downstairs."

"What if I do? That doesn't prove anything. Lots of people love a relaxing massage after work, and they don't have to be born between certain dates."

"But you do admit you enjoy a nice massage. Pity you've turned me down. I do a wonderful sensual massage in all those difficult to reach places."

Jay's whole body burned at the thought. This wasn't like her at all. She was torn between taking control of the situation or succumbing to this bohemian seductress, who was challenging her boundaries and changing her usual MO. "Do you work or are you a lady of leisure?"

Lia raised her eyebrow again. "I work for a charity, but there's no way I could afford to come here on my salary."

"Ah, your mother." *Idiot.* Talk about a mood killer.

Lia shook her head. "I really don't want to talk about my mother now. I'd much prefer to get to know you better...physically." She placed her hand over Jay's. "We've established neither of us is interested in relationships, so maybe we could have some fun upstairs while getting better acquainted?"

It sounded more like an expectation than a question. Jay was a confident woman, but Lia was in a whole different league. Usually, the invitation was a little more subtle, a little more innuendo, and less "let's do this." Desire and sense warred within her. She glanced at the brass captain's clock on the wall; it was getting late, and for whatever reason, a quick bit of sex tonight would feel empty and leave her even more lonely. She drained her glass and leaned forward so her lips almost touched Lia's cheek.

"Tempting though you are, I should be getting home. I have an early start and a big meeting tomorrow."

Disappointment flared in Lia's eyes before she settled to a neutral expression. "Maybe you could yield to that temptation another time. Now run along and tuck yourself up in bed with your cocoa." Her smile softened the sarcasm, but her body stiffened, and she withdrew her hand.

"At least let me settle your tab." Jay caught Alice's eye and indicated their glasses. Alice nodded. She must have anticipated that Jay would pay as she placed the receipt on a silver dish, folded down, and slid it across to her. Jay placed her platinum card on the tray and passed it back to Alice, who stepped away to ring it up.

"Thanks. I look forward to getting to know you better at some other time when you're not so caught up in big meetings." Lia rose.

"I'm here next Wednesday evening. Maybe we could meet up then?" Jay asked before she could think about it. "Are you sure we haven't met before?"

Lia quirked an eyebrow. "It must have been in a previous life, but you probably don't believe in that either." She leaned forward and feathered a kiss on Jay's cheek before exiting gracefully, her hips swaying like Jessica Rabbit.

Damn. Sometimes Jay wished she could be more spontaneous. Despite their vastly different ways of seeing the world, if they had indulged, it could never have been just a one-night stand. Lia wasn't someone she would fuck and forget. She was enigmatic, confident, engaged. Everything most women who passed through Jay's life weren't. Her logical scientific brain knew it was the correct course of action not to pursue Lia, but her libido rued the loss.

Chapter Two

LIA SHUFFLED HER FEET in the restless crowd, a mix of cold and excitement making her shiver. She stood tall and performed her grounding routine as if preparing for battle, which it was in a way: a battle for the planet. And so far, the self-centred corporates and oily politicians were winning, spiralling them into the flames of hell.

No one looked at her, as if they didn't want to catch her eye in case she insisted they also be pushed to the front. Funny how everyone talked big in the pub about taking action, but she always ended up leading the charge. If she was being charitable, she supposed it would be much harder for the others if they were arrested. They didn't have a wealthy family to bail them out, and they could lose their jobs.

She rolled her shoulders, ready to strike. She needed to limber up, be relaxed to be as quick and effective as possible. This had to be a hit and run affair. She didn't want a charge for criminal damage. She pulled her snood up over her nose to camouflage her face, although with her reddish hair and taller than average height, she tended to stand out. If they were to continue this type of action, she might need to invest in a balaclava.

An anticipatory buzz percolated through the crowd. People gripped their placards and coughed quietly in the cold morning air. Lia smiled at the great turnout. Her nerves tingled, and her heart seemed to swell in her chest. They were making a difference, challenging the attitudes of those in power, and changing the world for the better. It was better than sex. *Almost.*

The face of the woman she'd nearly bedded last night flashed through her mind. Jay was stunning in a corporate kind of way, with her expensive, tailored business suit, tantalising smile, intelligent brown eyes, and short dark hair that Lia wanted to tousle out of place and run her fingers through. Her intelligence was such a turn-on. When she spoke, her pronunciation was almost too articulated, as if she'd taken elocution lessons. Or maybe that was her way. Lia had guessed correctly that she was a scientist, so perhaps she liked precision in everything, including in her speech.

Lia was surprised to be rejected, as the air seemed charged between them, and she was sure Jay would have agreed. Jay seemed to want her, judging by the speed of her pulse and the desire flashing in her eyes, but she'd said no, for now. That stung. Lia couldn't remember the last time she'd been turned down. Women flocked to her, and even when she'd been rejected, she simply chalked it up to experience and moved on. But she didn't want to move on, or she couldn't move on, because she couldn't stop thinking about Jay. It wasn't Lia's over-inflated ego or simply the thrill of the chase either. She was sure that Jay was interested. Lia would rearrange her work schedule so she could be in London on Wednesday, although six days was too long to wait. She resolved to stay at the club more often. Her mother didn't mind it going on her bill; she always said she preferred to know Lia was safe rather than getting into trouble. Again.

She glanced around. This was trouble, if the gnawing in her stomach was anything to go by. Still, she chose to ignore it. She shook her hands and attempted to centre herself, inhaling deeply and imagining the breath circling through her chakras from the ground to the crown of her head, cleansing and clearing. Focusing herself was much easier after a long stay in an Indian ashram that specialised in meditation and yoga.

An inner calm settled within her. She was ready.

Across the porcupine panoply of placards on the other side of the road, Steve nodded to signal that the cars were on their way, and the chanting started.

"No more oil! No more oil!"

GREEN *for* LOVE

Signs were thrust high in unison with the shouting. This was her tribe, her people, building itself to a frenzy, united to fight for the planet. Lia had never had such a strong sense of belonging, not at school, not at university, and certainly not in her family. The noise swelled to an angry crescendo as a swanky car drew up. People banged their hands on its sides, and the driver slowed down, trying not to hit anyone, thank goodness. Their ploy to delay its progress for her to strike was working.

Blood rushed in her ears. This was her moment. She picked up the paint-filled balloons by her feet and nodded at Steve, who had his phone in position to film her. She stepped in front of the crawling car and aimed two balloons at it. The balloons burst with a satisfying splatter, and a nebula of magenta paint exploded all over the metalwork. The driver leaned on his horn and then slammed into reverse. Lia caught the eye of the woman in the back of the car, staring open-mouthed with apparent shock and anger. And recognition.

No way. Lia stared back, unable to take her eyes off the passenger. The last time she had seen those eyes, they'd sparked with desire and flirtation. Lia gulped. *Jay*. She could have gone to bed with her last night, certainly would have done if she hadn't said she had a big meeting today. Now it was clear. The traitor was a *petroleum* scientist. Lia had come close to sleeping with a woman whose values totally misaligned with hers, and they'd agreed to meet again. That wouldn't be happening now. If they'd had sex, Lia would have slept with the enemy, unknowing. How much more nauseous would she have felt now if they had? It was clear they were as compatible as water and electricity, though there had been an undeniable spark fizzing beneath the skin and arcing across the air between them. And just as deadly. Damn shame.

"Awesome! Did you see the look on that woman's face? She looked like she wanted to roast you on a stick," Steve said, tapping his phone. "I got it all on video. It's hilarious. I'll post it on the website after a quick edit."

Lia swallowed the bile rising in her throat and spun around to glare at him. "No. Don't target individuals. Just post the balloon and paint. It's the company we hate, not the people."

"What's got into you? Normally you think those at the top deserve everything they get."

He was right, but she couldn't do that. Once people appeared on their website, they were often targeted by trolls and sometimes harassed in person. Jay didn't deserve that.

Lia was sure she was ultimately a good person—she'd felt it in Jay's vibrations—even if she was on the wrong side of the argument. Lia didn't want that on her conscience. She wanted to bring down the system that made the rich richer, but she didn't want to hurt people, least of all the gorgeous woman who had turned her head yesterday. "Not this time. I don't want the driver or the passenger to be identifiable. Cut it after the paint hits the car."

They stepped out of sight of the shifting security cameras that Steve had scouted out beforehand.

"Suit yourself."

In the distance, a police siren sounded, and the crowd dispersed, melting into the shadows. Lia traded her snood and flat shoes for her Burberry trench coat and her heels she had in her bag, then she mingled with the crowd heading towards the city. Expensive clothes often meant she could blend in and look as if she was a bank executive job instead of a paintbomb-throwing protester.

Jay had definitely recognised her. She would amp up her future disguises. Would Jay tell the police where they could find her? Lia intuited that she wouldn't but had no idea why. They seemed to have established a bizarre unspoken bond that they wouldn't hurt each other.

Was she crazy to trust Jay? Probably, but she'd do so anyway. She always trusted her gut, and she wasn't about to start questioning it now. Though the disappointment that they wouldn't date didn't sit well, she'd stay true to her values and ideals. Great sex could be found anywhere. Finding someone who was committed to saving the world was a lot harder.

Chapter Three

An hour earlier

JAY SMOOTHED DOWN HER skirt and rearranged her blouse so the buttons were dead centre. She mentally rehearsed her speech as Neil, one of the company chauffeurs, drove her towards the HQ building. As they navigated the London streets, a thrill of excitement shivered down her spine. Riding in the back of a limo like this, with its interior adorned with more walnut and cream leather than she'd ever seen, was what she'd worked for all her life. It was affirmation that she'd made it.

Jay inhaled the aroma of luxury and settled back into the deep seat. She unclicked her briefcase with a satisfying snap and withdrew her notes, not that she really needed them. Oliver, her CEO and mentor, encouraged her to do as many talks and presentations as possible so that she would be comfortable when she took that step up to the board as Chief Operating Officer.

The traffic had become clogged as they traversed the city streets. Jay glanced at the clock set in the polished walnut that gleamed so brightly she could make out her face. "What time should we get there, Neil?"

"By my current reckoning, around 8:10. Don't worry. We'll have you there early so you can set up for your big meeting. Do you want to rehearse your speech again?"

Understanding and gratitude warmed her to her toes. He was such a considerate man. "Not this time, Neil, thanks. How's Marian getting on?"

Neil looked in the rear-view mirror and smiled. "Good, thanks.

Oliver has said I can borrow the car for her graduation. I couldn't be prouder."

He could talk about his daughter for hours, and she could do with the distraction. She needed normality after her encounter with Lia last night. Lia's willowy contradiction of appearance and breeding fascinated Jay. She'd been drawn to her cultured tones, mesmerised, as if by a siren's call. Jay was painfully aware that her own accent occasionally revealed a West London twang, despite years of coaching. There was something about Lia that hooked her in, like a sailor drawn to the rocks.

Departing from her usual MO had been strange and yet so natural, and she was really looking forward to exploring their connection further. There wouldn't be a soul connection, obviously, but maybe it could be something to stave off the loneliness a little.

Her notes creased between her fingers, and she smoothed them out, trying to eradicate the wrinkles, but they were as stubborn and permanent as her misgivings.

As they approached the city, the buildings grew in stature, towering and off-putting like the house prices. Oliver had said she could lease the company flat in Mayfair when she became a board director. She would be entertaining on a regular basis, and they didn't want clients visiting her tiny apartment near Tower Bridge, even if it did have a nice view.

She would love nothing better than to casually drop that she had the keys to the Mayfair apartment into conversation with that money-grubbing toe rag and head of commercial, Richard Worthington. There was a way to go until that was a reality, and Richard would do whatever he could to stop her from getting there. As the son of John Worthington, the Chief Financial Officer, he was also angling for the COO spot, but he didn't have the experience, knowledge, or gravitas for it. Although he'd been born into wealth, he reminded her of the barrow boys hawking their wares, always wheeling and dealing on the grey side of the law.

Neil cleared his throat. "Looks like trouble. Shall I go round to

GREEN *for* LOVE

the other entrance?"

She peered at the noisy mob ahead, their placards dancing like some grotesque puppet show. "Those bloody protestors again. Haven't they got anything better to do? No, go through them carefully. We shouldn't capitulate to their terror tactics, otherwise they've won."

Neil's mouth became a thin line of determination, as if he disagreed with her assessment. "Sure."

He edged forward, and her window was filled with angry faces mouthing obscenities at her. Jay's heart thumped as loudly as the banging on the roof and windows, but she did her best to avoid eye contact and keep her expression neutral. Neil slowly manoeuvred around them, trying to avoid catching their trailing limbs.

She was about to say, "Go back" when a figure dashed in front of the car, and terror gripped Jay's heart. "No!" she cried out as the tall figure pulled something from behind their back. Surely they weren't going to be shot. Almost before she realised what was happening, pink objects hurtled towards the car and burst with an explosion of paint all over the Rolls Royce. The perpetrator was clearly a woman. Some kind of scarf covered her face from her nose to her chin, and she wore dark clothes, but she hadn't really hidden her strawberry-blond hair and freckles. When Jay met her blue eyes, she knew that it was Lia.

"Oh," she whispered.

Neil reversed the car at speed, and Lia watched her as they pulled away.

"Hang on," Neil said and turned the car around to face the other direction. They continued to speed away from the altercation. "Are you okay?" he asked, his voice a bit shaky.

"Yes." Her heart rate slowed, and she licked her teeth as if trying to eradicate the disappointment and hurt. Lia must have come to London specifically for the attack. So much for being there on business. Had Jay been a distraction from the purpose of her visit? The discomfort that she was merely an afterthought did not sit well.

20   **E.V. BANCROFT**

Yet that was how Jay treated her conquests when she went to the club, so she couldn't complain.

Neil flicked the wipers and sprayed the windscreen, trying to clear a few splatters of paint.

"I should've listened to you and gone via the alternate route. I'm so sorry they've damaged the car. I hope it's nothing too major."

"It wasn't your fault. You didn't throw the paint. It would have been easier if they were eggs. I'd better warn the others if they haven't come in." He pressed the speed dial.

"Hi, Neil, is everything okay?" Marta asked over the car's speakers.

"We've run into protesters close to the front door, and they've thrown paint all over the car. Can you notify security to clear them away? And can you call the police and warn any other directors coming in by company cars to go via the back?"

"Of course. Are you both all right? Who are you driving today?"

"Jay."

"I hope she's not too shaken up."

Jay smiled. "I'm okay. Thanks, Marta."

Her smile fell as Neil turned the corner and navigated his way around the back streets to the rear doors. The knowledge that Lia was the perpetrator sat like a cannonball in her stomach. Even if they called up CCTV footage, it was unlikely they could identify her. Jay should inform Oliver and the police that she knew who she was, or at least how they could find her, via the club. She'd given Jay her name, if that was real, and her room number, and presumably the club had her contact details.

Lia's blue eyes had bored into her as Neil pulled away. What was in her expression? Surprise and anger, certainly, but also sorrow or disappointment. Or maybe that was just what Jay was thinking. But no one knew they'd met... She shook away the thought. She'd worked so hard to get where she was, and always put work first, before anything else except her mum's health, certainly before any relationship. She owed Lia nothing. They weren't girlfriends

GREEN *for* LOVE

or dating and there'd been no suggestion of more than another conversation. And yet, for some reason that was neither logical nor rational, Jay knew she wouldn't say anything, but she couldn't understand her motives.

Could she really live with herself if she gave them the details? Besides, she would need to explain what she was doing and how she spent her evenings and Jay really didn't want people like Richard ever finding out about her private life, even if the club was a respectable women's private club. He would be bound to make something out of nothing and use the information against her. Better to say nothing. She exhaled and sat back in her seat, which didn't seem as comfortable as before as she tussled between guilt and indecision.

"Well driven back there, Neil. Where did you learn to do that handbrake turn?"

"We all take defensive driving skills courses in case our passengers are ever a kidnap target."

"That's cheerful."

"Never had to use it in anger before. Given the bulk of the Roller, I think she performed pretty well. We didn't even take out any bollards."

"If they've got it on CCTV, maybe you could request it to show your grandchildren one day?"

He laughed, but his voice still sounded shaky. "That's a way off, I hope. Marian's only just graduating. We could do without any more excitement just yet."

Jay smiled and turned to the back door of the office building, steel and anonymous, with no handle on the outside. It was like the door that had been shut on her hopes of anything with Lia, whatever that might have entailed. An overwhelming sense of disappointment dragged at her shoulders. She had hoped for better. No, damn it; she was entitled to feel pissed off. Lia had played her, and Jay had fallen for it. She said she worked for a charity, not that she was an eco-terrorist. There was a code at the club. Maybe you didn't give up a lot of information, but you didn't outright lie. *Get a grip.* She took a deep breath. *Focus.* Emotions only degraded logic, and right now, she was working. She could do this.

***

"You cannot seriously expect us to start fracking. It's not scientifically proven to be safe and uses a huge amount of water." Jay didn't care if her voice was raised, this was one more item in this shit show of a day. She stood toe-to-toe with Richard as they packed up after the meeting.

He shrugged. "It's lucrative. Which you'd know if you cared about the bottom line and what the shareholders thought, rather than seeking some nerdy snowflake answer all the time. You may have Oliver's ear for now, but he won't be in charge forever, and then you won't have anyone batting for you and your flimsy ideas."

She clenched her jaw. "Oliver doesn't want fracking. It's risky and dirty. Why do you think those protestors attacked this morning?"

"You can't make all of the people happy all of the time. Protestors are no more than an inconvenience."

His look of complete indifference enraged her even further, and she wanted to shout out her frustration at his smug face. What else could go wrong today? She was still smarting from Lia's actions and Neil's upset at the car, which tugged at her guilt because she'd urged him to go on. She really didn't need this dickhead gloating over her as well. She took a deep breath and tried to calm down. "Magenta has always been transparent. We're working to evolve from within, not take huge leaps backwards."

"But all your innovations are years away from making a return— if ever. You're right that Magenta needs to evolve but not in the way you think." He picked up his briefcase.

She gripped the back of a chair. "Oliver will never agree to this."

GREEN *for* LOVE

She knew it was true for now, but her stomach churned at what would happen when Oliver retired. Everything would be okay if Oliver got his way and made her CEO. Then she would set the agenda and convince the board about the new technologies-led, eco-friendly strategy.

"Oliver already knows and is happy to proceed."

"He can tell me that himself." Jay snatched up her papers and strode out of the room, not caring if the door swung back in his face. Anger propelled her down the wood-panelled corridors to Oliver's outer office, where Marta looked up, clearly surprised at the hurricane appearing at her desk.

"Is he in?" Jay pushed open the door without waiting for an answer.

Oliver sighed heavily and turned away from his laptop. He returned to his neutral, professional demeanour and gestured for her to sit in one of his plush visitors chairs. "What's biting you?"

Jay gripped the back of the chair to anchor herself. "Did you know about the fracking?"

"Ah, Richard has got to you."

Her heart thumped so hard, she thought she might have a heart attack. "You knew but said nothing to me? What about Magenta being transparent? How we're transferring to net-zero by 2040?"

He raised his hand, probably as surprised as she was by her vehemence. Maybe it was her cumulative rage about everything that had happened today.

"Whoa. We might need to work on your sangfroid if you want to be CEO. This isn't like the cool, collected scientist I know. What's really bugging you?"

She deflated. "Did Marta tell you about the car?"

"Neil did. Bloody oil protestors. Fortunately, it was emulsion, so it'll come off. And with regard to fracking, Richard doesn't understand the optics of everything we do, and that we'll be held to account. Rightly so."

"So why the fracking? It's currently illegal, as well as potentially unsafe."

Oliver took a toffee from a bowl and offered her one. She shook her head, too angry to snack.

"Jay, if you want to take over, you have to consider all options, and you need to learn about balance. We're exploring all options. Richard is pursuing a hopeful lead in the northern wastes, where there are hardly any people to complain. It would create hundreds of jobs."

"When those protestors hear about this, they'll do more than throw paint."

"Ah, it's actions that matter. Don't tell Richard, but I have no intention of going ahead. I'm proud of the employees we look after, the good record we have, and our transparency. I'm not going to throw that away. But that doesn't mean I don't want the available information on all options."

Jay sank onto the seat, her fury dissipating. "Thank God. You don't know how relieved I am to hear you say that. I'd hate to face protestors every day because we've been hypocritical."

Oliver smiled at her, a genuine smile. She loved this man, her mentor and friend as well as her boss.

"Coffee?"

When she nodded, he placed an order with Marta. Moments later, she entered with a silver tray and two cups and saucers.

Oliver settled back in his chair and stirred in his sweeteners. "How's your mum?"

Jay held the cup above the saucer without bringing it to her lips. "About the same. She likes the new mobility car and finds it easier to get around. Needless to say, it's a lot more expensive."

"I'm sure she appreciates everything you do for her."

Jay took a sip. Perfect. Not too strong and just the right temperature. Marta was a star. "I'm only doing what she would do. She sacrificed so much for me."

"Yes, but don't you think you've repaid that debt? Live a little. Get a girlfriend. Or a dog. Get a life."

"I have a life, thanks."

"Working all the hours that God sends doesn't count as a life. I appreciate how devoted you are to Magenta, but there's more to life."

"I don't have time for a girlfriend or a dog. Have you seen how much travelling I do?"

He grinned. "I do sign off on your expenses, you know. The girlfriend could look after the dog."

She snorted. This was the first time she couldn't be completely open with him. She should have told him how to get to Lia so they could notify the police, but the words didn't come. Something inside stilled her conscience, normally her lodestone when it came to work and her life. Jay did what was right *because* it was right, irrespective of who may or may not be watching. But Lia had unsettled her highly tuned equilibrium, and she couldn't betray the trust she'd seen in Lia's eyes as Neil had sped away.

Jay swirled her coffee around in the cup. Caffeine wasn't the best solution for a headache but right now, she needed it.

Oliver straightened and resumed work mode. "Now, since you rudely interrupted me, perhaps you can give me an update on the hydrogen project."

Jay relaxed. In work mode, she didn't *have* to think about Lia's icy eyes glaring at her in shock and anger. She could bundle that away in the box marked, *never going to happen*. She had never put her personal life above her loyalty to her work, to Oliver, and she still wasn't sure why she was doing it. Her tightly ordered world had shifted, and she wasn't sure she liked the change.

Chapter Four

"ARE YOU SURE ABOUT this?" Steve whispered. "It's only been a couple of weeks since our last action. If they ID you, you're certain to be taken into custody."

"I don't care." Rage fuelled Lia's desire for tonight's work. The objective was more important than any personal consequences.

Steve held out the protective wadding to put down her trousers in case she was arrested. He ran his fingers through his hair, a tell that he was anxious. But she was the one taking the risk. She wanted to shake the government, and the power brokers, and the corporates, and rattle them out of their complacency. If they didn't do something, the planet would be lost. She detested the pandering to the self-serving capitalists who wanted only to gild their mansions and increase their bank balances. Come the planetary disasters, they would be in the best place to weather the storms, but most of the world's population would burn, or drown, or be forced to migrate to the habitable fringes where there would be more fighting as people struggled to live. *Wake up*, she wanted to scream at the powers that be.

Lia glared at him and by the light of her headtorch, he shrivelled a little. "I'm not asking you to do it. Things will never improve unless the companies are embarrassed and inconvenienced into making big changes. If you're not with us, you're against us."

Steve ran his fingers through his hair again, leaving it even more tousled than before. "Don't go all radical diva on me. I'm concerned for your safety."

Lia gave him a curt smile. "In war, there are always casualties. Besides, my parents will bail me out. Good upstanding members of society and all that." *Casualties of war...* Two weeks after meeting Jay, she still couldn't get her out of her head. Those mesmerising eyes behind those nerdy glasses, her intelligence, and her sexy laugh. How ill-fated that she was an enemy; she hadn't struck Lia as being a handmaiden of the devil, but Google told a different story.

Jay Tanner, head of science and technology, was one rung below main board level. Lia could understand her working for a company like Magenta to repay her university debt, but she was nearly forty-four. She'd clearly chosen to stay. What did that say about her values? She was a slave to money, cared nothing for the planet, unthinking—

"Lia, where'd you go?" Steve held out more wadding.

She took it from him. "Sorry. Thinking about the casualties of war."

"Ah, that woman really got under your skin. That's not like you."

"No, it's not. Let's do this." She stuffed the last of the material down the back of her trousers in case she was dragged off later, though she hoped it wouldn't come to that. No. It *needed* to come to that. They needed to hit the headlines.

Steve passed over a jar of Vaseline, and she rubbed it around her wrists. The preparation was a ritual, a meditation almost, like donning armour in medieval days. Tension gripped her stomach.

They slipped out of their tent and joined the rest of the group at the oil terminal gates. Seeing the others slipping out of the shadows caused excitement to buzz deep inside. Here was the group that was changing the world, one protest at a time. There was such a thrill to being part of something bigger. For the first time in her life, she'd found her purpose, her reason for being. She was here to do this for the greater good.

Lia and the others got on all fours on the roadway leading up to the terminal. The smell of solvents, mixed with the distinct petrol smell of distillate, hit her nose.

"Settled?"

She nodded, so Steve superglued her hands to the road, then

did the same for everyone else. A tanker swung around the corner; the driver blared its horn and the air brakes hissed like an enraged animal.

Steve yelled at him to stop and rolled the video onto their livestream. He approached Lia and shouted above the din. "Tell us what you're doing and why?"

"We're protesting against the use of fossil fuels which are killing the planet," Lia shouted.

The horns continued blaring like the angry honking of geese. From behind her, a van door slid open and shut. How had the cops arrived so quickly? She heard running feet, truck doors opening and slamming, and the heavy crunch of boots hitting gravel. Steve swung his camera towards the arrival of the TV crews.

"Great. The local TV station has arrived. Gives you another opportunity to say your speech." He melted into the background to continue filming.

The silhouettes of two big men blocked the security lighting. She braced herself for rough handling and hoped Steve would catch it.

"What the fuck are you doing? We're trying to deliver fuel," one man said.

"I know that. But until we stop the use of fossil fuels, our planet is on a trajectory to disaster," she said. The man spat in her face. She could do nothing but shake her head, so it didn't get in her mouth. "Go back to your tankers," she said.

The other man, his muscles straining at his shirt, raised his hand as though he was about to strike her but the other held him back. "Nah, look."

A reporter and her cameraman appeared with a microphone and pointed at Lia.

"It appears we have conflict here between the tanker drivers and the protestors."

The drivers retreated to their tankers, and Lia smiled at the camera. "No more oil," she shouted, and her fellow protestors joined in.

The tankers sounded their air horns to drown them out. In the distance was the unmistakeable sound of an ambulance. Its siren and blue flashing lights approached, getting louder and brighter.

"The protestors have glued themselves to the roadway, causing an obstruction not just for the fuel tankers but also for ambulances. There's already one here that can't get through." The reporter leaned closer to Lia. "Do you think you're justified in stopping people getting to the hospital?"

Damn. They hadn't anticipated this. "There are other routes. The planet is facing an emergency, but the oil companies are ignoring it. Until we stop fossil fuels, we can't do anything to bring down the temperature and that will affect all of us, not only one person."

"What if the person in that ambulance dies because they can't get to the hospital in time?"

"The onus has to be on the paramedic to find an alternative route."

"There's only one main road into this hospital, and you've blocked it."

Lia squashed down the anxiety in her stomach. She had to stay calm to get her message across. *Please don't let the person die.* "That's not the issue I'm addressing. The planet is on course for extinction, and we need to do something about it before it's too late."

"You'd let someone die? I guess you wouldn't send in a helicopter either as that uses fuel."

"Unfortunately, this kind of drastic action is the only way we can get the oil companies to listen."

The reporter turned away. "So, there you have it. According to these heartless protestors, the ends justify the means. Let's go back to my colleague in the studio, who has a statement from Essex police."

Heartless? Anger fizzled under her skin. "We do it because we care about the planet, about the future for everyone," Lia shouted, but the reporter had already moved away. Her body trembled involuntarily. Her hands ached from being in the same position.

The police force arrived in a flurry of sirens. Van doors slammed and weighty footfall echoed on the concrete before stopping in front of her.

"Blue 3 request firefighters for ungluing," someone said into their radio. He gave Lia a derisive sneer. "You're under arrest for causing an affray and obstructing the emergency services."

This ending was inevitable, and her day would only get worse, but her parents would bail her out in a few hours. She closed her eyes and tried to shut off the noise. What would Jay think about this? Lia shook her head to clear the thought. She shouldn't be thinking about her. The cause was more important than anything, including her personal happiness.

Chapter Five

JAY'S MUM WINCED AS she lifted herself from her wheelchair and wobbled to a standing position. She rushed to help, but her mum waved her away.

"Don't fuss. I've got to walk to get the strength back in my legs."

"But, Mum—"

"I'm fine. So much better now. I'll be back at work in no time."

That wouldn't be happening if Jay had anything to do with it. "You don't need to do that. I've told you that I'll look after you."

Her mum lurched forward one step and then another. Jay itched to rush in and help, but her mum had to practice using her prosthetic.

"Jay Tanner, you've done enough. I've never relied on anyone, and I'm not going to start now. You've already given me this house and you buy all the shopping. I really wish you'd let me pay rent."

How many times were they going to have this conversation? "I'm not going to charge my own mum rent—"

"But you're paying the mortgage."

"And I love that I can do that for you after everything you've done for me."

Her mum shooed her off and continued to cross the living room floor, clinging to the furniture like a drunk at sea. Eventually, she reached her La-Z-Boy reclining chair and lowered herself to a sitting position. She shuffled to make herself comfortable and sighed heavily with the effort she'd expended. Jay placed the remote control on a side table. Her mum would've been in a lot more pain if she'd stayed in her tiny council flat in Ealing. The La-Z-Boy wouldn't have fit up the stairs, and even if it had, it would've taken up the whole living room. Jay sat down on an old armchair, and her mum flicked through the channels.

"Let's watch the news. There's probably something about the protest at your refinery today."

Her mum seemed eager, as if there was nothing else to fill her day. That was the only downside of where she was; it didn't have the same sense of community as her old place, where she spent time playing cards and chattering with her friends.

Jay had heard about the protest at work and didn't need a reminder, but her mum had already switched on the news. She ought to be getting home, but she could always sleep in the spare bedroom, which her mum had set up for Jay. It was her less than subtle hint that she wanted Jay to live with her. But she wouldn't give up her flat; it was her independence. It was only forty minutes' drive home when the traffic wasn't too bad, though there was little to return to. No pets, no plants, no partner.

A twist of loneliness settled in her chest. Maybe Oliver was right. Maybe she should find herself a girlfriend, but her previous girlfriends hadn't been able to cope with playing second fiddle to Jay's career.

As the news headlines unfolded and Lia came on screen, Jay couldn't lose the thought of her, of their attraction, and then of her paintbomb attack. When Lia faced the camera, Jay's body reacted with a thrumming between her thighs. Lia's gaze bored into her, hard-eyed and angry and at odds with her casual flirting at the club, confident and oozing sex appeal. Part of her wished she'd slept with Lia and got her out of her system, so she could return to her normal, ordered life. Meaningless sex was like unwrapping a parcel; once she'd savoured and delighted in it, it no longer had any allure.

Onscreen, Lia shouted at the reporter. How could she think this was the right course of action? What did she hope to achieve?

Her mum shook her head. "I don't understand these people. How can they hold up an ambulance? It's so selfish."

GREEN *for* LOVE

Jay put her hand on her mum's arm. "I know, Mum, but they probably hadn't expected any ambulances." It did look callous, and Lia hadn't come across that way at all, or was that Jay's wishful thinking again?

"Whose side are you on?" her mum asked. "They're targeting *your* company. What will they do next? I'm petrified about you going into work, that I'll get a call to say you've been shot or something."

Her mum's protectiveness was sweet, but she was being overly dramatic. This wasn't America. Jay had hoped Lia might stop her activism after Jay had seen her and not told anyone where they might find her. That Lia had amped up the intensity of her protests seemed to be a direct snub. She patted her mum's arm. "I know, Mum. Sometimes it feels personal."

"You've always worked so hard and never harmed anyone. You shouldn't have to worry about your safety."

"I don't normally go in by car." Despite her affected nonchalance, Jay was drawn to the incident playing out on camera. She really shouldn't care if they hurt Lia when removing her, but she winced at the rough handling. Jay stood to avoid witnessing it and scooped up the jug to pour her mum some water. She placed it on the side table.

Her mum shook her fist at the screen. "They should lock them all up and throw away the key."

"Maybe we need to get better at our PR. They're winning the media war by getting more attention. We're researching greener alternatives, but that doesn't hit the headlines."

"Nonsense. They shouldn't lie in the road and block it. It causes problems for innocent people. What would have happened to me if the ambulance had been delayed?"

Jay shuddered and handed her mum the glass of water she had ignored. "I know, Mum. It doesn't bear thinking about."

Her mum took a sip and raised her glass to the arresting officer. "Good. Serves 'em right."

She should be relieved that they were getting arrested, the same as her mum was. Instead, a pang of pity ran through her.

Her mum put the glass down, obviously intent on continuing her rant. "We need oil. Where would we be without medical plastics for my prosthesis? All the single use plastics used during COVID, and oil to heat our houses and transport our goods? It's not practical."

"I'm with you, Mum, but we do need to change. Oliver and I are trying to persuade the board we should look at being net-zero by 2040. That's what we're planning for." Would that impress Lia? Probably not. She should have written her off by now and moved on to the next conquest, but she really didn't want to go back to the club. It was as if Lia had ruined the place for her forever. No, that was absurd. Jay had already been feeling like the club wasn't quite doing it for her anymore. There simply wasn't an alternative. So she needed to find one. It had nothing to do with Lia, who was an irritating thorn that would eventually break off and be gone.

The real issue was exactly what Lia's group was protesting. Maybe they could bring the net-zero timeline forward if they implemented the pilot studies that already showed great results. Surely, that would soften Lia and her friends a bit, and it would be better optics for the media. These action groups weren't going to go away any time soon. She would talk to Oliver about it on Monday. And if that earned her a few bonus points with a certain tall, bohemian enigma, all well and good.

Chapter Six

THE OUTER POLICE STATION door clanged behind them, and Lia sighed. She'd never been so terrified in her life. It was much worse than boarding school, and that had been a horrendous experience. The constriction and humiliation of a few hours in the cells left her considerably weakened and less sure of her actions. She stood up to her full height. No, she hadn't been humiliated. This was the price of furthering the cause, as unpleasant as it may be. She rubbed at her fingers where the solvent had left her stripped skin raw and stinging, then she gently pulled at some remaining glue as she walked towards the car park.

The puddles reflected the orange security lights, and a lone figure stood by the car, isolated in the way only possible in empty car parks at night. Lia waved at her mother, but she didn't wave back, and her mouth was a thin straight line of disapproval. Her mother marched towards Lia but didn't kiss her in greeting.

"This is not happening again, Cordelia. You're bringing shame on the family name," she said through gritted teeth.

She'd expected a punishment lecture. It was the first time she'd been held in the police cells, and all she wanted was to go home and have a shower. "Thanks for picking me up." Lia used the smile that had always got her own way as a child, but the flash of irritation on her mother's face suggested it wouldn't work this time.

"You're not going back to Bristol. You're coming with me to Northumberland. You're fortunate I was already in the UK." Her mother spun around to return to the car.

"What about work?" Lia asked and followed, having to use her full stride to keep up with the flurry of footsteps.

38 E.V. BANCROFT

"Text them and say you'll be taking a long weekend at home and will be back next Tuesday."

"I'll try." Lia attempted to text and walk. If her only real punishment was a trip home, she'd take it. She pressed send. "Okay, I've asked."

Her mother unlocked the car and slid into the seat as if she couldn't get away from the police station quickly enough. Almost before Lia had snapped her seat belt on, she nosed the car out of the parking spot.

"You're mixing with the wrong sorts in Bristol. It's such a hotbed of activism. I can't believe you volunteer to work for that tiny little charity of yours and give away all your income from the estate." She glanced over as Lia snapped her mouth shut. "Yes, I know about that, and I know that you live in some tiny little hovel provided by the charity rather than somewhere more appropriate. You should know that Tim is proposing that your share of the income be transferred into a capital refurbishment fund for the estate. The roof in the main hall needs replacing. He makes a good case."

Lia gripped the grab handle hard and tried to keep her voice even. "It's not his money to use; it's mine. If he didn't keep buying the latest tractor and farm equipment, he would have enough to repair the roof on his house. He could get contractors in, but no, he wants to have something he can bomb around the lanes in and show off to his mates."

"Which is part of the reason I'm in England. I need to check how things are going on the estate and reassure your father, who's sitting in France stressing about it, and that's no good for his heart."

"So you don't trust Tim either." That was a revelation. Her brother had always been the sensible and responsible one, according to the family. It was no surprise when her parents left him to run their estate when they retired to France. They were concerned she would fritter away the income and neglect the husbandry. But they were wrong. She loved the land. Gramps had instilled a love of the hills, dunes, and salt plains of the Northumberland coast in her.

She had always hoped she would live up there, amongst the

GREEN *for* LOVE

barren dunes and the castles steeped with its history of battles and flip-flopping between countries as raiders stole brides from over the border. She longed to shiver in the cold Northumbrian air, smell the salt, and throw her arms wide to the vast open skies. Going home wasn't a punishment; it was a reward.

"Cordelia, did you hear what I said?"

"Sorry, Ma, what?"

"Listen, will you? I said this is the first and only time we'll bail you out. You need to grow up and start taking your responsibilities seriously. You're very lucky that your boss is so indulgent of you; most places wouldn't let you take time off willy nilly—"

"He's also a member of No More Oil, and I work for Bristol Green Energy, an environmental charity, so in a way it is doing the work—"

"Nonsense. The charity's doing something positive. Protesting is nothing but a nuisance, and it's destructive."

"That's not true. The power of a million voices has to be heard by government. They have to change their views and do something soon to stop the climate disaster that's coming."

Her mother's tight-lipped huff signalled the end of the conversation, and she turned up the radio. For hours, they spoke only to discuss where they should stop for coffee.

During the interminable drive, Lia's mind drifted back to being hurt that Jay worked for Magenta. She was strangely sure that something could have developed between them. It was odd how many times her thoughts drifted back to her, after they had first met.

"Any new girlfriends on the horizon?" her mother asked as if she'd been listening to her thoughts.

"No, I thought there might be someone I wanted to get to know better, but it looks like it won't be going anywhere."

"You're looking for perfection, and that doesn't exist."

Okay, so her mother *had* guessed her thoughts. "Are you saying I should settle for second best?"

Her mother pulled onto the motorway again. "No, it's just that you have such an impossibly high standard."

"I want the best—my soulmate, and I'm not prepared to compromise."

Her mother's demeanour had softened over the journey, and she shot a glance at Lia that was a mix of sorrow and affection. "You might end up very lonely."

"I'm too busy with my job and my activism. I don't have time to be lonely." That wasn't entirely true. If it were, she wouldn't be obsessing over Jay. Hell, she wouldn't have been in that bar in the first place, looking for company to staunch the ebb of isolation eating at her.

"I do wish you would tone that down, dear. Or at least not get into trouble when you do it. It gives your father palpitations, and he can't afford to have another heart attack."

Lia sighed and sipped at the herbal tea she'd bought at their last stop. "Don't try and guilt trip me into stopping. It's important. The survival of the world depends on it."

"But does it have to be you?"

Lia pushed her reusable mug into the cup holder in the centre console. "We should all be doing our bit."

"But not everyone gets arrested. I know you don't believe me, but this really is the last time. Even our friends in France saw you on TV lying down in front of that ambulance. I've never been so ashamed in my life."

Lia inhaled a cleansing breath and released it slowly, imagining her anger dissipating on the puff of air. "I didn't know an ambulance was going to turn up. And I checked; it was a woman giving birth and the mother and baby were fine."

"But it was always a possibility. You still need to consider all the possibilities and consequences, Cordelia, even though you think you have the moral high ground."

Lia stared out at the passing fields. "Can we change the subject?"

GREEN *for* LOVE

"Sure."

Her mother turned up the radio again, and they sat in silence as the miles hummed by, until they pulled off the A1, not far from the main part of their estate.

Lia bundled out of the car as it pulled into the drive, hardly waiting for the engine to stop.

"Where are you going?" her mother called after her.

"I need to ground myself."

"What about saying hello to your brother and his family?"

"Tim will be out somewhere on the estate, Abby is at school, and Diana won't want to speak to me anyway. She's probably at a spa getting her nails done or shopping with her friends. I might grab a spare Barbour though and some boots. You can come with me if you like."

Her mother shook her head. "No, it's too cold. Remember I'm used to the heat of Southern France now. I'll make myself a cup of tea, sit by the fire, and read."

Lia nodded. "I'll bring in your case later." She was glad of the jacket as she walked up the long slow climb with an easterly wind blowing hard from behind her, pinching her exposed skin. In August, the hillside would be covered with the delicate pink of calluna heather, but now the landscape was bleak, partly covered with clouds sagging against the hills with latent rain. Her skin tingled with the cold, and she felt alive in a way she only could here.

She carefully weaved her way through the path to the old bird hide Gramps had built. Hundreds of migrating birds seethed in a frenzy of feeding. The entrance to the wooden bird hide was partially overgrown, indicating no one had been here for a while. She would bring Abby up here again. Sadness tightened her heart that Tim never took the time to bring his daughter to such a magical spot.

Lia stared out through the open slits and pulled out the old binoculars that had once belonged to Gramps. The outer case was scratched, but the lenses were still good and clear.

She could almost see him now, when he would smile down at her and put his fingers to his lips. She closed her eyes and let the memory take over...

He nodded towards the binoculars set up in the hide. She approached the lenses and stepped on a small box, careful not to disturb the stand. With the naked eye, she saw what looked like grass but through the binoculars, a whole new view opened up in a circle of awe. Two cygnets, all fluff and greedy mouths, peered over the side of a nest, demanding attention.

"Mute swans. They're the only ones that breed in the UK," Gramps whispered, seeming to be almost as in awe as she was. "Aren't they fabulous?"

Lia shook her head to clear the memory and wiped a tear from her cheek. Now Tim was hellbent on bringing the marginal fields into higher yield. He didn't care about leeching the soil, destroying the habitats, and displacing the wildlife. She felt so powerless, she wanted to weep. Even pouring her trust income into charities didn't assuage her guilt.

She would continue to fight him and his cronies on the deserted Northumberland sand dunes, in the boardrooms, and on the front line of the oil refineries, even if that brought her into conflict with the likes of Jay.

Chapter Seven

ANTICIPATION RIPPLED AROUND THE large conference room. Jay mentally rehearsed her speech, her first at an annual general meeting, and willed the last few shareholders to hurry through the doors so she could get on with it. Every person was having their credentials checked by bouncers who wouldn't have been out of place in a US presidential campaign. This was nerve-racking enough, but after the increase in demonstrations, they couldn't be too careful. In her peripheral vision, a willowy figure with strawberry-blond hair moved to one of the few remaining seats. Jay's heart raced, and her traitorous body throbbed. Their eyes met, and Lia glared at her. Why did she have to look so hot when she glowered like that?

Her brain caught up with what Lia's presence might mean, and a cold shiver quelled her arousal. She scribbled a quick note to Oliver. *Strawberry-blond woman in the left aisle, seat two from the back, is the agitator from the refinery.*

He looked up at Jay before turning to speak to one of the bodyguards behind him. The bodyguard spoke into his mic, and one of the bouncers at the back of the room approached Lia. Her mouth pinched, and she ruffled through her bag, pulled out some paper and showed it to him. He must have been satisfied because he retreated to his original position, speaking into his mic as he strutted in the way that only extremely muscled, taut, and fit people can do. The bodyguard whispered something to Oliver.

He shielded his lapel mic and whispered, "She's a bona fide investor."

Great, hostile investors were just what they needed. Lia threw a

44 E.V. BANCROFT

look that was pure poison. The image of Lia stretching across the bar in the private club, revealing her cleavage as her shirt stretched over her breasts flooded Jay's mind, and she licked her lips. Life could be cruel, wrapping her enemy in such a stunning package.

But she wasn't going to be intimidated, and she smiled as though completely unconcerned.

Alistair, the chair of Magenta Oil, rose and tapped the microphone. "Good afternoon, ladies and gentlemen. Welcome to the annual general meeting of Magenta Oil PLC. We have some important votes to cast today, so I'd like to get started. I will now pass you over to Oliver, our CEO, who will review the past record-breaking year," he said.

Oliver rose. When Oliver spoke, people listened, and when he entered a room, people turned towards him. It certainly helped he was over six foot, solid, and could also turn on the charm. Jay had been modelling her style on his for years. She'd become proficient at the schmoozing, though she couldn't stand the wild assumptions people made without having the requisite evidence to support their theories. It seemed to be getting worse, not only in the business world but politically, where truth and evidence counted less than optics and soundbites.

For the first hour of the meeting, everything went well, almost lulling Jay into a sense that she'd worried unnecessarily. Maybe Lia was here to gather information rather than disseminate her biased viewpoint? Jay snorted at her naivety. *Who was she kidding?*

Oliver smiled encouragingly at Jay.

"I'd like to hand over to Jay Tanner, our head of science and technology, to outline the exciting scientific research we're doing," Alistair said.

Jay inhaled and stood, hoping her trembling knees wouldn't be obvious. The round of smattered applause surprised her. "Thank you. As the chair said, we're working to net-zero by 2040–"

"That's too late. We need to make changes now to stop the planet from boiling over into catastrophe. We can't continue

GREEN *for* LOVE

business as usual," Lia shouted.

Her chair scraped as she stood, rending the peace and grabbing all the attention, as people twisted in their seats to stare.

Damn you. "We're working hard to make changes, and we will expedite them. We've been exploring fuel efficiency and the use of hydrogen in vehicles—"

"Fuel efficiency is like trying to row the Titanic. You need to stop investment in fossil fuels."

There was a scatter of applause, presumably from Lia's friends and other hostile investors. Jay didn't want this to devolve into a slanging match. "We're also exploring biofuels—"

"They take up land that's needed for food," Lia said loudly.

Security guards surrounded her, ready to throw her out if she created chaos. Oliver would hate that optic. If they acted against Lia now, it would look like they were silencing the opposition.

Jay pressed her fingers against the white-clothed table in front of them to stop her hands shaking. "If you know your history, you'll find that at the time of horsepower, one of the four crop rotations was for animal feed, used to power transport and agriculture. So up to twenty-five percent of land has historically been used for energy." They were slipping into a tit for tat argument, and there seemed to be nothing she could do to stop herself from engaging and slipping to Lia's level.

Oliver stood. "I suggest that Jay heads up a working committee with relevant external stakeholders to research alternatives and how feasible it is to bring forward the net-zero timeline. I invite our eloquent shareholder to join that working committee. Please leave your contact details at the back of the room if you would like to be involved, and we'll contact you. Now, I suggest we move forward to the next item on the agenda."

Jay slumped in her seat, her cheeks burning. Oliver had been forced to hijack her presentation to keep things on track *and* had dumped a ton of extra work onto her. A working committee with external stakeholders was a sensible idea, but how was she supposed to work with Lia when they approached the world so differently? Despite her misgivings, her heart pulsed faster at the thought.

"Next item on the agenda. Purchase of land for development," Alistair said.

"What does that mean, development? Do you mean renewable energy or not?" Lia asked.

Alistair focused his attention on her. "As it is stated in the meeting notes, each site will be evaluated on its own merits, and then the optimum strategy will be followed. That is an operational matter to be decided by the board."

"You're just green-washing. You have no intention of developing renewable energy—"

"Thank you for your comments. We welcome your input in the working committee, where these items can be thrashed out in detail. In the meantime, I'd like to keep to the agenda. Thank you."

Surprisingly, Lia kept quiet, whether that was because Alistair had promised her a say or because the nearby bouncers were intimidating her, Jay didn't know, but she was glad for the reprieve. Her body thrummed to see Lia again, even if it would only be to verbally clash swords. She schooled a neutral expression for the rest of the meeting, belying her heart skipping like an excitable child.

How could she still want to see more of Lia when she had just embarrassed her? Her head had no answer, but her heart pulsed hard and fast. No, that wasn't true. She admired Lia's courage to hold fast to her convictions, to stand up for what she believed in, to have such passionate beliefs. It was so much more direct and honest than everyone else she dealt with.

Of course, that was going to make working with her as much fun as working with an angry snake in a cage.

Chapter Eight

Three weeks later.

JAY TAPPED HER NAILS on the desk. How dare the damn woman be late after having made such a fuss at the AGM? Everyone else was here, even Professor Ian McBride. She warmed to him immediately when he held her gaze and didn't play the normal handshake war, vying for dominance. He merely shook her hand with respect and equality.

The strains of Malaguena echoed through her brain from the paso doble dance she learned at her dancing class last night. Their dance teacher had said it was like a bullfight, and with the fast strings and quick tempo, she could believe it. Her dance partner and friend, Adam, had been particularly flamboyant as he stamped his feet like a matador. She smiled at the memory, but it faded when the conference room door banged open and Lia strode in, glowering with a scowl as intense as any classical guitar player.

"I did not expect to be molested on my way in by your so-called security," Lia said.

Her eyes flashed in a way that was seductive, and the spark rippled down to Jay's core. Lia's unapologetic confidence and passion was hot, and Jay felt a twinge of envy that she would never have that innate power. But this was her workplace, where she had earned her power. "You can't blame them after the scene you caused at the oil refinery and in the AGM. They have to be sure you're not going to throw paint or glue yourself to a wall." Jay kept her tone cool and professional. This was her domain, and she was in charge.

Lia slammed down into an empty seat. "Your chair invited me to make a contribution. You should hold your attack dogs off."

Lia was like the bull that made a pass at the cape but failed to make contact. "Fine, I'll speak to them afterwards and assure them that you'll be a calmly contributing member of this process." She waited a beat as Lia's eyes narrowed. "Now, can we get on? You should have read the scope of the committee. We need to agree on a report which I'll present to the board. Are there any comments before we open discussions for alternative research areas?"

Lia tapped the pencil on the notebook provided in an agitated beat, taut and ready to pounce at the first opportunity.

"You said the intention is to be net-zero by 2040. That's too late to hold back the temperature rise and all the climate change that's already in progress. I'll send through links to scientific research papers as that's the only thing that will satisfy Ms Tanner." She glared at Jay before addressing the room again. "There's going to be mass migration, drought, and food shortages. Oil companies have a responsibility to stop all fossil fuels and find alternatives now."

Lia gesticulated wildly as she spoke, creating a vortex that was sucking the others in. Lia's passion was a powerful pull on a physical level. She was equal parts interesting, intriguing, and infuriating.

Jay cleared her throat. "We're looking at alternatives, but currently there is insufficient infrastructure to provide all transport through electric vehicles. Besides, there's a shortage of the resources needed for EV batteries. And we need plastics for many uses, including medical and food packaging. Aviation doesn't have a viable alternative fuel source yet, so we can't simply stop production of fossil fuels with no proven and sustainable replacement."

Jay stared at Lia, whose mouth was clamped into a hard thin line. This was like the dance last night, circling around the counterarguments. She almost expected Lia to stamp her feet in anger.

"If I may cut in?" Ian asked. "We should be aiming for net-zero

GREEN *for* LOVE

as soon as possible."

A flash of anger forced Jay to breathe in sharply to regain her composure. She wasn't being fair to Ian; his input was reasonable and the kind she welcomed. Perhaps she was more agitated by Lia's presence than she liked to admit. Jay turned to Ian and smiled. "While that's laudable, if Magenta stopped producing all fossil fuels, the shortfall would be filled by other companies using dirtier fuel and who don't have our values. Despite what you may think," Jay caught Lia's gaze, "we are ethical and transparent, unlike many of our competitors. We've redirected resources to improve items such as carbon capture and storage and increased fuel efficiency. My favourite is hydrogen fuel, which produces water vapour and warm air as waste products." She raised her hand when it looked like Lia was about to interrupt. "And I know we need the infrastructure, but it's more convenient than electric battery cells for cars because it only takes about five minutes to refuel. We should be seeking to spread hydrogen fuel around the country."

Ian nodded. "But you have to use about six times as much electricity to produce hydrogen as you do for electric batteries."

He was what they were hoping for: thoughtful and challenging.

"Exactly, and that's why we're researching how to improve the efficiency of the hydrogen fuel."

Andrea, another shareholder, raised her hand. "Do I understand this right? You could produce hydrogen using fossil fuels, and it would be cheaper than using solar. Is that correct?" Andrea frowned when Jay nodded. "So, what's to stop Magenta using fossil fuels to produce hydrogen and pretend that it's clean energy—"

"Quite." Lia smacked her hand on the desk. "Greenwashing, as I thought."

Jay gripped her pen. "No. We're only using blue and green hydrogen for this research. We *do* have integrity."

Lia clearly didn't believe her. Not wishing to stare into her eyes, Jay scanned the other committee members with a forced smile.

"We're happy to hear other suggestions for areas to research and develop in the next few years, so we can become net-zero as soon as possible. I'm happy to come and visit projects that are up and running to see what's being done."

Ian handed over a list of areas to consider.

Lia raised one eyebrow. "Seriously? You'd come out of your ivory tower and actually see what's making the difference on the ground?"

Challenge accepted. "I'd be delighted." Each time she and Lia made eye contact, there was a spark of passion, anger, and arousal intermingled. There seemed a connection between them, like a tether, although that was ridiculous woo woo and the kind of thing Lia might say.

If Lia would soften her adamant intensity, Jay was sure they could work together well. If only she could harness the tempest that was Cordelia Armstrong-Forde.

Chapter Nine

LIA STORMED OUT OF the building, glad to escape the self-satisfied smugness of the other committee members. She rushed to the Underground, her footsteps slapping on the pavement and her bangles jangling like discordant wind chimes. "Bloody woman," she said to Christian when he answered her call.

"Good afternoon to you too. I take it the meeting didn't go well?"

Lia ignored the amusement in his tone. She increased her pace, adopting the standard London speed of fast and intense. "It was fine, but there was a lot of grandstanding and greenwashing. All 'Magenta has integrity and is transparent and is looking to be net-zero by 2040.' I said that would be too late, but they came up with all the usual bullshit about not being able to stop now because other companies with less integrity would simply fill the gap."

"That's probably true."

Tightness gripped Lia's temples. "Whose side are you on? They need to stop *now*." Lia stepped around a newspaper vendor and down into the bowels of steaming humanity. The Tube wasn't the most pleasant way to travel, but it was currently the most ecologically friendly. "I'm going into the Tube now, so the signal might drop out."

"Sure. Before I forget, I need you to attend a meeting next Tuesday with the council on making Bristol homes draught-free."

She swiped her Oyster card. "Sorry, Christian, no can do. I have another No More Oil planning day."

He took a sharp intake of breath. "Lia, I need you to do your work. The work we pay you for here at the charity: the one you're supposed to be an employee of. The trustees are on my case about the amount of time you're spending on activities. Your last TV appearance didn't go down well."

A slight unease fluttered in her stomach. She never thought Christian would challenge her; he agreed with what she was doing, which was why she'd worked with him in the first place. "At least people are talking about the real issues. And by investing in the major oil companies, we can disrupt company meetings. Do you think they know their dividends are used to fund the activism? I love the irony that they're paying to have us glued to the gates."

"Not all publicity is good publicity."

His response was too quick, as if he'd had this discussion with someone else and been fed the words. Part of her felt sorry for him. She wasn't an easy person to manage, but this issue was too big to be silent, easy, and compromising. Sometimes, you had to do the uncomfortable to make the change. Better a few minutes' discomfort than a lifetime of regret for inaction. "We're approaching a tipping point in public opinion. I'm happy to arrange a meeting with the council on another day, and you know I always make up the hours."

"It's not only the time, although having you here during the hours you signed up for would be nice. The trustees are petrified the charity name will be dragged through the media—"

She pounded down the stairs to the platform, heading for the optimum position for the doors. "But we're doing great work raising funds to upgrade the ancient housing stock."

"I know that, Lia, and you're brilliant at extracting cash from the wealthy."

Lia's train arrived with a hum of the rails and a swoosh as the doors opened. She boarded and squashed herself in, pulling her scarf over her face to limit the smell of other people crushed against her. "Yeah, it helps to have contacts." The signal dropped as the train entered the deep tunnels.

The meeting had been better than she expected. Several times,

GREEN *for* LOVE

she caught Jay watching her, and arousal had stirred in response. Jay was wrong in so many ways, but she was impressive and sexy in her power suit. She'd worn a red jacket, possibly to emphasise her dominance. Would she be dominant in bed, or was she just a little mouse? Lia smiled as she clung to the overhead straps of the carriage. It would be interesting to find out. There was an undeniable buzz between them, something more than just sexual chemistry.

Lia closed her eyes and tried to ground herself, not easy in a swaying carriage. She imagined the energy of her chakras responding when she pictured Jay. There was definitely red and orange, but as she made her way up her spine, the one that resonated most was green, the heart chakra. That equal mix of blue and yellow, sky and sun, the fresh new approach, and it sometimes meant love. No, that was ridiculous. Jay was infuriating and wrong, and her values were all messed up. It must be the fresh approach. Jay challenged her. Yes, that was more likely.

Lia rolled her shoulders. The train stopped at the next station to let a swarm of passengers off and on. The doors closed, and the seething mass of bodies settled to fill the space. It always surprised her how people could be so quiet when commuting, but their emotions leaked out in energetic waves. Anxiety, anger, anticipation all crowded in on her, invading her emotional space. She closed her eyes again, shutting out the world and people's energies, imagining she was in an impenetrable glass dome. The emotions dimmed, and she could breathe again.

Why was she still drawn to Jay despite them being on opposite sides? To be fair, Jay had chaired the committee meeting well, letting everyone have their turn, and she'd listened to Lia's point of view. But Lia wasn't interested in gentle words. She wanted action and results. She wouldn't trust Jay or Magenta as far as she could throw them, and subsequently, she couldn't seriously contemplate doing anything with Jay, however appealing.

Perhaps while she was on the committee, she would tone down

her activities and stay in the background, for the sake of a little peace between them. Not because she'd actually backed down, of course, but as a little node to Jay's silence over her balloon-bombing. She imagined getting a nod of approval. There was something about the way Jay had looked over her dark-rimmed glasses to fix Lia with a stare that had made Lia's insides melt. She still felt like a puddle, and it wasn't from the heat in the carriage.

"Paddington, next stop."

She was looking forward to going back to Bristol and organising Jay's visit as part of the fact-finding mission for the committee. The prospect of having time with Jay had her energy quivering in anticipation. Maybe there were more advantages to being on this committee. She could do a two-pronged attack by sending links to the impacts of climate change and by having direct input onto the committee. Now that she had Jay's work email, she had access to her. Getting to know Jay a bit better was certainly a major benefit. Not that she'd ever let on. Much better to keep her cool. Her heart did a little happy dance that she could discover more about Jay without seeming keen or interested.

Chapter Ten

JAY SMILED WHEN SHE saw Lia waiting at Bristol Temple Meads train station. At the committee meeting, Lia had warned her to wear old clothes as they were visiting some allotments and old houses belonging to the poor.

"People will be suspicious of someone dressed in full-on business attire. You need to dress down. Can you do that?"

Patronising git. If only Lia knew that Jay had been brought up wearing charity shop clothing that her mum had to shorten and take in long before such things were trendy.

Jay wore black jeans, trainers, and a turtleneck top under her walking jacket, and she hoped it struck the right note between professional and appropriate. Adam had said she looked good, and he was her go-to consultant on all things fashion-related. Also, if they were going to stand outside at an allotment, it could get very cold. She reminded herself this wasn't a date but an opportunity to collect evidence from which she could make recommendations to take back to the committee.

The doors opened, and Jay stepped off the train, wariness and excitement warring for dominance.

"Hi. I hope you're happy to walk in those, they might get dirty." Lia pointed at Jay's brand-new designer trainers.

Clearly she wasn't one for niceties or chitchat.

"I'm fine." Jay hitched her rucksack onto her back. "I enjoy walking, and I get out into the country when I can." Not in her exclusive Lavair trainers though. Maybe she should've worn her tatty tennis shoes; they would have been more in keeping with Lia's footwear.

"You do?" Lia asked.

Jay nodded. "When I was at university, I did a few of the long-distance walks, like the Ridgeway and the Pembrokeshire coast path. I don't get much time now."

"Too busy making money?"

If they were going to spend the whole day together, she hoped Lia would be less hostile. Maybe a little honesty would bridge the gap. "No. Most of my spare time is taken up looking after my mum, who's in a wheelchair. I take off one evening a week to go ballroom dancing."

Lia's eyes widened, and she blushed, perhaps with shame or embarrassment. "Sorry, that was uncalled for," she said softly.

"Yes, it was. If we're going to make the most of the day, perhaps we could drop the judgement and enjoy being outside and in each other's company. You seemed to like me when we met the first time."

"That was before I knew who you were," Lia said.

"You don't know who I am, Lia." Jay closed her eyes and counted to ten. This was going to be a difficult day. "Let's get going."

Lia spun around and led them out of the station to a bus stop. Her hair bounced around her shoulders and glinted more coppery in the morning light as she flounced down the street like she was in an advert for a hair product. Jay had to stop objectifying her. Her outer shell belied a radical heart, and although Lia believed in her goals with an admirable passion and tenacity, Jay couldn't condone the methods she used to raise their profile or the narrowness with which she viewed the issues. She was stubborn, and Jay knew what that looked like. She'd been called it many times, although she preferred to describe it as strong-willed.

At the bus stop, the electronic display showed there was a three-minute wait for the next bus.

"If you like nature, I don't understand why you work for an evil company."

"Magenta isn't evil. It's open and ethical, and my job is to look at

GREEN *for* LOVE

future-proofing the business by researching new technologies and eco-friendly solutions. How is that evil? We could only be focusing on the bottom line, on heinously high profits for the shareholders, and million-pound salaries for the execs. But we don't."

Lia waved her hand. "There won't be a future if you continue to drill for oil. If you really wanted to prove you weren't driven by money, you'd leave and find another job."

Jay swallowed her anger before responding in as measured a tone as she could muster. "It's much easier to affect change from the inside. Oliver and I have altered the company's direction, and Magenta has the influence and the capital to invest in new technologies. Besides, Magenta is all I've ever known—"

"That might've been fine when you were younger, but what are you, a couple of years older than me? Forty?"

"Forty-three, and age has nothing to do with it. I work hard, and yes, I earn a good salary. But I've got two large mortgages so I can pay for my mum's place as well. I shouldn't have to justify myself to you. *I've* worked for everything I have." She sucked her cheeks in and blew out a breath. She *was* justifying herself, but Lia should know that she was more than just her job.

Lia shrugged. "There are other well-paid jobs."

God, she was like an infuriating looping TikTok rant. No matter what Jay said, she didn't seem to listen. What was the point? Lia held her hand up, and the bus stopped to let them on. Surprisingly, Lia paid for them both. They sat down beside each other, and Jay inhaled Lia's woody perfume. She was instantly aware of Lia's lithe hips pressing against hers, causing a buzzing below the surface where they touched. *Focus.* She couldn't be sidetracked by her libido.

Jay cleared her throat. "Like I said, I feel strongly about the environment, in a different way from you, obviously, but we're making constructive solutions, and we don't have to lie down in front of ambulances to make our point and get things to happen."

Lia flushed. "That was an unintentional consequence. Without those kinds of demonstrations, you wouldn't be talking to me now."

I almost wish I wasn't. "That's not true. You were invited onto the committee because you're a shareholder, and we want to explore other opportunities. Otherwise, I wouldn't be here with you on a Friday morning when I could be doing a million other things. So maybe instead of attacking my career choices, you could tell me about the projects you're working on."

Lia had the grace to look slightly sheepish before her eyes gleamed, and she seemed to shift from wary to enthusiastic. It was fascinating to watch, like a chameleon, except they normally tried to fit in with their surroundings, and Lia seemed to want to stand out.

"First of all, we're going to visit local houses where we've organised a draught-proofing project. Did you know that the UK has the draughtiest housing stock in Europe? Did you get the link to the *Guardian* article I sent through? What we're doing is a step further than roof insulation. We employ ex-prisoners and the long-term unemployed to carry out the work. Most of them are grateful for the new start, and we've had lots of other people ask if they can join."

Lia chattered on with passion and earnestness throughout the journey, and Jay marvelled at her transformation from hostile to engaging. Jay's gaze was drawn to her lips and hands as she gesticulated.

"Here's our stop," Lia said and hurried to the front.

Jay swung her backpack over her shoulder and rushed to join her on the pavement. They approached a concrete tower block tagged with obscenities and entered the lobby. A chain hung across the metal doors of the elevator, with a handmade sign indicating it was out of order. Lia sighed and walked up the stairs, and Jay followed. The waft of stale urine and spicy cooking, shouting from within apartments, too-loud televisions, and the exposed corridors that let in grime and cold—all of it slammed into her like slivers of shattered memory.

GREEN *for* LOVE

On the third floor, Lia stopped and knocked. There was a shuffling behind the door and the hacking cough of someone who sounded like they were on fifty cigarettes a day.

"Who is it?"

"Lia Armstrong."

Interesting that the full name had been dropped and even her accent seemed less pronounced. So maybe she was a chameleon, trying to fit in. Who was the real Lia?

The chain scraped, and a woman's face appeared in the crack of the door. The door shut again, and the chain rattled as it was drawn back. She didn't open the door fully, but enough, like a slender entry to a cave. It looked so dark inside, and Jay had to take a steadying breath against old emotions.

"Hi, Elsie. I brought you some carrots from the allotment, and I've brought Jay Tanner to show her the draught-proofing work we've done. I messaged you yesterday." Lia proffered the paper bag she'd been carrying then turned to Jay. "Elsie was instrumental in setting up our community allotment, but she can't work on it now. She's still suffering from long-COVID and gets tired if she does any physical work."

Jay peered into the gloom and looked straight into the bright eyes of the slightly stooped woman. "I'm sorry to hear that, Elsie. If it's not convenient for you today, we can come another time."

Elsie coughed again but not as brutally as before. "Come in. Today's fine. It's not as if I'm going anywhere."

Jay stepped in behind Lia after she'd caught her look of surprise. Clearly, Lia didn't expect her to be nice, or respectful, or kind. Talk about prejudiced. The television was on, with *Escape to The Country* booming too loud.

"Lovely to meet you. My mum loves this programme. Sorry to disturb you. I hope it's not a nuisance," Jay said.

"Not at all. Any friend of Lia's is a friend of mine."

She wouldn't go that far. Lia could barely be civil, let alone friendly.

E.V. BANCROFT

"Cheers for the carrots," Elsie said. "You can't beat them fresh with the soil still on. They last longer if you don't wash them till you need them."

"I can believe it."

Lia smiled at Elsie with an indulgence that made Jay wonder if they had this conversation regularly. Why couldn't Lia treat Jay with the same respect and warmth? Underneath the external, rather delicious package was a complex intriguing woman that Jay would like to get to know better. Not for the sex, but because she warmed to this kind, considerate woman, so different from the screaming harridan who demanded immediate and impossible action.

She preferred Lia's fire that warmed and shed light, rather than the conflagration that raged and destroyed, but it was all part of her. Though what Jay preferred was irrelevant. Theirs was a working relationship, nothing more.

Normally, Jay was so cool and objective, but being close to Lia had her skin tingling with nervous energy, and she was unsure whether it was the allure of the unobtainable or the appeal of the inappropriate. She wiped her glasses on her turtleneck and replaced them, needing to shift her thoughts. She concentrated as Lia showed her the industrial sealant and the draught excluder around all the windows.

"We've set up a community energy scheme. There are solar panels on the roof and an energy storage unit in the basement. It can't supply the needs of all the residents, but it's helping to reduce the reliance on the grid. We've also done a deal to purchase only green electric, and we checked the companies' credentials, before you ask. I don't believe in greenwashing."

A ghost of a smile crossed Lia's face, and she lit up in a delightful way that pulled Jay in, but she was here to do a job. Jay never had problems focusing on the task, and she wasn't going to start now.

"Outside, we have a solar-panelled car port and an electric, communal city car."

On the estate where Jay grew up, a communal car was what

GREEN *for* LOVE

the local gang used as a getaway car. She shuddered, her heart going out to Elsie. Thank goodness her own mum didn't have to live this way anymore.

Lia turned to Elsie when she'd finished her tour. Jay was impressed by the facts and statistics Lia rolled off. She might be overzealous, but she knew what she was talking about.

"Thank you so much, Elsie. I'll see if there are any potatoes ready next time I come, and I'll do some reiki healing on you too," Lia said and headed to the door.

Jay held back her laughter. Surely Lia wasn't being serious. You didn't heal long-COVID by waving your hands around someone's body.

"Thank you, dear. Lovely to see you and your friend," Elsie said.

Jay nodded, unable to speak without scoffing. Maybe whatever the healing entailed helped a lonely old woman, but why not be honest and admit it was about the comfort of human touch, which was scientifically proven, rather than dress it up in some ridiculous trickery? She sighed. *Civil. Be civil. She doesn't have to think like you.* "She's a sweetie," Jay said as they made their way to ground level, their footsteps echoing on the bare concrete stairs.

Lia nodded. "She is. She used to love spending her time in the allotment. She only goes when the weather is nice now, when she can take a picnic and stay all day."

"I wish we'd had an allotment when I was growing up," Jay said quietly. The cramped living conditions, the noise and feel of this place, and the stench of poverty had thrown her back into her childhood.

"What do you mean?" Lia asked.

"I grew up on an estate much like this." The revelation made her blink and mentally kick herself for revealing too much, leaving her exposed for Lia to peck at like some vicious crow.

"So you've worked hard to escape," Lia said.

Jay thought she caught the slightest hint of admiration, though it might have been wishful thinking. Unwanted tears formed at the back of her eyes, and she blinked them away. This visit had touched on emotions she thought were deeply hidden in the recesses of her mind. But she wasn't in that place anymore and neither was her mum. She stiffened and drew in a deep breath. "What's next?"

"We're off to the country to see a solar company and solar park." Lia smiled. "It's about a three mile walk from the bus stop."

"All the more reason to have transport, whether that's petrol, electric, or hydrogen. Who has two hours to waste walking there and back?"

Lia raised an eyebrow. "Too wimpy to walk?"

They locked eyes, and the spark between them returned, like two rivals eyeing each other up before a chess match, pitting their wits against each other. Lia had made her opening gambit, and Jay matched her with her pawn. "No, but I do have a train to catch back to London this evening, so you'll need to keep up."

A slight smile flickered at Lia's lips. "I'm taller than you."

"I'm a fast walker, like most Londoners."

"Fine, let's pick up the pace then."

Lia strode towards the bus stop, her bangles jangling and her green skirts billowing out like sheets on washing day. Jay lengthened her stride to keep up, not wishing to concede any advantage Lia may have with her extra height.

They were quiet on the bus, and Jay mulled over what she'd seen. The work of Lia's charity was impressive and what they were doing on a micro scale was making a difference to people's lives, like Elsie, who'd said her bills had dropped even though energy prices were increasing. That was a real win. And Lia had been kind, thoughtful, and knowledgeable, showing the different layers to her personality, the warm sandstone as well as the hard volcanic rock, and Jay had to admit she liked them all.

When they stepped off the bus, Lia set off at a fast walk down a lane without looking back. There was no way Jay was going to allow Lia to beat her. She overtook her, smiling as she accelerated past. It was worth it just to see Lia's wide eyes.

GREEN *for* LOVE

Lia quirked an eyebrow at Jay, then increased her pace and retook the lead.

"Who do you think you are, Lewis Hamilton?" Jay called. "If you even know who he is."

Lia swung around. "Of course I know who he is. Formula One is one of the worst offenders because it glamorises fossil fuel consumption."

"There's an electric formula for cars, and Formula One has been great for technological innovation." Jay shot past again, practically at Olympic walking speed. They must have looked a sight, two middle-aged women competing like they were on the school playground, but she didn't care.

Lia jogged past her, her shoes slapping on the pavement. "The Nazis sponsored technological innovation too. That doesn't make them good people," she said.

Jay increased into a jog and matched Lia's pace so she could talk as they ran. It was wonderful to stretch her legs; it had been forever since she'd been on a run, and she couldn't remember the last time she'd done this in the countryside. She changed her stride to the lope of a long-distance runner, grateful she'd elected for trainers and not caring if they got muddy. "Are you against all technological change? If so, you may as well live in a cave."

"No, of course not. But I hate that the only measure is economic growth. There should be environmental impact and social impact measures too."

"I agree," Jay said.

Lia turned her head. "You do?"

"Yes, of course. We should be held accountable for long-term impacts and for non-financials."

Lia scowled and edged her pace up a little. "That isn't what Magenta says."

"No, but Oliver and I have been discussing how we can incorporate all of that into quarterly reports. Unfortunately, the CFO and his son aren't keen." Immediately, she wished she hadn't said anything. It was no secret, and there *had* been a press release about exploring the options. Was it a betrayal of Oliver and Magenta? There were moments when it was easy to forget that Lia was considered the enemy.

As if Lia had also had the same thought, she started to run faster. Damn her graceful and beautiful long legs. She was like a gazelle—if a gazelle wore trainers and a skirt. Lia pulled ahead, so Jay held her backpack straps and sped up. "I wish I'd put a sports bra on," she said as she pulled level again.

Lia grinned after taking a long look at her breasts. "Do you want to slow down?"

"Not at all. I can keep this up all day, despite the obvious impediments."

"Wonderful impediments they are too," Lia said.

"Thanks." Jay caught sight of a blush burning Lia's cheeks. There was no way Jay could maintain this run without the proper clothing. Her ample breasts moving on the offbeat were too uncomfortable. She clasped her arms over her chest. Damn her if they weren't going to run all the way there.

For the next couple of miles, there was nothing but the sound of birdsong and the even rhythm of their trainers on the lane. It was beautiful to see the different spring greens and catch the whiff of fresh air. The slight breeze cooled the sweat gathering in drips on her forehead and her back, especially where her backpack clung to her shirt. Lia was obviously fit, and running in a skirt didn't seem to bother her at all. She'd just pulled the material up so she didn't trip. Jay wondered if Lia knew she had a constellation of freckles on both her calves... her taut, muscular calves. Were her legs as smooth to touch as they looked? What was she thinking? She shouldn't be looking.

Jay saw a sign advertising Solar Solutions. Through the wooden gates, there were a couple of buildings, one of which looked like a timber-clad home and the other, an office or workshop. Both gleamed with banks of photovoltaic tiled roofs. Lia increased her

GREEN *for* LOVE

speed again, and Jay pushed herself to keep up until they both arrived at the glass door, puffing and laughing.

Lia touched first and did a little victory dance. "Beat you."

"Only because you have longer gorilla arms," Jay said.

Lia grinned. "That was fun. Thank you for being a good sport."

"I love to run, but usually without luggage and when I'm wearing proper attire." She didn't miss Lia's appreciative glance again.

"I was wearing a skirt. Don't try playing the 'I would've won if I'd worn a decent bra' trick with me."

They laughed and locked gazes. Lia was so close, staring into her eyes. It was there again, that pull, like they had a covalent bond between them, sharing an electron that wanted to draw them together into a singular molecule.

Lia blinked. "I don't know about you, but I'm very sweaty."

"You mean you don't normally run here?"

"No, I come by bike. Sometimes I use the community Nissan Leaf."

Of course she did. That made sense, but why hadn't she offered to transport them around in that all day? It would've been much easier than the schlep to the different sites. Jay suspected it was bloody-mindedness to prove a point, or dare she think that it was so they could spend more time together? "I don't suppose they have a shower?"

"No, sorry. If we have time, we could stop by my place and shower, although you said you have a train to catch."

Jay was unsure whether it was a thrill or the cool breeze on her sweaty body that made her shiver. She was intrigued to know where Lia lived. A cottage with a large garden and lots of vegetables maybe? She'd bet money on Lia being a vegetarian. "Can we take a rain check this time? Thanks for the offer."

"You're welcome," Lia said.

Lia stepped back, and their connection fizzled. This couldn't just be one way, surely? Jay needed to focus; she'd never been to a business meeting quite so sweaty and unprepared. She smoothed down her hair and wiped her glasses with her sweater, which felt way too hot after her run. But she couldn't exactly strip off.

Lia pushed the door open. "Hi, Noor. We've got a meeting with Gavin. Is he free yet?"

The woman at the desk nodded towards the door as she continued to type. Anyone who could touch-type properly was impressive. Jay was very much a hunt and peck typist.

They entered an office that was light and airy, all glass and golden timber. Sunlight filtered through leaves outside, dappling a greenish glow in the room. The aroma of sawn timber scented the air and gave the place a serene feel.

Gavin crossed the room and kissed Lia on both cheeks. His face creased into a genuine smile. "Lia, lovely to see you. So, this is your visitor. Ms Tanner, is it?"

He put his huge hand into Jay's for a vigorous handshake and gave her a similar, welcoming smile.

"Welcome to Solar House. As you can see, our whole building is designed to be a comfortable working environment and to generate more energy than it consumes. We have fully integrated photovoltaic panels and roof lights." He pointed to the ceiling where light streamed in. "Did you notice the meter when you entered? That shows the energy we're producing at any time."

His enthusiasm was contagious, and Jay found herself being swept along as they toured the facilities, and he pointed out how they blended in with the surroundings.

"This is the future for office buildings and houses. We've also retrofitted many homes, farms, and factories." He brought them back to a conference room, and they all sat. "I understand you work for Magenta Oil."

Jay nodded and stiffened in her seat, waiting for the admonition and judgement to come hailing down.

"Is it true that you're researching alternative fuel sources?"

"Yes." She relaxed her shoulders a little and explained what she was working on. "It's about following the science, looking at the

GREEN *for* LOVE

whole life cycle and realising it can't be done instantly. Everything needs to be planned, and tested, and measured." She couldn't resist the subtle dig at Lia who seemed to want everything halted immediately without considering the consequences for jobs, the economy, and modern living. Or rather, she didn't care about the consequences.

Gavin nodded. Lia didn't respond, as though she was absorbing it all, perhaps gathering information to make the next attack. Unless she'd decided to give Jay a chance. Maybe now was a good time to impart the information she wanted to register with Lia. "Magenta is planning to install the first hydrogen pumps into ten fuel stations early next year. Before you ask, it will be blue hydrogen, with the intention of eventually swapping to green hydrogen." Jay grinned at the look of surprise on Lia's face.

"Really?" Lia asked.

"I told you that we're looking to futureproof the business *and* the future. So there is a plan." Jay smiled. Lia stared at her and half returned the smile with a slight uptick in her lips, her eyes boring into her own as if trying to pan for the truth.

They may not be lovers, but if they could move from enemies to friends enjoying banter, that was real progress, and Jay would take it with open arms.

Chapter Eleven

GAVIN TURNED TO LIA. "When would you like that lift home and back to the station for Jay?"

She smiled at him, wishing he hadn't been so obvious, not wanting to admit the plan was to cadge a lift back. Because they had run, there hadn't been the opportunity to point out the environmental features along the way. Ah well. Next time. She shook her head. Who was she kidding? There would be no next time.

Lia had enjoyed seeing another side to Jay, one that was kind to people. Lia had been surprised to find out she had a disadvantaged background. Guilt and admiration tugged at Lia's heart. There was far more to Jay than she first thought. She'd listened with interest and asked intelligent questions, which Lia had expected, but she'd also spoken to Elsie as an equal, when Lia had assumed she would be arrogant and condescending. Perhaps she could accept that Jay had good intentions, even if she was still wrong.

"Would you like to come back for a shower before your train home? My flat isn't far from the station, and now that we're taking a car back, we'll be saving a bit of that time you were so worried about."

The wide-eyed expression on Jay's face almost made Lia laugh, and Jay didn't respond immediately.

"Okay, yes, please. My friend Adam is going to check in on my mum tonight, so I have a late pass. He talks to her about *Strictly Come Dancing* and *EastEnders* so she's happy, although Adam spends most of his time dreaming he's dancing with the guys on the show."

Lia warmed to Jay dropping personal details into the conversation. She would love to get her hands on her birth chart so she could find out so much more. "Great. If you're free now then, Gavin, should we go?"

He nodded, and they walked out of the building towards the company van. The three of them sat on the bench seat in the front.

"It fits standard solar panels in the back," Gavin said. "We've been retrofitting a number of industrial buildings, a strategy which has huge potential."

"Would solar be able to supply all the electric needs of a big industrial plant?" Jay asked.

"Not normally, no, but with additional support on batteries and heat pumps, we can get to net-zero and even carbon negative in some cases. We're working with companies to make them SBTi net-zero compliant."

"That's *Scientific* Based Targets initiative," Lia said.

Jay gave a tight smile then she turned to stare out of the side window. "Yes, I know."

By the way Jay gripped the door handle, Lia had pushed her too far. She nudged her slightly, and Jay turned towards her, frown lines causing furrows between her eyes deep enough to plant carrots. Lia smiled. "I wasn't trying to patronise you. I wanted you to know that I understand the science too."

Jay's frown softened, warming Lia's heart. And those eyes, so intense and sharp, almost stopped Lia's breath.

Jay blinked. "What you've shown me today is impressive, but it's such small scale. To be effective, it needs to be rolled out nationwide. That won't happen unless there's the political will to change—"

She started to wind up like a spring again. "Maybe if politicians weren't in the pockets of the oil lobby, they would actually do the right thing—"

Jay held up her hand. "What I was going to say is that political will needs to be changed from all sides, internally, and through

GREEN *for* LOVE

lobbying, and from the general public. But alienating everyone by guerrilla tactics won't help."

Rather than explode with the torrent of invective that gushed up from her gut, Lia centred herself. "We'll have to disagree on that, because it's only through mass movements being kept in the headlines that change happens."

Jay shook her head. "The only way? No. All interested parties need to work together to effect change."

"I agree, Jay," Gavin said. "We need to roll out nationally and internationally. If you have any sway, please try and change the minds of the powers that be."

Jay smiled at Gavin, and Lia wanted it directed at her too. What was happening? She was always the strong, confident one—some would say cocky—but her fiery self was being cooled by Jay's logical, genuine responses. "I've halted my radical activism for the duration of the committee," Lia whispered.

Jay's face brightened, and she stared into Lia's eyes. It dawned on her that she wanted Jay's approval. She stared ahead, confused, surprised at herself, and yet pleased she had revealed something personal too. "That doesn't mean I agree with what Magenta is doing though. We need to stop all fossil fuels now," she said, needing to re-establish herself at the top.

Jay shook her head. "That isn't practical, but we're working towards it as you'll see when you come to the research lab."

Lia was fully aware they seemed to be repeating the same conversation. But she'd keep having it until change became inevitable, even if it made her frustrating. Even if she lost out on cultivating something with Jay because they couldn't see eye to eye. But as she looked at Jay, who was smiling as they passed a herd of deer, a tiny niggle at the back of her mind wondered if that cost might be awfully high.

***

When Lia opened the door, her heart sank as she realised how untidy and tiny her place was. Familiarity caused indifference. It was very different seeing it through someone else's eyes. And despite everything, she wanted Jay to be impressed, although she didn't want to inquire too closely into her motives for wanting Jay's approval. She snatched up a discarded towel and stuffed it in the laundry basket. "Sorry about the mess. I didn't expect a guest tonight."

Jay shrugged. "No problem. I have a small, one-bedroom flat in London, so I know about space constraints."

Lia crossed the room in three strides. "Herbal tea? The shower is through there. I'll get you a clean towel. Do you need a change of clothes?"

Jay flushed a little. "Maybe a T-shirt or sweatshirt?"

Lia placed a towel, a Greenpeace T-shirt, and an old, faded university sweatshirt on the chair outside the bathroom door. She closed her eyes and leaned against the door jamb, imagining the cascade of water washing over Jay's toned body. She had enjoyed running behind Jay and admiring her butt, and the way she squashed her breasts to stop them from jiggling as she ran had almost made her stumble.

The water turned off, and Lia hurriedly stepped away to sort out the tea, annoyed she was acting like a fool. After a few moments, the bathroom door opened, and Jay stood there with her hair tousled and looking casual in Lia's clothes. Lia was sorely tempted to take her hand and lead her to the bedroom. Without her usual heels and makeup, Jay stepped into her androgyny in the most delicious way, as though her corporate skin had been peeled away to reveal the shiny, true Jay beneath. This casual, softer Jay had her arousal clicking up a notch or two. Lia imagined threading her fingers through her soft short hair and brushing up the undercut. She sighed and pulled down two mugs. Hot and spicy ginger seemed appropriate.

She moved the unfolded laundry from the chair onto her bed

GREEN *for* LOVE

and switched on the fairy lights, then turned on the aromatic wick. It was an indulgence, but she loved the clove and cinnamon scent, and she was sure Jay would too.

"Smells like Christmas," Jay said when she stepped into the kitchen area. "I didn't know you'd been to Bristol Uni."

Jay indicated the logo on the sweatshirt she wore, which emphasised her breasts which filled the sweatshirt in a rather delicious way. Lia's mouth felt dry, and she consciously raised her gaze to Jay's face. "I started on the economics course but dropped out in my final year when my grandfather died." Lia blinked to hold back the emotion, still present years later when she thought back to that terrible time in her life. "I was very close to my gramps. He taught me all about nature and the countryside, and I missed him dreadfully. I fell apart for a few years. I'd done an environmental economics module and knew that's what I wanted to devote my life to, not graduate into a merchant bank like most of my contemporaries. It was my old tutor who got me in contact with Christian, my boss at the charity, and I've been there ever since, working for them and living in their flat."

There was so much more she could say, and she tamped down the emotion that came rushing up unbidden. She had already said too much, left herself exposed, open to ridicule. She was sure she couldn't trust Jay, and she was foolish to let her guard down.

Lia smiled to cover her anxiety and indicated Jay should sit on the small sofa and handed her the tea. It would be so easy to slip into the empty seat beside Jay, but she elected to place herself at a distance on the kitchen chair. They sipped their drinks, and the silence became heavy and tense like a storm about to break.

Jay placed her mug down and looked around the room. "Do you have a thing about Christmas, with the lights and all?"

Lia detected the slight twang of a London accent as though Jay was letting down her guard and relaxing. "Not really. I love the scent and sights, and they make the place feel special all year round."

74

E.V. BANCROFT

Jay tugged her fingers through her damp hair, trying to curl it into shape. "Think of all that extra electricity you're burning."

Lia canted her head to one side, unsure whether Jay was teasing but convinced when the edges of Jay's mouth curled up and her eyes glittered with amusement. "It's all solar and battery storage given that this is a charity flat, and it's been insulated to within an inch of its life. Some energy is also fed back to the grid which earns the charity a tiny amount of revenue each year."

"Okay. I've had the talk all day about the wonderful work you're doing. I get it. Tell me something interesting; tell me more of your story."

Lia glowered at the implication that energy wasn't interesting and rolled her shoulders, which had tightened at the thought of her family. "My family's farm is in North Northumberland, not far from Lindisfarne and on the flight path of the migrating geese. We've got some grasslands where they spend the winter. My gramps built a hide and shared his love of birdwatching with me. There's nothing like the fascination of watching them settle, and squabble, and feed. I always try to get up there at least once over the winter period to watch them, but I miss the passing of seasons."

Jay had stopped brushing her fingers through her hair. "You clearly have a passion for nature and Northumberland. Why don't you live there rather than the middle of a city?"

"I can't watch my brother destroy the estate." Lia didn't hide the irritation in her tone. Jay raised her eyebrow, and Lia sighed. "My brother lives in the hall with his family, and all the farms have tenant farmers in. They're all working the land."

Jay blinked a couple of times. "Wait. Hall? Farms, plural? How big is this place?"

Lia felt like she was showing off, and she hated that. She detested the boasting of Tim and his landowning friends, more concerned with the shooting and fishing than nurturing the environment. Yet he was supposed to be the sensible one and she was the flaky one, the one who couldn't be trusted. "Big enough, but I'm not

GREEN *for* LOVE

welcome there anymore. My brother, Tim, wants to run the estate to maximise profit in the short-term rather than nurture the land for the long-term."

"I can't imagine that goes down well."

Was Jay siding with Tim? "What do you mean?"

Jay raised her hands. Lia wouldn't be calmed down like some puppy. She felt her defences surrounding her like the walls of the Northumberland castles designed to keep out attackers.

"I wasn't being judgemental," Jay said. "I only meant that must be hard to witness, given how strongly you feel."

Lia relaxed a little, but she was still wary. Despite her aura, which seemed pure, Jay still worked for the establishment intent on destroying the planet. She was no better than Tim and all his tribe that she detested so much. The tribe who had mocked her at boarding school and who seemed to continue to university: arrogant, entitled, wealthy. Lia wanted nothing to do with them, and that included her family.

"Lia, are you okay?" Jay asked and seemed genuinely concerned.

She shook away the old memories that slept in a hole she'd created in her soul just for them. "Away with the fairies," Lia said, grinning when Jay's eyebrow quirked slightly. She didn't need to know the details of Lia's past. She smiled. "I only go up there to see my niece, who I'm very fond of, and if I have to attend a family event. But now that my parents have retired to France, I don't need to go north. I love my flat and allotment, and I have friends here." She didn't say that most of those friends she had made through her environmental activities, and they actually had very little in common outside their activism, which meant she spent a lot of time alone. She checked her watch. "I'll walk you down to the railway station. We probably need to leave soon if you're going to catch your train. I'd offer you supper, but I'm strictly vegetarian, and I suspect you're a meat-eater."

Jay frowned. "What was it you said when we met? That's a lot of assumptions to make?"

"I wouldn't need to make assumptions if you gave me your birth details. I know you're a Taurus, but where's your moon?"

"I don't believe all that guff—"

"You won't mind providing the information then, since it won't tell me anything." Lia handed her a notebook and pencil. "When's your time, date, and place of birth?"

"I don't know the time. I'd have to ask my mum, but this is silly."

Even so, she wrote down the details in small, neat handwriting. Her cynicism was no more than Lia had expected. "We'll see. Now, if you don't want to get all hot and sweaty again, we need to leave now."

"Sure. Thanks for the shower, and the tea, and for the loan of the clothes. I'll give them back to you at the next committee meeting."

As they walked to the station, Lia itched to get back to feed Jay's birth details into her astrology programme. It would give her more information on how to approach her. And she could use all the strategies she could get if she wasn't going to fall for her.

Chapter Twelve

LIA GROUNDED HERSELF WITH a few deep breaths. She needed all her confidence to enter the lion's den of Magenta's refinery. That wasn't the real problem though, was it? She needed all her confidence to remain open and non-judgemental. This was the reckoning for inviting Jay to her work and passion in Bristol. She had stayed in London last night and half expected Jay to be in the club bar. She wasn't, of course, and Lia had acknowledged her disappointment.

The train pulled into the platform, the doors opened with a satisfying hiss, and she stepped down. Her nose was assaulted by the pervading heaviness of pollution. How could this be good for people? It must be affecting their lungs and mental health. This was such a waste of time. How could coming to an oil refinery help her understand what Magenta were doing? She tamped down her exasperation. *Be open and observe.*

She exited the station to the car park and saw Jay waiting, wearing a dark trouser suit and bright blue blouse that matched the colour of the car beside her as though it was all coordinated.

Unbidden, her heart quickened, and there was an insistent throbbing between her thighs. Stupid body, lusting after someone so inappropriate. Jay did look gorgeous though. There was something about the way she carried herself, confident and commanding, in business attire she wore like she was born to it. The more intimate knowledge of Jay's background made her even more enticing because it had been so carefully curated.

"Hey," she said when she was close enough and held out her hand. For a moment, she thought Jay was going to kiss her cheek as she leaned forward, but she pulled back and they shook hands formally.

Jay's hand was soft and her grip strong but not bone-crushing. Confident, like everything else about her. Her fingernails were unvarnished and closely cut, as though establishing that she didn't waste time on such frivolities as vanity. With looks like hers, she didn't need adornment.

"Thank you for coming," Jay said. "I hope you're going to find this interesting. First of all, do you notice anything strange about this company car?"

"No, I don't tend to drive, so cars don't mean much to me."

Jay was almost bouncing on her toes with excitement, and it was difficult not to be drawn in by it and harmonise with the same energy, like a tuning fork vibrating at the same pitch as another. Maybe that's what their attraction was. Despite everything, they harmonised and resonated on the same wavelength. She must be misreading it. She'd have to consult their composite charts tonight.

"It looks like a normal car, doesn't it?" Jay patted the bright blue bonnet.

"Yes?" It felt like a trap.

"This car is a Toyota Mirai, powered by hydrogen fuel cells. The only emissions are water."

Did Jay think she was a sucker? Who would believe anything spouted out by big corporate? Acting like it was a solution took away from the actual issues. "But you still produce the hydrogen by fossil fuels, don't you? So, it's not exactly environmentally friendly. It's why they call it grey hydrogen because the overall impact is still negative."

Jay opened the passenger door for Lia to get in. A part of Lia enjoyed the old-fashioned chivalry. The other part reminded her that she wasn't here to be wooed.

"I told you we're looking at alternative ways of producing hydrogen."

They buckled up and Jay checked her mirrors before pulling out.

GREEN *for* LOVE

"So why did I have to come to the refinery? Couldn't you just tell me that in London? I could smell the pollution when I arrived at the station."

The car was quiet, like any electric vehicle, but Lia wasn't about to admit she was impressed.

"Our research huts are at the back of the refinery. I wanted to show you what we're doing with hydrogen production. We'll need to blend it with liquified natural gas to pipe it around the country—"

"Which is still a fossil fuel. This feels like smoke and mirrors. And how many pumps are there where you can get hydrogen?" Lia crossed her arms, determined to stick to the topic and not focus on how strong and capable Jay's hands looked on the steering wheel.

Jay flinched but recovered with a broad smile. "At the moment, there are only about one hundred pumps for hydrogen in Europe, but Magenta are linking up with other fuel companies to expand on that."

As they pulled away, Lia looked at the industrial zone they were driving through. *Be open, listen, and don't judge until you have all the facts.* She repeated like a mantra.

They were welcomed at the security gates, and the guard checked Jay's identity badge and her driving license. They had certainly enhanced security since her crew had glued themselves to the road outside. There were more flood lights and numerous alarms signs too. "Don't you have dogs on security anymore?" Lia asked, wondering if it sounded casual enough.

Jay flashed her a wary look. "Yes. The guards walk the rounds with dogs overnight. As you can see, security is tight, particularly after your incursion."

The comment wasn't barbed and merely stated the facts, but a flush burned up Lia's neck and face. Damn her pale complexion. Wanting to get Jay to like her competed with doing what was right. What was right didn't include bedding someone who could distract her from changing the world.

"It's a twenty-four-hour operation with different shifts, so there are always people on site."

Lia cocked her head to one side. Was Jay trying to warn her off from repeating their protests? Jay drove slowly around the huge tanks and pipes of the industrial complex, and there was even a fire station and a fire engine peeping out.

Lia pointed at it. "It shows how dangerous the substance must be that you have your own fire brigade."

Jay frowned and then focused on the road ahead. "No. What it shows is that we care about the safety of our people and the surrounding area. That's precautionary, and we've never had to use them. Didn't you see the sign coming in saying it had been 473 days since the last incident? We take safety very seriously."

Lia was fed up with her bullshit party line. "Shame you don't take the environment seriously."

Jay sighed. "Are you going to be antagonistic all day? I thought we'd got beyond that." She nodded toward an area they were passing. "We're even working on wind turbines that are more bird-friendly."

Lia pushed down the guilt at deliberately needling Jay. She didn't want to like her, to be absorbed by her, to be drawn to her, but that was no reason to be a complete jerk. She smiled. "Where I come from, we have migrating birds coming down to feed in the winter, and there are thousands of them, so we definitely want anything bird-friendly."

"Good. We're here." Jay switched off the engine and sped around to open Lia's door again.

She steered her towards the old Nissen huts that looked as though they'd been there since the Second World War. Obviously, they didn't waste money on expensive buildings for the research department. Lia noticed that the chain link fencing at the back of the huts was old. No upgraded security there.

Jay introduced Lia to her fellow scientists and displayed her hydrogen pilot plant as if she was demonstrating how her baby could walk. Lia was impressed. They were clearly taking alternative

GREEN *for* LOVE

fuel seriously. If they could get Magenta to shift to net-zero even ten years earlier, it could make a huge difference. Maybe working together could be fruitful after all. And she certainly wouldn't complain about having to spend more time with Jay. Their eyes met, and Jay gave her a sweet grin. Lia smiled back. Maybe she still had some things to learn, and that knowledge could always be useful down the line when they scheduled their next protest. As she looked at Jay, who still looked excited, her stomach turned. She was trying hard, and she'd be hurt if Lia showed up at the gates with another protest.

But the end was worth the means, right? It bothered her that she wasn't sure anymore.

Chapter Thirteen

THE NEXT COMMITTEE MEETING went well. The reports from the visits had been well received, and Jay smiled at the positive reaction. Lia raised an eyebrow in a way that was both sardonic and amused, and Jay shivered involuntarily. "Thank you for all your input. We're making great progress. We can take the suggestions you've made and incorporate them into the first draft of the report. Oliver is very happy with what I've told him so far. I'll send through the draft before we reconvene in a fortnight. Does that work for everyone?" AT NODS AROUND THE table, she pulled the meeting to a close and started to gather her papers, aware that she was being watched. Her heart rate spiked with Lia so close that she could detect the scent of essential oils that reminded her of when they met.

"I want to make some more suggestions," Lia said. "You need to put in an earlier date to get to net-zero."

Jay flipped from arousal to annoyance in a second. "We agreed in the meeting to keep it as it is."

The door clicked shut as the last committee member left.

Lia smiled. "True, but that doesn't stop me from trying. And talking of dates, are you free for lunch? There were some interesting facts that I found from your birth chart, and I'd like to explore them with you further."

Annoyance warred with curiosity, and curiosity won out. "Sure, I'll let Marta know that I'll be out for lunch. We can go to my regular place. I'll book a table."

Twenty minutes later in the restaurant, Lia whipped up her serviette and placed it on her lap.

"I'll email you a copy of your birth chart and interpretation, and you can see if it resonates with you."

Jay blushed, imagining Richard seeing a copy on her work email. "I'll text you my home email. Please don't send it to work."

Lia raised her eyebrow. Was she mocking her? "So that means you are interested then? I see from your chart that you've got sun conjunct Chiron in Taurus. That means you have a lot of hurt about your father."

Jay's jaw tightened, immediately regretting letting Lia pry. "That's speculation based on your observations and knowledge. You know I've never mentioned a second parent. How do you know I have a father? It could be a second mum or non-binary—"

"You're right, I should say second parent. Okay, you carry a wound around your second parent."

Jay sighed, unsure whether to feed into this nonsense. "My dad left Mum when she was pregnant, so I'm not sure hurt is the word. I never knew him. We've been a happy little family of two ever since, despite Mum working three jobs to give me what she could. So the hurt is for my mum."

Lia's expression didn't falter as if she didn't concede the logic. "Ah, the pain is because you don't know your father. Your sun in Taurus means you're very stubborn and won't back down." She raised her eyebrow, and her eyes twinkled. "You've just demonstrated that."

How could Lia be so infuriating and alluring at the same time? The slight frown between her brows was cute, and the way she sucked in her bottom lip when she concentrated was causing pulsing in more than her heart. Yet the nonsense she spouted was unbelievable. Did she think Jay was duped by this punt and prod to find out more about her? She straightened her knife and fork so they were perfectly aligned with the plate. "If you want to know about me, you can ask. No need to ask gaseous clouds millions of miles away."

"Could I trust what you tell me, Ms 'I'm a scientist but actually I'm a senior executive in a major oil company responsible for polluting

GREEN *for* LOVE

the planet and destroying our future?'"

Jay tightened the grip on her cutlery. This again? "Have you seen or heard nothing at the committee meetings and visits?"

Fortunately, the waiter Dominic came over. "Jay, how lovely to see you again. What can I get for you and your guest?"

She smiled, glad for the reprieve. "Hi, Dominic. I'll have my usual. Lia, what would you like?"

Lia slapped the menu down on the table. "Do you have something vegetarian with low air miles? And still spring water. I don't trust tap water that's been through three kidneys and stuffed full of fluoride."

Dominic's smile faltered a little at the ferocity of Lia's request. "The whole menu is vegan and low-processed. We get our fruit and veg from local markets, so choose whatever you like without worry. And one bottle of spring water coming up. I'll give you a few minutes to decide."

After he left, Lia rewarded Jay with a dazzling smile, and it tingled Jay's nerves to her toes. She would do whatever she could to see that again.

"You regularly come to a vegan restaurant?"

"I come here because I love the food, and I invested in the restaurant as part of their crowd-funding drive. They're opening another premises near Liverpool Street later this year that will be even closer to the office." Jay inhaled. She had said Lia could ask anything. "It also has the advantage that none of my colleagues would be seen dead in here, so I'm not going to run into them in my downtime."

Lia's mouth hung slightly open. "Wow. I didn't expect that. You are a contradiction."

"Pot and kettle come to mind," Jay said and was grateful for Dominic returning with their drinks. "Have you decided what you want?"

"What do you recommend?"

"I always go for the swede gnocchi. It keeps me going when I don't have time to eat later."

"Is that because you're eating something else at the club?"

Jay felt the heat of blush from her chest to her hair roots. Not that she was ashamed. "Two of the swede gnocchi, please, Dom."

He nodded and left.

"What I don't understand," Lia said, "is how somebody as intrinsically good as you could work for an evil company and also pick up married women in an expensive club. It doesn't ring true."

Maybe it hadn't been such a good idea to come for lunch. "I know you think the company's evil, but they gave me a chance in life. I would never have got out of a council flat in Ealing if it hadn't been for the Magenta scholarship. And yeah, I'm happy to help women exploring their sapphic side, but I never initiate the sexual advances, so I don't consider myself a marriage-breaker, if that's what you're implying. Come on. You're from the same class. You know that most of those marriages are commercial alignments of their various estates. The men are off having affairs, so why shouldn't the women? They get their needs met, as do I. No complications, no harm, no foul."

Lia nodded as if conceding the point. Jay took a sip of her water and decided to be blunt. "I'm feeling very exposed. I don't have access to the same information, or should I say same assumptions, that you do."

"What would you like to know? I thought you grilled me when you came to my flat. I'm more curious why you don't hang out with your colleagues much."

Visions of Richard sneering at her at their last management meeting came to mind. He was mediocre and envious as well as entitled, a toxic mix in any situation. She much preferred it when she spent her days hob-nobbing with her fellow geeks. That was a safer topic to light on, rather than the power politics at play. "Have you seen most scientists? They don't do socialising. They're wonderful for completing a task but don't want to include others. I've been accused of that myself but with Oliver's mentoring, I've

GREEN *for* LOVE

been working on the social side. I seem to be good at the mediation and finding the middle ground, although I detest the office politics and backstabbing."

"But you're in the corporate world. That's a prerequisite."

Dominic returned with their food quicker than expected, and Jay thanked him. She decided to keep her responses general. She didn't want to provide any further ammunition for Lia. Her guard was crumbling enough with all the time they were spending together. "True. Get lots of people competing for the top jobs, and there's always jostling for position."

"Not where I work. Christian, my boss, lets me do what I want as long as I deliver the funding and get the projects completed on time."

Jay took a bite of her gnocchi and stifled a moan of delight. She loved the food here, and it was nice to share it with someone. "Doesn't he set parameters and goals?"

"Yes, but I always blast through them. It helps having a wide net of contacts, most of whom like to believe they're doing something to give back and help the poor."

Confidence clung to Lia like expensive perfume, difficult to define but wafting around her like luxury, and she could imagine Lia taking anything she wanted. How she wished she was as confident. Mostly, she felt like an imposter, an outsider, someone tolerated, not feted. "Tell me more nuggets you gleaned from my birth chart then."

Lia dabbed at her mouth with her serviette, and Jay stared at her luscious lips as they curled upwards in a mischievous smile.

"Well," Lia said. "You love status, money, and the good things in life, and you fear losing them. Your Mars in Leo is very determined, and because it is on the descendant, it's ambitious, and you think yours is the only way."

"That's not true. I've been very open in listening to what you and Ian have proposed–"

"Your Aquarius on the descendant wants freedom, but you

have an internal conflict between affection and freedom. Hence, you seek out comfort at the club but don't want the commitment of relationships."

A shiver went through her at how surprisingly accurate Lia was. "You're making this up from the bits I've told you already."

"No, really. I'm happy to let you have a copy of your chart, and you can ask any astrologer worth their salt." Lia fixed her with an intense gaze. "Do you believe in love?"

"What is this, twenty questions?" Seeing the expression of disappointment on Lia's face, Jay sighed. "If you mean the all-embracing, Hallmark movie sentimentality, then no, I don't."

Lia visibly swallowed. "What do you believe in?" she whispered.

Jay ate her gnocchi to give herself a moment to consider her response. "I don't know. It's not something I've given a lot of thought to. I believe love is a verb. What you *do* for somebody else on a daily basis. It's not great passion or grandiose statements but the consistency of little acts of kindness and respect. Always respect." But what would it be like to be in the throes of great passion? The thought made her shift uncomfortably.

Lia nodded. "Lovely. The interesting thing I wanted to tell you is that by looking at our combined chart, called the composite, I can see that we've known each other in a previous life."

"I don't believe in past lives," Jay said and placed her cutlery down on her plate. "Tell me about *you*. You're clearly passionate and idealistic, yet you seem to want to hide your background. Why?"

Lia exhaled, and her shoulders slackened as though she was releasing her armour. "I've never felt like I fit in. I never met the expectations of my family, especially when I dropped out of uni and wouldn't marry one of my brother's friends—or marry any man, for that matter."

"Was that when your gramps died?" Jay asked between mouthfuls.

Lia nodded. "In addition to losing my beloved gramps, I'd

GREEN *for* LOVE

always hoped he would let me be the guardian of the estate, to continue it in a way he held dear. He didn't. I trusted him to let me look after the geese, but he instructed that my father, and then my brother, should manage the estate. Nobody trusts me to make a real contribution, and although I've worked in the charity sector for years, I've always thought I should be doing something bigger and even more important. Working with No More Oil as an on the ground activist gives me that, but I wouldn't expect you to understand."

They ate in silence for a few minutes, while Jay debated whether to continue this line of conversation. But she wanted to understand. Letting the family line of inquiry go seemed like a good idea though. "I understand that you care about the planet. What I don't get is why you targeted Magenta in particular and why so radically?"

Lia pulled her lips and cheeks in sharply. "Surely you remember the Magenta oil spill in the Norwegian oil field about twelve years ago?"

"Of course. But plenty of safety measures have been put in place since then."

Lia's glare was so hard, Jay wanted to shrivel in her seat. Damn, she'd ruined lunch. She pushed away her plate.

"I don't care what bullshit you told yourselves. I saw the impact on the geese coming over, polluted and exhausted. I saw the dead seabirds washed onto the beaches. It's not something I could forget. Not to mention the contamination of local water sources and the destruction of habitats."

Jay put up her hands, but Lia's glare was pure poison. "Okay, I see why you would be so angry with Magenta, but why the escalation now?"

Lia tossed her serviette down. "Because nothing is being done about it, and it's getting worse every year. The planet's heading for a disaster which will impact everyone; the whole ecosystem will change and have a devastating impact on so many species. It makes me want to cry, but crying doesn't solve or change anything. It's only by taking direct action that the issue is kept in the headlines for people to talk about. I'm not doing it to further my career or my bank balance. I do it because I care about the world."

"I get that, and I admire your passion—"

"But you won't do anything to change—"

"I'm trying to change things from the *inside*." They weren't getting anywhere with this discussion, and people at the tables around them were giving them strange looks.

Lia snorted and seemed to be wrestling for control of her temper. "History has shown very few things change from inside; there's usually a catalyst from outside that shifts the status quo."

Jay didn't know whether this was accurate or not and made a mental note to research it, but at least Lia seemed to be calming down.

Lia sipped her water then placed her hands palm down on the table. "Sorry. You asked me a question, and I didn't reply rationally. Your logical brain must be screaming now."

Jay mirrored Lia's movements. Oliver had told her that it helped to build rapport. "Actually, I'm more interested in having a relaxing lunch with you so we can get to know each other better."

Lia coloured, the slightest blush giving her a pink glow. It was very charming.

Lia's eyes sparkled. "Tell me more about you. You're clearly ambitious. Where do you hope to end up? CEO?"

Although Jay was unsure whether Lia was teasing her, she felt she ought to be open. "Eventually, yes, when Oliver retires in about three years' time. But in the meantime, he's mentoring me to take over as Chief Operating Officer in eighteen months. So yes, I'm ambitious."

"It's obviously something you're very sensitive about. I admire your work ethic and that you care for your mum. And I like your kindness. You're a most delectable package." She motioned towards Jay's body, then touched her forearm.

GREEN *for* LOVE

Jay's skin erupted in goosebumps, and her heart picked up a pace. For a few glorious seconds, she basked in the admiration. Was this how it felt to be the recipient of genuine and personal affection? She was usually the one to make the moves, and it was disconcerting that she was being manoeuvred this way. "I need to get back. Shall we share the tab?"

"I'll take it. But don't you feel that connection between us? That energy flowing, despite our differences?"

Lia was nothing if not direct. Jay, however, had no idea how to respond in a way that didn't suggest there could be more between them. "Yes? No. I need to get back. Thanks for lunch. I'll see you next week at the committee visit. I'm happy to give you a lift there. I'll text the details to you." Jay snatched up her jacket and escaped into the fresh air, if the London air could ever be called fresh. Why had she agreed to lunch with Lia? She should have known it would unsettle her. That's what Lia kept doing. If she wasn't doing it by trying to bait her, now she was doing it with the hocus pocus stuff. Jay could do with a whisky, but it would be a long afternoon before she could relax at home and try *not* to think about Lia's smile.

Chapter Fourteen

"This is more like it." Lia's whole body tingled with excitement as her energies became aligned. She stretched her hands up to salute the sky in the Urdhva Hastasana pose. This was a place to practice yoga, clean and fresh, and to revel in life. Not only was it wonderful to stand in the Bedfordshire countryside but also the project was exciting, genuinely inspiring, and forward thinking.

In the middle of a group of committee members, Jay pointed at the arrangement of short wind turbines, dwarfed by half a dozen conventional turbines. "These are the vertical wind turbines."

The series of twenty or so much smaller wind turbines were arranged in formation, with blades spinning slowly. Having already researched the information, Lia was impressed that they had modelled the same principles as geese flying, or fish swimming, disrupting the turbulence and harnessing that energy more efficiently. She could imagine them in Northumberland.

"We're now taking the optimum arrangements from our computer models and trialling them in the real world."

"They look like little merry-go-rounds," Andrea said.

She was such an airhead. Her facile comments and lack of understanding of any environmental principles made Lia want to throttle her, but Jay laughed politely.

"Some of the modelling we've done shows that individually they're less effective than a single horizontal wind turbine." Jay smiled at Andrea. "A series of horizontal wind turbines produce a lot more turbulence, which impacts the turbines behind, so they need to be spread out much further. The vertical turbines don't affect the air in the same way, so they can be clumped much closer together in a smaller footprint. This means we can produce more energy per hectare of land."

"That's fascinating," Ian said, taking photos on his phone.

"I need to ask that you don't publish any of those photos as this is still a research project," Jay said,

"Of course, but I'm interested in the findings of your trial." Ian put his phone away.

"I'm sure that can be arranged. I'll clear it with Oliver first."

"Thank you," Ian said.

"I thought you couldn't get planning permission for onshore wind farms in England now?" Lia asked with what she hoped would be an innocent expression. She knew full well what the laws were.

Jay's smile dazzled. "Not at the moment, but this is an existing site, and we're lobbying government, explaining that the footprint and noise levels are much lower with vertical turbines."

Lia bit her tongue. Of course Magenta would have the ear of the government, but she was genuinely impressed with what Jay's company were doing.

"Research by Stanford University has shown that not only do the vertical turbines improve the power of a traditional wind farm, they also have a much lower threat to wildlife. We've had no reported bird or bat strikes in several years."

That got Lia's attention, much as the movement of Jay's mouth did as she spoke.

"We're also experimenting with different blade colours to see if that makes a difference but at the moment, we can't tell—"

"Bats are blind. They won't care," Lia said and grinned.

Jay blinked at her and seemed to try not to laugh. "Correct, but as the vertical blades are around the same profile, they don't seem to be as confusing to their echolocation as conventional wind turbines."

Jay was impressive. She wasn't just one of the bosses who learned the headlines; she seemed familiar with the tiniest detail and handled all the questions with humour and good grace.

GREEN *for* LOVE

Their eyes locked. Jay faltered slightly in her explanation and licked her lips. Lia smiled. Oh, that attraction was definitely mutual.

Jay continued, leaving Lia to observe the earnestness of her demeanour, the way her hair flopped over her eyes and she had to push it behind her ear, only for the next gust of wind to tug it out of position. It was adorable to watch.

This trip had been worth the early start. She was in London for meetings tomorrow with big potential donors, which could make a huge difference to her charity. Part of her wondered if Jay would go to the club herself tonight; that could be interesting.

"If there are no more questions, shall we go to the pub and get out of this wind?" Jay asked and had an enthusiastic response. "Okay, follow me. The Plough is only five minutes away."

As she and Ian fell into step, Andrea said, "Ooh, isn't this exciting? Going to a pub on a workday. Won't your boss be cross if you spend time out?"

How could Jay be so patient and not tell her to stop prattling?

"Not at all. He knows how important this committee is, and he's looking forward to seeing the recommendations. I hope you can see we're serious about our research into renewables."

"It's very impressive, Jay," Ian said. "I love that you're optimising the energy per hectare while minimising the impact on the environment."

"Thank you, Ian. I appreciate you saying that."

Was that a dig at Lia? "I'm blown away—pun intended," Lia said, and Jay turned back to reward her with a glorious smile that made her clit quiver and her toes tingle.

It didn't hurt that Lia could watch Jay's tight ass in her jeans as they made their way back to the cars. She needed to keep her libido in check. This was a business outing. She was also being very superficial. But Jay *was* the whole package: intelligent, kind, and thoughtful, as well as being hot. Their energies meshed, but their values didn't, and that was a problem. Lia sighed softly at the unfairness of it.

"Would you like to come back to London with me?" Ian asked as they approached the vehicles.

He looked so eager, as though he wanted to chat for days. It would be lovely, but she wanted the opportunity to get to know Jay more. "Thanks, but I need to pick Jay's brain about the impact on wildlife."

"Challenge me about it, you mean," Jay said and stiffened, as if she was waiting for an attack.

The others laughed.

"Probably. But you'd hate it if I accepted what you said without evidence, you being such a stickler for science." Lia met Jay's gaze. The intensity in her expression made Lia's breath hitch and something seemed to pass between them... An understanding, a slight lowering of the defences.

They looked at each other for too long, and the tension between them dissipated as Jay unlocked her car.

After they'd eaten lunch, Jay thanked everyone for their contribution, then the various committee members dispersed. She was the epitome of a smooth senior executive, making everyone feel welcome and valued. But Lia couldn't help wondering which Jay was the one comfortable in her own skin.

When they got into Jay's car, Lia asked, "What's the range of this car?"

"That's part of today's test. It's seventy-five miles each way, plus driving in London, so in theory, it should be feasible to do it in the four-hundred-mile range advertised. If not, I'll be looking pretty embarrassed on the side of the road."

They laughed, and Jay pulled away and settled into driving.

"You're incredibly patient with Andrea," Lia said as they joined the A1.

Jay flashed her a glance then returned her attention to the road. "She's trying so hard to fit in and enjoys the perks of being on the committee. Perhaps she's a Taurus?" Jay grinned.

Lia wasn't going to rise to the teasing and leaned back in her

GREEN *for* LOVE

comfortable seat. "She's bored and lonely, but she irritates me with her irrelevant questions and comments."

"Her husband is one of our biggest individual shareholders, and he asked that she be welcomed onto the committee, so I couldn't exactly refuse."

"Don't you hate being polite to people you don't respect?"

Jay shrugged and indicated to overtake a lorry. "I always try and treat everyone with respect–"

"That's not what I asked."

Jay pulled into the fast lane and accelerated smoothly. It was all so precise; she'd probably calculated the exact speed she needed to accelerate to optimise fuel consumption.

"I know, but it's not my place to make judgements about people. Being kind and respectful doesn't cost me anything."

Seriously, was Jay really some saint working in the devil's business? "Oh, come on, everybody makes judgements. We all have a sense about people."

Jay gripped the steering wheel and stared at the traffic ahead. "I hate it when people judge me, so why would I do it? And if someone doesn't respect me, should I be okay with them being rude or unkind to me?" She glanced at Lia. "That doesn't sound very woo woo, if you don't mind me saying. You say all this zen stuff, but you're as judgemental as the rest of them."

Lia realised she was grinding her teeth, so she relaxed her jaw. Was Jay right? Was Lia being hypocritical, spouting zen but really treating people insensitively? She didn't want to become like her mother. "By 'them,' do you mean my class? I've always tried not to be as judgemental as my brother and his cronies. I hate their entitled criticism, arrogance, and complete disrespect for the environment. You seem really sensitive about where you grew up, but I admire that you've worked your way up. You know what you're talking about, and you're trying to make a difference."

"Now you're taking the piss." Jay's mouth had become a hard line, and she focused on the road ahead.

"Believe me, I'm not." The ensuing silence created a strange tension in the car, with only traffic noise as they overtook several lorries. Lia was grateful she wasn't driving, but Jay didn't seem to mind.

She stared out the window for a few minutes and then at Jay, who was sitting rigidly, focused on the road ahead. "There's a strange vibe. Have I upset you somehow?"

"After all you've done to embarrass and annoy me, now you're worried if you've upset me?"

Lia squirmed in her seat. She supposed she deserved that. "It's not personal. It's never been personal. I admire and respect you, and I think we've established from the beginning that I'm attracted to you, so I don't understand why you're suddenly all emotional."

"I'm not."

Lia stifled a laugh and stared pointedly at Jay's hand gripped so tightly around the wheel that her knuckles were pale.

Jay glanced at her. "Okay, but you're deliberately pushing my buttons and mocking me."

"I'm absolutely not mocking you, and I'd rather like to push another of your buttons. You're delightfully hot when you're riled up."

Jay scoffed. "You did *not* just say that."

Lia felt her arousal spike, despite herself. Where was her control? She deliberately and slowly relaxed her fingers around the grab handle. "I did, because I want you to know that your Steve Jobs look is incredibly sexy."

Jay smiled and shook her head before pulling into the slow lane. "He's been dead a long time, so I'm not sure that's as sexy as you think it is. But it's better than you being down my throat the whole time, so I'll take it."

Lia grinned. The words of her psychic kept drifting back to her: *"You'll meet your soulmate this year. It will be through work. In fact, you may have already met her."* If it was true, the Universe was having a laugh making her soulmate be a senior executive in an oil company. No, it couldn't possibly be that.

Chapter Fifteen

AFTER TWO AND A half hours of trying to wrangle disparate views in the committee meeting, Jay decided enough was enough. Lia and Ian frowned at her over the papers. Jay smiled to ease the tension. "We've split into two factions here, those who believe we've gone far enough and those who would like to see a more radical approach. So we can make progress on drafting the final report, I recommend we insert what we can get through the board right now. If we go for the more radical solutions, I can guarantee that the whole report will be rejected."

"You're kicking it into the long grass," Lia said.

Jay leaned forward. "No. We can think about revisiting it after the successful pilot phase."

The rest of the committee, including Ian, murmured agreement. Why couldn't Lia just be pragmatic and accept some progress? Nothing was quite good enough. She wanted the end of oil in its entirety, and there was no middle ground.

They glared at each other, and Jay felt alive, her skin tingling. There was a slight twinkle in Lia's eyes, as if she knew she was turning Jay into a puddle of want. It was a game to her, a fencing bout, but people could still get hurt.

Maybe it wasn't. She was passionate and determined to do whatever she thought was best for the world. Jay wished she had half of Lia's conviction, even though it was tricky being on the receiving end of such stubbornness. It meant she couldn't let her guard down, as much as she might wish it were otherwise.

Jay rolled her shoulders to release some of the knots built up over the meeting. "We'll insert a paragraph in the final report, recommending the committee reconvene next year to consider more radical solutions. All those in favour?"

Everyone but Lia raised their hands.

Jay smiled. "Carried. One dissension to be minuted."

She thought Lia would be angry, but the widening of her pupils seemed to be indicating something else. Desire? "If there's no other business, I'll close it there. We have one last meeting to finalise the board report in a fortnight. Thank you for your time and expertise. Don't forget to put in your claims for hours and expenses with Marta as you leave."

There was the hubbub of chatter and shuffling papers and scraping of chairs and salutations like a school class being dismissed.

"Lia, can I have a word, please?" Jay asked. By the worried glances other people sent Lia, they clearly thought she was in trouble. It was Jay who was in trouble. She couldn't get Lia out of her head, and she spent most of the meeting being conscious of Lia's every move and comments. When they were apart, she wondered what she was doing and how the charity was going. She'd considered calling her several times to see if she wanted to go to dinner but had talked herself out of it. Jay didn't date. And she certainly couldn't date Lia, who was picking away at her sane, ordered, scientific life, and she didn't know how to stop it.

Maybe asking her to stay behind was an error. But she wanted to warp time, to slow down and soften those glares, to snatch more time with Lia and get her smiling. Jay adored her smile. Could there be something between them?

Finally, the chatter subsided, the door clicked shut behind the rest of the committee, and the room settled with a hush as if it was exhaling. Lia sat upright and alert, and for once, even her bangles were still.

Jay needed a segue into what she really wanted to ask. What she was planning was something so alien that she may as well ask Lia to take a rocket to the moon. She elected for safer territory,

GREEN *for* LOVE

where she could anticipate the reaction. "I know you want us to go further, but it's better this way. We can make some real progress." Seeing Lia inhale as if she was about to launch into an attack, Jay hurried on, "But I don't want to talk about work. Are you still in London tonight? At the club?"

Lia nodded and her shoulders lowered a little, but her gaze was still intense.

"I wondered if you wanted to join me at my dancing class tonight. It's only a social dancing course, but my partner can't make it. And it's fun."

Lia stared at her as if she'd just asked her to rob the Bank of England. Had she completely misread the situation? Then she smiled, and her whole demeanour changed. The armour was gone, and the soft, warm soul beneath shone through.

"Where is it?"

"Near the city. I know it's not ideal for the Mayfair club, but I could pick you up and drop you off." *In for a penny...*

Lia canted her head as if deciding what to do. Jay couldn't bear the idea of being shot down. So much for sophisticated senior executive? She picked up the remaining pads and pens. A lot were gone, but if people wanted them as souvenirs, so be it. It wasn't coming from her budget. As usual, thinking about work was easier than thinking about romance.

"Okay. What time does it start? What should I wear?"

Jay's head snapped up. "Come as you are. We can put special socks on your shoes so you can slip on the dance floor." At Lia's look, she smiled. "That's a good thing, trust me! In fact, come back to my apartment and have dinner. It won't be anything special. Probably pasta."

"Thanks, that would be lovely. I confess I'm intrigued to see where you live."

Had Lia been thinking about Jay beyond work? That was interesting. "I bought a tiny riverside apartment a few years ago near the Tower of London before prices shot up. It's easy access for the office and not too far from where my mum lives. I can pick you up about five, if that's okay?"

"No, I'll come by Tube rather than pollute the planet. Text me your address."

Jay wondered if she should say that it wasn't a date. Or that it was. Or that it didn't mean anything. Or that it could. For fuck's sake. She was saved from saying anything when Lia headed for the door.

She smiled as Lia gave a little wave before she left the room then slumped into her chair. What was she thinking?

***

Later, as Lia looked out of the balcony windows, Jay wondered what she thought about her apartment. She loved the view from the balcony towards Tower Bridge and the river, and towards the city from her bedroom, although that had recently been obscured by new apartment buildings.

"Great view. This must have cost you a pretty penny."

"It feels like I'm renting it from the bank. Working in London is expensive."

"Why don't you change job then? Or is that a sore subject?" Lia smiled and stepped closer to the window, her breath fogging up the glass.

"I love my job. I get to control my day, set my own targets, and it's amazing when we make major technical breakthroughs. Living in the city is the price I pay for that." And loneliness, but she wasn't about to admit that.

Lia wiped the condensation from the glass. "I couldn't cope with being so close to so many other people. All this noise and pollution. Yuk."

"But Bristol is the same," Jay said.

"It's much smaller, *and* it's not my home. Northumberland is my home, with its bleak ruggedness of heather moors and windswept

GREEN *for* LOVE

beaches."

She had a look of such longing and wistfulness that Jay wanted to reach out and hold her.

"I bet this is wonderful at night." Lia traced her finger over the glass and smiled.

"It's pretty with all the lights, but I'm glad the bedroom is at the back of the house."

Lia raised her eyebrow. "Just the one bedroom then?"

"Yes. Although this is a sofa bed if ever anyone stays over." Not that anyone ever did. She had no time for friends, apart from Adam, and she never brought women here. She went through to the kitchen area. "Would you like a drink while I cook?"

"Just water, thanks. I don't want to be uncoordinated when I'm dancing. Did you say it was a course?"

"We're doing the cha-cha-cha at the moment. It's one of my favourites. I love the Latin dances."

Lia leaned against the window and looked her over. "Ah. Are you an expert?"

"Not at all. Adam's an amazing dancer. The new guy he's dating must be serious because dancing is sacrosanct to him. He normally leads, but I'll lead this evening." Jay stopped what she was doing and looked up. "Unless you'd like to lead?"

"I'm at a disadvantage because I don't know how it differs."

That wasn't an answer, but Jay was happy to let it be. She set down her glass. "Let me show you the steps. I'll put *Havana* on by Camila Cabello. It's nice and slow." Jay slid open the balcony door, and the sound of the city rushed around them as they stepped onto the terrace. She stood beside Lia. "Follow me. That's right, slow, slow, cha-cha-cha. You've got grace. Continue doing that, and I'll mirror you and lead."

Jay stood in front of Lia and looked up into her eyes. Lia frowned as she concentrated and counted. She was so close, their breath mingled, emulating the closeness and slow twining of their bodies as they moved. Their heartbeats and breaths were in sync, shallow and fast, and it had nothing to do with the exertion and everything to do with the excitement racing around her body.

They glided around the balcony. There wasn't much room, but they blended together well, and Lia pressed closer, her breasts brushing against Jay's chest. Arousal shot to all her nerve endings. The lights of the city below came on like fairy lights, and she lost herself in the moment. The closeness and the touch made her body tingle, a soft breeze sent goosebumps over her exposed arms, and Lia stared at her as if she was trying to read her thoughts.

Jay blinked a couple of times and pulled away, unsettled by how perfect the moment felt. "I'd better cook, or we won't have time to eat."

"Maybe you can show me a bit more here," Lia said. "I'm getting very comfortable."

Jay wasn't sure if Lia was talking about dancing or simply being together. Either way, she didn't care if they went out or stayed here to dance. When she danced, she wasn't the dutiful daughter, or the scientist climbing to the top in a misogynistic work environment, or the lesbian who hid from relationships. When she danced, she lost herself in the concentration of perfecting her steps and her posture, in the joy of the music and movement, of being in the moment.

She had freedom and grace with Adam, but the intensity and arousal amped up with Lia, and she could lose herself. Yet the turmoil in her emotions screamed at her to wake up. Professionally, Lia would do what she could to block Jay at every turn. And Jay had worked far too hard to get involved in a relationship with someone who could—and would happily— tear it all down.

Besides, Lia wanted a soulmate. She believed in forever, in people meant to be together, dictates given by the stars. That was simply nonsense invented by romance novelists and greetings card companies to make money. No, taking this further was a terrible idea. They should go.

Yet Jay was drawn back into the dance, her resolve dissolving

GREEN *for* LOVE

in the warmth of Lia's closeness. What could be better than this? Each step they took in sync, every twirl of the choreographed routine formed a bond between them.

"What do you love about dancing?" Lia asked when Jay paused for a second to let Lia follow her footsteps.

"It's a way to get into my body, to concentrate on what I'm doing and forget about my cares and stresses for a few hours. Open out for the New York, outside arm extends. Perfect."

Lia mumbling the count was adorable. Jay couldn't help but smile when their gazes locked. Her heart beat faster, and her breaths came short and shallow.

The music continued, but they stopped dancing. Jay's smile slipped as Lia stared intently at her lips. Desire flooded her, and her clit started to throb. Lia's lips parted, and Jay met her halfway. The kiss was so soft and sensual that Jay stifled a moan. It was everything she hoped for and more as Lia's tongue trailed across her bottom lip, seeking entrance. Her pulsing arousal fired through every nerve in her body. She couldn't get enough. Lia cupped her breast, and Jay melted into her, trying to get as close as she could. Pleasure tingled along her skin as Lia pulled her closer and brushed a nipple. Jay arched, wanting more, wanting to make love to this gorgeous woman.

But they were in full view on her balcony, probably silhouetted against the light spilling from the lounge. Warning bells sounded in her head, and she pulled back, breathing hard and fast, her heart thumping. "What do you want?"

"I want you to fuck me."

Jay's core throbbed at the words that seemed extra crude in Lia's posh accent.

Lia smiled as she stared into Jay's eyes. A slight shadow flickered over them, and she sighed. "But maybe not now. We need to go to the class, and maybe I'll be able to keep myself from fucking you on the dance floor."

"Sod dancing. Let's go to bed," Jay said.

Somehow those words seemed to break the magic spell, and Lia shook her head as if she was trying to clear it. Her shoulders dropped, and she looked away.

"We shouldn't take this further. You're a wonderful kisser and despite everything, I find myself so pulled to you that I can't stop myself. But we can't. I know it's because we knew each other in a past life that I feel myself drawn to you. Our energies resonate, but it can't last. Our composite chart says that we could learn a lot from each other, but you need to learn to love yourself first. And I need to learn how to trust and compromise."

Jay held back any biting comment at all the astrological mumbo jumbo. She did love herself, didn't she? Annoyance flickered across her consciousness. How dare Lia presume to know her better than herself? She had no idea. This was getting way too intense and woo woo for her. "I've already told you I don't do relationships. What about two adults having some fun together?" Jay asked, although a little voice at the back of her head squealed that she wanted more than that.

"I don't know why, but this feels so much more than just a one-night stand. You'll go back to being a bigwig in Magenta oil, and I'll go back to my charity and my activism. We're always going to be rivals and honestly, I don't want to end up in a bloody heap like Romeo and Juliet."

Cold disappointment slid down Jay's body, cooling her ardour and freezing the fire of desire. Lia was only saying what Jay had been thinking, and yet her body refused to listen to logic. "That's a bit dramatic. It doesn't have to be so black and white. If you didn't do your activism, maybe we could still see each other. That was probably the best kiss I've ever had in my life, and I want more. It doesn't have to be serious; it's just sex. I'm not asking for connection." Jay knew she sounded pleading, but she didn't care. She didn't want to let Lia go.

Lia stepped back into the lounge. "I can't *stop* my activism. For your sake, I put a halt to it when I was working for your committee,

GREEN *for* LOVE

but I don't know what will happen if the recommendations aren't implemented. You can't ask me not to care about climate change, about the future of the Earth. It's who I am."

Jay slapped her hand on the balcony railing. "I'm not asking you not to care. Has nothing you've seen or heard made a difference? Don't you trust me?" Jay went back into the lounge and slid the balcony door shut, like closing any chance of something between them. Her body felt like osmium, and she forced her legs to move.

Lia held Jay's gaze. There seemed such sorrow and desire in her eyes, as though she was battling within herself. "I trust your belief that Magenta's different, and I can see that you've gone through hoops to come to a compromise, but until the changes are made, it's all hot air. And you say you're not looking for connection, but when I have sex, I'm always looking for an energetic connection, even if it's just for that moment in time. I like you, so a connection would be inevitable, and that won't do. Our lives are too incompatible. I should go. Sorry if that means you don't get to your dancing."

"I don't really feel like going now. It doesn't matter." Jay snatched up the remote to close the blinds and stabbed the button far harder than was necessary.

"It does matter, I can see that. You're a wonderful dancer. You completely captivated me, and I forgot myself for a while. Honestly, despite everything, I'm still drawn to you. There's nothing I'd like better than to kiss you again and follow you into your bedroom." She smiled ruefully. "We've been here before, only you pulled back last time."

"I wish I hadn't. I wish we'd had sex, and then maybe I wouldn't have this overwhelming attraction to you that I can't curb. It's not logical and I hate it." Jay rammed the remote in its holster on the wall.

Lia stepped forward and lifted Jay's chin until they looked deep into each other's eyes. "Do you know how hard it is not to kiss you now? You have me twisted up inside. I..."

Lia dropped her gaze to Jay's lips again and pulled her in for another kiss, more searching and frantic than before, as though it could be the last time. Maybe she could persuade Lia to stay. They could get this out of their systems and move on. She kissed harder and deeper to sear it into her memory.

Eventually, they came up for air.

Lia cupped Jay's cheek. "I don't know what to say. I can't get enough of you, but I should still go. I need to process what's going on in my head and heart. Can I call you tomorrow?"

Without waiting for a response, she kissed Jay on the cheek, snatched up her bag, setting off her bangles like an alarm, and left.

Jay touched her tingling lips. This was madness. She never chased anyone or even thought about them after sex. But Lia was pouring disquiet and uncertainty into every cell of her body, and she seemed to be drowning.

She wanted more of those kisses but was caught in the madness of curbing her loneliness by having sweet sex when it was the last thing she needed, like having chocolate instead of protein.

She admired Lia: her fire, her passion, a woman who knew her own mind and didn't play games. But Jay didn't have time for anything more than sex, and she didn't want arguments every time she mentioned her job.

So she had to let Lia go. But why was it so hard?

Chapter Sixteen

LIA SAT IN THE club's light and airy dining room the following morning and sent Jay a text. "Can we talk? I can stay at the club until Friday night."

Her phone rang a couple of seconds later, and she gulped down her feelings along with her herbal tea before answering.

"Hi. I'm not entirely sure it's a good idea, but yeah. Can we meet up for lunch today? I've got the day off and have to drive to my mum's house to take her shopping. We could do lunch before I drop her shopping off."

Lia checked her watch. She had some work phone calls to make but had the rest of the day free. "Sure. Lunch will work. Same place as before?"

"Great. Twelve thirty?"

"Perfect." Lia ended the call and went back to her room to meditate before she set to work. She began sifting through her feelings. *Jay, Jay, Jay...* Lia had no one to call, no one to chat about these things with. And that lack of connection was a problem. She closed her eyes and recommenced her meditation.

She had just begun chanting when the Darth Vader theme tune her niece Abby had assigned to her mother because "Grandma's scary" sounded on her phone. Lia didn't disagree. So much for not calling when she was working. Not that she was at work yet, but still. There was no point ignoring it, as her mother would continue calling until she answered. "Ma, how are you both? How's France?"

"Warm. I'm calling because Tim tells me you've been interfering with what he's doing at the estate."

Lia slammed her fist on the floor, her zen moment of calm

replaced in a heartbeat. "Little tell-tale, running to Mummy. If he's got a problem, he should talk to me directly and not hide behind your coat-tails. How old is he, seven?"

"I asked him how it was going, and he said you complained he wasn't doing a proper rotation system—"

"He's not. He's leeching the soil." Lia adopted the Wonder Woman position with her legs apart, grounding herself to deal with the onslaught of her mother's judgement and criticism.

"I'm not going to get into an argument with you, Cordelia. It's his business to run as he wishes, and he can sell off redundant land if he wishes."

Icy fingers of dread crept around her heart as her mother's words sank in. "He's selling land? Which piece? He can't do that."

"You'll have to ask him. I have no idea; he said it was redundant. But that's irrelevant. It's his decision to make. You're too irresponsible to be trusted with the business. Dropping out of university to waste your time on an Indian retreat like some sixties hippie and working for fifteen years at some tiny charity where you get arrested often enough that you probably have a cell named after you—none of that screams capable business manager, Cordelia."

She and her mother had very different ideas of trust. "What you mean is you'll trust me if I follow your rigid expectations, but the moment I think and act for myself, you don't like it. That's not trust—that's control."

Her mother let out an exasperated breath. "Don't be so dramatic. Besides, you're clearly not interested in investing in the business since you give away all your income."

"It's none of your business what I do with my money. It's mine to do with what I want." The barb nestled deep in her gut. She had never felt tethered to the earth since Gramps died, not really. And despite all her yoga and energy work, she was adrift and alone in the world. The only time she felt any camaraderie was when she was engaged with No More Oil, but even other activists had no idea who she really was. Not that she would tell her mother that.

GREEN *for* LOVE

"He's wrong. Gramps would hate what Tim's done to the estate. He's destroying the land like we're destroying the planet."

"Not this again. I don't want to hear another diatribe."

Every word was like a smack that stung, another weight on top of all the other rejections she'd had since she hadn't met their expectations even as a child. Lia had to finish this call, get out of here, reground herself by walking in nature. "I've got to go." She hung up without waiting for a reply. She needed to talk to Tim and arrange a visit. She couldn't let him do something drastic and disastrous. Steeling herself, she called him.

"Finally," Lia said when Tim picked up after the third successive call.

"Some of us are busy providing food for the country and contributing to the economy, not sticking ourselves in front of ambulances and wasting police time."

That incident stuck to her like gum on her shoe. "There's no point telling you I didn't know there'd be any ambulances. It's important to challenge the destruction—"

"Spare me the lecture. Was there a purpose to your call? If not, I'll get on with my day."

"Driving around in the latest Fendt tractor isn't working, whatever you tell yourself. The tenant farmers and the contractors are the ones doing all the work. What piece of land are you selling?"

"A redundant piece that's not productive. I'm not discussing the estate with you. You'd have me ripping up all the fields to provide wildlife havens—"

"Which is what you're doing with the grouse moor and then letting the gamekeepers poison the birds of prey."

"I've never condoned that—"

"But you haven't denied it either. That's illegal as well as being immoral." A sharp pain in her palms indicated she needed to uncurl her fingers. She inhaled deeply to recentre herself. "I'd like to come up and see you and Abby if you're free this weekend."

"No can do. We've got some of my uni friends here for a shoot."

Lia shuddered. His friends were loud and boorish, and she didn't like them. "Perhaps the weekend after?"

"No. Diana has got a shopping trip planned, and we're going to see about getting Abby into boarding school near Newcastle."

"Do you have to send her away? She doesn't want to go. You know how school screwed me up. Why would you inflict it on Abby? At least let her go to the local day school."

"No. She'll be boarding."

He was so smug and stubborn. It may be a family trait, but she hoped she wasn't as arrogant as he was. She smoothed down her shirt. "In that case, apply for Cheltenham Ladies College so she can be closer to me."

"Can you imagine how humiliated she would be if her weird aunt who always gets arrested walked in the gates rather than drove in?"

She shouldn't have pushed him. It was like baiting a bear. She could imagine the disdain written on his face. They were so different she couldn't believe they came from the same gene pool. Now Abby was being forced into the same upper-class mould. She closed her eyes, wishing she could help Abby to break free from the fortress of expectations and judgement. Abby was too sensitive for the viciousness of school, just as she had been. She blew out a breath, trying to expel her frustration. It wasn't something she could change now. "So when can I visit?"

"How about the weekend after that. I'll check with Diana to see if she has anything else scheduled. I'll let her confirm with you." He ended the call before she could reply.

Lia hated his big brother power play. He thought if he delayed her enough that she'd give up, but he should know better than that. Surely he knew she would want to see what he was doing now that their parents had emigrated. It didn't matter that she didn't really have a say in anything. In her heart, it was still home.

Lia stared at the yoga mat mocking her. There was no way she could meditate now. Her heart rate was too high, and her energy

GREEN *for* LOVE

was boiling below her skin. She would walk through Green Park until she calmed down enough to make her work phone calls and then make her way to meet Jay. It was probably about four miles, but she needed the rhythm of her feet on the pavement to ground herself. It wasn't the hills or beaches of Northumberland, but it would have to do.

Nearly two hours later, flushed with the exertion, she sat down in the restaurant and Dominic brought her an herbal tea. She called her work contact. "So, you can do the transfer before the end of this week? Great, thank you. It will make a huge difference to our customers as well as helping to save the planet." Lia ended the call and rattled her bangles in delight. If she hadn't been in such a public place, she would have done a little celebratory dance.

She was still smiling when Jay came rushing in. Without thinking, she rose to hug her. The warmth of closeness and Jay's spicy perfume enveloped her, and she inhaled deeply.

"That's a wonderful welcome," Jay said, her gaze a little wary.

Lia regretted being so warm. If they couldn't go anywhere, it wasn't fair to Jay to give her hope, but it felt so natural. "I've just had some great news about the charity. I've just secured our third biggest donation ever." Lia did her utmost not to notice the tight jeans Jay was wearing, or the way her grey turtleneck sweater stretched taut over her breasts. She seemed more approachable, more androgynous, and incredibly appealing. But Lia shouldn't be thinking that way, she reminded herself as she picked up the napkin.

"That's wonderful. Congratulations. Is that for a specific project?" Jay asked.

"Yes. It's for a solar farm on an old industrial site by the motorways. It will produce enough electricity to make a profit that can be reinvested in further projects and help cover the charity costs. The council have already preapproved planning, so it'll be up and running within a year." Her heart skipped a beat. Christian would be delighted, and maybe the trustees would remember exactly how invaluable she was. That was one in the eye for her mother. If only they could see the difference she made.

She looked up to see Jay staring at her. "Sorry, did you say something?"

"Yes. I asked if you knew what you wanted."

"Same as last time. That was delicious."

Jay's smile reached her eyes, and she seemed to glow as she called over Dominic. Lia didn't know whether the delight was because Lia appreciated the same food as Jay or because she loved the attention. With Jay's Saturn in Leo, she would feel unlovable, so any sign of affection would soothe her.

Lia wouldn't say that aloud, of course. Jay made it clear that she thought astrology was rubbish. She would have to be more subtle about slipping it into the conversation. Subtlety wasn't Lia's strong point, but if they were going to be friends, she may need to be less direct in her communication, or at least soften it a bit.

Could they *be* friends? Jay was interesting and a challenge, and Lia loved adventure. Anything to stave off the boredom. It's why she had been stultified in the ashram. "Has Magenta decided to exploit any more oilfields today?" she asked, just to get a response. Jay was easy to wind up, and it was better to annoy her than to admit that she wanted more than friendship. "Sorry." Lia felt like a schoolboy pulling the hair of a girl he fancied.

Jay scowled. "Why would you say that? I told you what I was doing today."

Well, she got a reaction, but it didn't give her the distance she sought. She needed to take back control of this conversation, and the best way was to ask questions. "Surely, being a senior executive, you're in constant communication?"

"I check in, but that's not relevant, is it? I'm on my day off. Clearly, we're too different to have anything between us, and to be honest, even friendship will be hard if you're constantly on my back about my work. So what happens from here?"

So Jay was going for the direct approach, which meant Lia

GREEN *for* LOVE

didn't need to hold back and could be truthful. "I don't know." Even as she spoke, her stomach churned. She couldn't give up what she believed in, the camaraderie of her fellow activists, her sense of purpose. "We could try being friends, but I don't know if we're too incompatible. Because you're right; I can't just ignore what you do for a living."

Jay gnawed at her lip, and an awkward silence stretched between them, interrupted only when Dominic brought their meals.

When he left, Jay said, "Perhaps we could try. I enjoyed our time together, even if you do make constant digs about Magenta, and by extension, me. Could you try to be less antagonistic?"

"I enjoy teasing you. I get bored easily, and you amuse me. It's my sun conjunct mercury in Aquarius. And I know you won't believe that."

"Patronising much? And talk about not taking responsibility for your words."

Lia raised her hand. "I wasn't trying to irk you. Shall we eat before this gnocchi goes cold?"

She picked up her cutlery and after a beat, Jay did the same.

Jay closed her eyes and moaned at the taste as though she enjoyed the sensuousness of the food. Despite her instructions to be platonic, Lia's body throbbed at the sight. It was tempting to touch Jay, but she resisted the urge.

They navigated to safer waters for conversation, talking about Jay's dancing, and Lia's allotment, and the new project, and it all felt normal, easy, and genuine.

Jay's phone buzzed. She checked it and frowned. "It's my mum. Do you mind if I take it?"

Lia indicated for her to go ahead, and Jay stepped away to take the call in private. Lia waved at Dominic for the bill, and he nodded.

After a few minutes, Jay returned and sat down again. "My mum's run out of milk and needs a cup of tea. In her world, that's a disaster. I said I was having lunch with a friend, and she asked me to invite you over too. Would you like to come?"

Was that hope in Jay's eyes? Lia centred herself to tap into her own feelings. Did she want to meet Jay's mum? It felt like a rush to meet the parent when she didn't even know if she would see Jay again. Why was Jay so keen, or was it just convenience? She'd said her mum was ordinary, as though that was a bad thing, and Jay seemed ashamed of her background. But Lia had only admiration for Jay, and she wished she could say that without coming over as patronising. Jay was so far removed from her council house upbringing now, but sometimes it seemed she was still an eight-year-old poor kid having bread and margarine for tea again and staring out at a world that had already written her off.

"Sure, why not?" Friends met friends' parents, and overthinking things wasn't useful in most situations.

They shared the cost of the meal and left a generous tip, and then walked in silence as they made their way to the underground car park where Jay had left her vehicle. Lia would have preferred to go by public transport, but that would have been impractical with the shopping, and it was very clear she was on Jay's territory now.

Jay stopped at a hybrid Toyota. It wasn't fully electric, but it was better than diesel. The silence was slightly awkward again. Perhaps Jay regretted her offer to bring together two very different parts of her life.

Lia stared at Jay's profile as she concentrated on the road. She had such beautiful features but was so much more than a pretty face. Jay had an inner strength that had probably come from having to fight for everything to prove her worth and confidence from knowing she'd worked for everything. And if all else failed, she seemed strong enough to pick herself up and start again. Despite her serious scientific demeanour, she had a sense of humour, and Lia found herself captivated by her contrasts and contradictions. What appealed most was her energy, so soft and vibrant, and Lia was pulled into it like a moth to the light. Rarely had she seen such a

GREEN *for* LOVE

pure aura in someone, and she wanted to be around it to let it burn away some of the loneliness that had seeped into her soul. "Tell me about yourself and your mum," Lia said.

Jay shot her a glance. It was like a reward for not torching her again like a scaly dragon. Did that mean Jay was the princess? Lia smiled at the thought. She couldn't imagine Jay with a tiara or ball gown. "I'm waiting."

Jay slowed down for traffic. "I'm debating whether you're trying to get ammunition or if you're genuinely interested."

"Ouch." Had she really been that harsh? There was only one answer. "I am interested. I was awake all night trying to work out what I want, what would be best for both of us." She hadn't meant to spill her inner thoughts, but she needed to explain.

Jay accelerated then slowed for a bike that slipped in front of her on some kamikaze mission. "When we went to see Elsie, I could easily have been stepping back into my childhood home. As a kid I promised myself that I'd work hard and escape and get my mum out so she could live the life she deserved. Then she fell down stairs at her cleaning job and broke her back, and part of her foot had to be amputated. Although she's in chronic pain, she'd still have to work because of changes in the disability allowance. I subsidise her living costs, so she doesn't have to work."

Lia's cheeks burned with the embarrassment that she'd had life so easy. They remained silent for most of the rest of the journey through North London. Lia couldn't comment with any genuine sympathy, and she didn't want to come across as patronising, a word which had stung at lunch. Lia waited in the car when Jay ran in to the shop to get the things her mum needed, and her thoughts slammed into one another like bumper cars. She'd had it so easy but now she was doing something that mattered. That didn't mean she had any real idea of what it was to not know whether she'd be able to eat the next day or not.

Jay seemed lost in thought, and a comfortable silence remained for the rest of the trip. Finally, they pulled up on a drive in front of a sweet-looking home. An adapted mobility car sat on the left, and Jay squeezed her car in beside it. Lia had to shimmy to extricate herself without knocking the other car.

Jay put both cloth shopping bags on one arm, rang the doorbell and then unlocked the door. "Hi, Mum. It's only me. We've got a visitor."

Lia followed, and Jay turned the deadlock behind them.

"Why did you come now, eh? I haven't had time to hoover," her mum called from another room.

"It's all right, Mum. I'm sure Lia won't mind, and I thought you were desperate for tea."

Lia trailed Jay into a sitting room that was bulging with bookcases and a large TV. There were a lot of classics on the bookshelves, which was surprising. Why, she couldn't say, and she was once again reminded of her preconceived ideas about people and how she judged them.

"I don't mind in the slightest," Lia said. "Don't get up." She crossed the room quickly and stuck out her hand so Jay's mum didn't have to rise from the La-Z-Boy recliner. Her mum's handshake was limp and frail. Lia wondered if breaking her back had also broken her spirit, but presumably not, given how bright and fierce her eyes shone. Her face was lined from years of pain and hard work.

"I mind. I'm Susan, by the way, as my daughter seems to have lost her manners."

"Sorry," Jay said from the kitchen. "I wanted to pop your frozen stuff in the freezer first." She entered and leaned against the door jamb. "I'm sure you're quite able to introduce yourselves."

In her own domain, Jay looked softer. It made Lia want to hug her. Instead, she played with the folds of her skirt, unsure what to do with her hands.

"Sit down, Lia. I'll make tea after I've put the rest of the shopping away."

She disappeared again and Lia sat, wondering what she could talk about. If she treated Susan as she did Elsie, she'd probably

GREEN *for* LOVE

be okay, but then she and Elsie always talked about the garden. Presumably Susan couldn't do the gardening. "How long have you lived here?"

"About seven years now." She lowered her voice a little. "Jay insisted I come. She's a good girl, but I miss my friends. We used to play cards every week, and this area is too snobby to have a social club nearby. Where did you meet?"

Lia couldn't say. Throwing paint all over Jay's company car wasn't going to make a good impression and neither would a woman's club. What was safe? What had Jay said to her mum about her?

"We met at a bar," she said finally, hoping it was close enough to the truth.

Susan clapped her hands. "Oh, does this mean you're Jay's girlfriend? She hasn't brought home a girlfriend for years. Are you going steady? I always thought Jay was too busy working to have a girlfriend. Although your face looks familiar. Have we met before?"

Lia put up her hand to stop Susan from straying into difficult territory. "No, it's nothing like that. We've been working on a project together, which is coming to an end."

Susan's face fell, and she didn't respond, but studied Lia intently. If that wasn't uncomfortable enough, the cold hand of dread clamped around Lia's heart as she realized how Susan recognised her.

Susan slammed her hands on the arms of the chair. "It's you, isn't it? That awful woman who screeched at the reporters and wouldn't move out of the way of the ambulance."

Susan's smile was replaced by a thin, flat line. Lia had never been embarrassed by her eco-action before. Never. Not even when her parents said it brought shame on the family. But in the face of Susan's ire, she shrank like a plant from an inferno.

Jay entered the room again, clearly having overheard the conversation. "Mum, Lia has been working with me at Magenta. She's done a great job on the committee and has put all of that behind her."

Lia gripped the arms of the chair and had to take a couple of settling breaths. She may regret blocking the ambulance, but she didn't regret pushing the issue into the headlines. How dare Jay try and change who she was or make assumptions about her, but now wasn't the right time to argue.

"But that person might have died in the ambulance."

Lia cringed, wishing she could disappear. Maybe this hadn't been such a good idea. Her knuckles bleached white, and she made a conscious effort to relax her fingers and centre herself.

"What have you always said about giving people second chances?" Jay asked. "Besides, Lia's my guest, so I expect you to be nice. She works for this brilliant charity in Bristol that insulates people's homes and puts in solar panels and heat pumps to reduce their electric bills."

Jay thought it was brilliant, did she? She'd never said that to Lia. She couldn't contain her smile. Or maybe she was doing the maximum PR for her mum's sake. She glanced at Susan, who seemed to be softening. Susan nodded as if to say she accepted her.

Lia smiled back. "If you can't play cards locally, can you do it online?"

"No, I've never got on with computers. Jay bought me an iPad, but I keep getting stuck and can't get back to where I want to. It does my head in."

"I have a friend, Elsie, who Jay has met. She likes cards too. I reckon she's a bit of a card shark." Lia could imagine Elsie and Susan's energies comingling in companionship, if they could understand each other with their strong accents, Elsie's with her broad Bristolian and Susan with her West London twang.

"Maybe we should get them together. Mum's a bit of a devil when it comes to cards too." Jay propped herself on the arm of the recliner.

The affection between them was palpable. Lia wished she had

that sort of easy relationship with her mother, and she pushed down the memory of the difficult conversation this morning. Seeing the devotion Jay had for her mum, Lia could feel the knot of judgement being pulled apart. Jay was clearly a good person. Life seemed more nuanced than Lia wanted to admit. Perhaps there was no black and white when it came to the environment, just different shades of green. She couldn't voice that; it was too costly to admit she might be wrong, and that there might be other ways of getting to the goal. Why did Jay have to unsettle her so? She should hate her for what she stood for, who she worked for, but Jay was more than her job. She was a kind, hard-working person who was confusing the hell out of Lia. Her world was being tilted, and she didn't like it.

Lia stared out of the window to avoid looking at the devotion between Jay and Susan. Jay's wasn't the face of a villain, which meant Lia wasn't the martyred hero. She shook off the unusual self-doubts. When she wasn't with Jay, she was doing exactly what she needed to. Wasn't she?

Chapter Seventeen

JAY LEANED AGAINST THE bar and accepted the whisky that Alice gave her. She surveyed the sea of sofas and silver hair and raised her hand as Mrs Battersby nodded at her. Jay grinned. The woman looked so prim and proper, no one would believe she was a dominatrix in her spare time. In the other corner, the honourable Lady Chestergreen smiled at her, fluttering her eyelashes. Jay had accepted that invitation before, but her policy of no action replays was still in place.

Today she was meeting Lia, even though she knew full well she was starting to swim in deeper waters. Friends shouldn't meet up at a place where sex was the expectation. Lia was turning her world upside down. She couldn't stop obsessing about her, wondering what she was thinking, what she was doing, what trouble she was causing.

Falling for the posh girl was stupid. Not that she was falling, per se, but the fact that she wanted more time with her suggested something deeper. Was this what happened when she wanted someone but couldn't sleep with them? Was this just an obsession that would fade if the itch was scratched?

Jay looked at her watch. Lia was late. The thought flitted across her mind that maybe Lia had been detained by the police again. She sipped her drink, and the smoky taste burned down her throat, just the way she liked it. A sound behind her made her turn, and Lady Chestergreen laid a perfectly manicured hand on her shoulder.

"Jay, my dear. I haven't seen you in here for a while. Does that mean you're free tonight?"

Jay flashed a false smile, trying to push down the thought of the animalistic sex they had shared many months ago. "Lady Chester—"

"Marjorie." She flapped at Jay's forearm as if Jay was being playful and teasing her, then settled her fingers around Jay's hand, gripping it possessively.

Why had Jay ever welcomed the ministrations of this predator, who was married to one of the wealthiest peers of the nation? The thought of being in bed with her now made Jay shudder. She turned to face Marjorie, determined not to be bulldozed into bed.

"Marjorie, I'm very flattered, but I'm meeting someone. But thank you for the offer."

Marjorie's eyes hardened even though her smile remained in place. "How disappointing. You were a lovely kink. If ever you feel lonely, just look me up." She moved in to kiss Jay on the mouth, but Jay turned her face barely in time to offer her cheek.

"Oh." Lia's voice came from the other side of Lady Chestergreen.

Marjorie, her hand still on Jay's shoulder, reached out to Lia, not missing a beat. "Cordelia, how are you? How is your mother? Are she and your father settling in France? How's his health now? Is he fully recovered?" She looked from Lia to Jay and back again, and her eyes narrowed. "I didn't know you were a thing. Does your mother know?" Not waiting for a reply, she squeezed Jay's shoulder. "Remember what I said, Jay. Cordelia." She nodded to Lia and made her retreat to the double doors at the back.

"Something you want to tell me?" Lia asked with an amused grin.

"Not here. Drink?"

"Normally I have water, but I'll have whatever you're drinking," Lia said, glancing at the whisky as she sat down on the leather bar stool.

"Are you sure you know what you're letting yourself in for? It's Ardbeg, perhaps the peatiest of the whiskies."

"You don't think I can cope?"

GREEN *for* LOVE

"Is everything a challenge with you?" Jay waved at Alice, indicating two glasses of the same.

"When it comes to you, yes."

Lia stared at Jay with an intensity she found both thrilling and daunting. Then Lia broke into a smile, and Jay's heart melted a little more. This yearning was dangerous to her rule of never getting involved.

Alice brought two more glasses, and Jay raised her glass. "To friendship and the end of a great project."

Lia clinked her glass, staring at Jay the whole time as she took a large gulp of the drink. Her eyes widened slightly, and Jay was sure Lia's colouring pinkened, but she swallowed and smiled.

"Do you like it?"

"Wow, that's strong and has a very deep afterglow." Lia still fixed her with her intense gaze, her pupils expanding. "It's not unlike you. Smoky, hot, and leaves a warmth in my stomach," Lia said, a hoarseness in her voice that could have been either the whisky or desire.

Jay wasn't convinced it was a compliment but decided to take it anyway. Lia leaned forward so their faces almost touched, and Jay could smell the whisky on her breath.

"I've tried so hard to get you out of my head, but I find myself pulled to you, and I'm helpless. It can't go anywhere. We're too different. We know that. But I crave being with you. You're the last person I should be interested in, yet here I am, wanting you despite knowing full well that it could be disastrous for my heart. And after our little dance the other week, I'm sure you want me."

Jay nodded, unsure she would be able to speak in her normal voice. Was this really going to happen? Should it? It shouldn't. God, she wanted it to. Lia put her hand on Jay's thigh. Where it touched set off sparks below the surface of her skin.

"Give me five minutes then come up to my room, eighteen. On the second floor." Lia knocked back the rest of the drink in one swig and hopped off the stool. She thanked Alice and exited the lounge, waving to a few of the women playing cards at the table.

Alice raised the bottle of Ardbeg, but Jay shook her head. She needed to look calm for the audience in the lounge, but the adrenaline of anticipation needed an outlet. Lia wanted her. A thrill shivered through her. After she drained her glass, she stood.

Alice winked at her, as though this was her normal routine. But this felt so different. It mattered. Lia mattered, despite her constant chafing about the environment. Compelled, she headed up the stairs to Lia's room. All thoughts of friendship, of boundaries, and of difference were shoved aside. This simply had to happen, consequences be dammed. Jay paused at the polished oak door to settle herself and knocked gently.

The door opened, and Lia tugged her in, shutting the door behind them and pushing Jay back against the door. She knit her fingers into Jay's hair.

"I want you," she whispered into her ear, and the soft warm breath caused Jay to moan a little.

Lia trailed kisses from her ear across her cheeks until their lips met. Jay almost expected them to sizzle with the heat. Lia's lips were soft, in contrast to the concentrated desire emanating from her. Jay relaxed into the kiss as Lia licked her bottom lip and traced her teeth along it. She opened her mouth and yielded, letting down her defences so all the pent-up lust could come tumbling out.

She wanted Lia with an intensity that had been squashed since Lia had visited her in her flat. Desire raced through every nerve in her body shouting, "Wake up, wake up," and she was—awake, alive, and humming with anticipation. Lia's hips pushed against Jay's, grinding in a way guaranteed to set her off.

"Stay the night?" Lia whispered.

The weeks of pent-up lust silenced her brain from thinking and her mouth from declining. Her senses were alive, and she was surprised when she murmured, "Yes," and leaned in closer.

"Please tell me you want this." Lia placed her hands on either side of Jay's face, stirring Jay's desire.

GREEN *for* LOVE

Her intense attention made Jay wet, made her want to tear off her clothes and submit to Lia's touch. "I've wanted you from the moment I heard your passionate speeches. Feisty, fighting for what you believe, like a modern-day Boudicca." Jay cupped Lia's face and pulled her close. There was nothing chaste about the kiss; it was all energy and passion. Lia ran her fingers up and down her back, tugging and pulling at her shirt. Jay was surprised her blouse had already been undone and was slipping off her shoulders.

They stopped kissing for a second for Jay to shrug it off, and Lia pulled her top over her head. Her bangles clattered.

"Hold on," Lia said and slipped them off, like removing her armour. "Let's take this to bed."

Lia grasped Jay's hand and pulled her so hard and fast, Jay almost lost her footing. She pushed her onto the mattress, and covered Jay's body with her own. The sensation of their breasts brushing hardened Jay's nipples, and arousal surged through her body. She arched her back as Lia tweaked her nipples, wanting to get as close as she could, to feel the electric charge that jolted all the way to her core.

"God, you're so hot," Lia said and breathed over Jay's nipple, causing Jay to writhe and give a sharp intake of breath. Lia opened the top button of Jay's trousers. "These need to come off."

Jay raised her hips to shimmy out of her trousers, not caring where they landed. She pulled down Lia's skirt and panties in one swoop, and they cascaded to the floor.

Surprisingly, Lia's triangle at the top of her thighs was bright ginger, much deeper than her strawberry-blond head of hair. She shivered and licked her lips as they rolled back onto the bed with Jay on top.

"Beautiful," Jay said and curled her fingers through Lia's coarse hair, slick and glistening. Lia moaned as Jay fingered her folds, and Lia opened her legs wide, rocking her hips, bidding her enter. But Jay didn't. She fluttered her fingers over Lia's inner thigh. She wanted to savour this moment, this coming together.

"Don't tease."

Lia tried to pull Jay's hand higher, but she circled Lia's clit, drawing out the sensation till Lia clutched her tight.

"For fuck's sake, just fuck me."

So much for the posh girl now. Lia's desperation amped up Jay's arousal, and the scent of sex enveloped them both. "What, like this?" Jay pushed a finger between her lips, into the wetness that made her moan.

"More."

Jay thrust two more fingers in, setting up a hard rhythm, with Lia rocking her hips in time, their breaths fast and ragged. This was fucking to forget, fucking to forgive, fucking to form a bond. She flicked Lia's clit and felt her own desire, hot and wet between her legs, as Lia clutched Jay's hand and bucked and shouted her name. Her abandon turned Jay on even more. Like magnesium burning in oxygen, there was a blinding white light as Jay climaxed just seconds after Lia, without even being touched. She shuddered and collapsed on Lia.

When she'd recovered a few minutes later, Jay laughed. "Well, that was embarrassing. I've never come before without being touched. You make me so wet."

"Give me a second, and I'll rectify that."

Lia kissed Jay and rolled her over. Softly, taking her time, Lia traced her fingers over Jay's skin, causing a rush of heat that melted the last defences between them. She didn't know if this would be just one night or maybe even a few weeks, but Jay didn't care. She had never had such wonderful, explosive sex before, and she knew she wanted it again, differences be damned. Her reaction was surprising and terrifying.

Jay stared deep into Lia's eyes, and for the first time, amongst the lust and dark desire was the softness of affection. A confusing cocktail of fear and excitement rushed through her. Lia liked her, was in bed with her, had come for her, and was now circling Jay's throbbing clit and feathering kisses along her neck, her breasts,

GREEN *for* LOVE

her belly, and lower. She released hot breath onto her clit, sending her into a spasm of desire, and Jay stopped thinking. There was only this moment.

Lia's soft licking beckoned an orgasm, which expanded in every cell of her body and spasmed as lightning shot through her from her hair to the tips of her toes, every nerve blasted in bright light.

Afterwards, sated and sprawled across each other, Lia chuckled. "That was a revelation, but I should have guessed you'd be hot in bed. You're an amazing lover, even if you did fight me for top."

Jay resisted the urge to giggle but joy bubbled up anyway. "You've got to be kidding me. I let you take control since it obviously means so much to you." Jay curled her finger around Lia's coarse ginger hairs. "This was a surprise. You must have Celtic blood."

"I think it's fair to say there is absolutely Scottish ancestry."

Jay laid her hand across Lia's flat belly, warm and slick from their previous activities. There was always a sense of accomplishment when she was lying in bed with one of the upper-class women from the club, but this was different. With them, she had a touch of remorse—even though they approached her—and an ache of loneliness afterwards. She knew more about Lia than she ever had any of the others. "Are you proud of your ancestry?"

Lia kissed the top of Jay's head, which felt both comforting and arousing. "Not so much proud, but I feel it in my bones. I feel it in the whinstone rocks and the heather moors. I feel it in windswept sand dunes, and beaches, and the solid rocks of the castles."

Jay tickled her, and Lia squirmed. "You're such a romantic. You obviously love it. Why don't you live up there?" she asked.

Lia sat up sharply, all softness in her expression gone. "Tim has responsibility for the estate, and I can't bear to see what he's doing to it, how he's destroying it by bleeding it dry. And I guess I simply don't feel welcome up there anymore."

Damn, she hadn't meant to get Lia agitated. She wanted her to be calm, relaxed, and comfortable in their post-orgasmic glow.

"Could you live somewhere else that's not on your land?"

Lia slumped back at Jay's gentle pulling and sighed. "I'd still know what was going on, and it would drive me to distraction."

"And you're not one to take things lying down, unless you're being glued there." Jay chuckled at her own bad joke.

"That's terrible."

They laughed, and Lia kissed Jay softly on the lips, stopping her from uttering anything else inane. She stared into Lia's eyes, or rather, she stared through them into the depths and complexities hidden from view.

"Tell me something," Lia said. "When we first met, I was surprised my seduction techniques didn't work, and when you rebuffed me, I wanted you even more. Why didn't they work? You seem to have availed yourself of some of the other club members. Why not me?"

Jay squirmed at the direct question, one she didn't want to answer. "I hoped you hadn't noticed."

Lia raised her eyebrow. "Being accosted by Marjorie in the bar, you asking if you knew my mother with a look of panic on your face... I don't need to be Sherlock to work it out. So why didn't you succumb to me?"

Jay sat up and crossed her arms over her chest. "I was unnerved. I still am. Something told me we could be more than a one-night stand. But I don't do more than one-night stands."

The gleam in Lia's eyes was positively wicked. "Ha ha. You admit you have intuition?"

Jay rolled her eyes. "I'm not admitting anything. Science has always been about a flash of a spark and then trying to disprove it hundreds of times."

Lia caressed Jay's jaw with a tenderness that was almost too soft to bear.

"So I was a flash of a spark, or rather, what we have is a flash of a spark?"

Jay wanted to backpedal, to hide, to rewind this conversation. She knew a few moves out that there was about to be checkmate.

GREEN *for* LOVE

"It's not logical. We shouldn't be compatible on any other level than sex."

Lia traced her index finger over Jay's lips. "Yet here we are."

"I know." *Checkmate.*

And yet, the night passed in a succession of hard sex and harder orgasms before they finally crashed into sleep, sprawled across each other in a tangle of limbs.

The light peeping in at dawn caused Jay to stir. Lia's arm was spread over her belly, and warm breath caused the hairs on the nape of her neck to stir. Her eyes shot open. She rarely stayed over, and it took a second for the memories of last night to come flooding in. No wonder she felt tired. She was delightfully sore in intimate places. She yawned and carefully extricated herself from Lia's arm so she could freshen up in the bathroom.

When she came out, Lia was sat up rubbing her eyes. Her hair looked more reddish in the light and was a mass of curls that made her look so cute and vulnerable, Jay was tempted to slip back under the covers and cuddle her, even though she wasn't the cuddling type.

"What time is it?" Lia asked.

"Just after six. I need to get ready for work."

Lia's smile faded. "Were you going to leave without saying goodbye?"

There was a disappointment in Lia's tone that caused Jay to falter. That was what she normally did, and for the first time, she felt guilty, as if she'd used the women she'd been with. But she didn't want to use Lia; she wanted to impress her. "I was going to let you sleep and call you later to see about meeting up again. I've got a locker downstairs in the gym, so I can shower and change there." She also kept a change of work clothes along with her gym kit. But she didn't want to tell Lia that. It seemed important that Lia didn't know how often she entertained women here, even though that was how they'd met.

"So you just love 'em and leave 'em? Am I just another notch on your bedpost?"

Yes. No. I've never felt like this before. Lia wasn't just another of the one-night stands for quick release. What she didn't know was why. She wanted Lia on a deeper level. If she had hoped her feelings would dissipate after sleeping together, she was sorely mistaken. Her crush was becoming a problem, and she needed to squash it immediately. "I thought that was understood. I'd like to meet up again, but if we don't, no hard feelings, I hope." Even as Jay said it, she shrivelled a little inside. "We said friendship, and this was a temporary thing, a way to deal with our attraction and put it to bed." She looked away from the hurt in Lia's eyes. "We knew it wouldn't go anywhere."

Lia nodded, lay back down, and curled into a ball with her back to Jay.

With a sigh, Jay silently gathered her things and closed the door quietly behind her.

Chapter Eighteen

LIA PULLED AT THE peapods causing the lattice of vines to distort. She placed them in a bucket and repeated the process in mindful activity. She loved harvesting what they had planted, nurtured, and grown. She felt most at home with her feet in the soil: grounded and peaceful, not raging at the oil giants and politicians. There was something honest about dirt under her fingernails and the glisten of dew on the spidery vines. She turned and waved at Elsie, who was concentrating on shelling the peas, cracking them open and sliding her thumb down with a swoop efficient from years of practice.

Elsie coughed and waved her off. "You don't have time to look up and wave, young lady. We need to finish by the time my programme starts."

But she was smiling, and Lia knew she wouldn't mind if they missed the first minutes or missed it altogether when they could spend the day outside, with the birds twittering and the bees pollinating the flowers. Lia checked the rest of the peas; they weren't quite ready yet.

Soil slipped through her fingers. Rich and deeply composted, it crumbled like cocoa. There was nothing she liked better than nutrient soil. She inhaled the earthy smell, the smell of happiness. She was closer to her gramps and Northumberland when she had her feet in the soil and the wind reddening her cheeks.

She decided to help Steve, who she had *volunteered* to cut down nettles on the steep railway bank. The allotments committee had agreed to plant the banks with wildflowers for the bees, but it would take a couple of seasons to establish the real rewilding.

Her phone buzzed in her pocket. She frowned when she saw it was a text from Jay, with a link to some scientific research probably bigging up the ecological impact of hydrogen. When she got home she would send a counter argument. The scientific tit for tat they'd started—the only area where they seemed to communicate well—was as enjoyable as slapping down playing cards with friends, and she looked forward to the next missive.

Lia rose and brushed the soil from her skirt. She ought to buy herself a cheap pair of jeans. She didn't want to wear her branded moleskin trousers in their community allotment, as they marked her as a rich outsider. But she supposed the air around her legs was cooling on a warm day doing heavy work.

When people knew she had money, they became suspicious. Class issues were still alive and well, and she didn't want to be treated differently. It wasn't her imagination, or even a guess. When people around her thought she was from money, they shut down. She hated the division it caused between her and the people she was trying to save the planet with. So she downplayed it as much as possible, even if she wasn't being terribly authentic. But lately, after spending time with Jay, she'd begun to feel like maybe that was part of the problem. Maybe that failure to let people see all of who she was meant her chakra was getting blocked. She turned her face to the sun. It was too nice for heavy thoughts.

She nodded to Fred, who loved to cultivate flowers, and made her way over to drop off the rest of the peas with Elsie and pick up a pair of worn gardening gloves. "Are you okay here if I go and help Steve?"

Elsie smiled. "I am. When I've finished these, I've got my paper. What could be nicer than sitting outside on a lovely autumn day? You take all the time you need."

Lia walked over to where Steve was hard at work, sweating as he tried to pull out some ivy that clung to the side of the bank. As her co-planner for the No More Oil protests, she knew him best, and she'd asked if he wanted to come help today, even though

GREEN *for* LOVE

they'd never spent time together outside the protests before. She was surprised when he accepted. "Need a hand?"

"Yeah, hand me that spade. I'll need to dig down a bit deeper. Tenacious buggers, aren't they?" He wiped his forehead with the back of his hand. "When you invited me to Bristol this weekend, you didn't tell me it was going to be back-breaking work."

"You did offer." Lia thrust the spade into the soil below where he was tugging. She expertly pushed it down further with her foot and levered up the roots.

"You're made for this," Steve said as he stepped back to give her room.

"I lived on a farm all my life until I went to Bristol."

"By farm, you mean your family's huge estates up in Northumberland?" He grinned and discarded the weeds onto the wheelbarrow ready to be taken to the compost heap. "I can't believe the landed gentry are happy their daughter has been arrested, and more than once."

Lia dug the spade into the soil again, giving herself time to think. "No, they're fed up with bailing me out. But they can afford it, so it's easier for me to do than anyone else."

"Don't you think someone else should take their turn? The authorities seem to have you in their crosshairs now."

Anger flashed through her, igniting the dry tinder. "Not you as well. I said I'd stop during the report, but I don't trust Magenta won't delay the implementation indefinitely. When they don't do as they said, we'll need to push the point home, to make it clear we won't put up with them making it look like they did something, only to let it fade into obscurity."

Steve raised his hands. "Don't shoot me. I'm only the messenger. The committee is a bit concerned that you've become a bit too high-profile." He yanked at another vine. "The latest media coverage seems to be more about you than the cause."

She'd seen the article he was referring to, complete with a photo of her glued to the ground. It said her family had chosen

E.V. BANCROFT

not to comment, but that wasn't the point. "What the fuck do you mean? We're getting publicity. We're getting people to talk about the impact of fossil fuels. I can't believe what you're saying. This isn't you."

Lia snatched up the wheelbarrow heavy with nettles and brambles and stalked off. She shouldn't argue with Steve; he'd been there with her all the way. But didn't the committee see this was way too important to worry about bad publicity? She ran the wheelbarrow up the plank to pour the weeds into the heap behind it then twisted it to shed the last few tendrils clinging to the sides. They needed to grasp the nettle to make their point. She crushed the plants in her hands and tossed them onto the heap so they could decay and mould down to rejuvenate the soil. Lia rolled the wheelbarrow down to the ground and gave herself time to recalibrate.

Standing with her hands on her hips, feet solidly placed on the ground, she tried to centre herself. Even Elsie didn't approve, although she said if ever Lia was in trouble with the police, she could always stay with her. But they both knew Lia had never lived in somewhere this small. They'd laughed, but Lia had been struck by Elsie's kindness.

She closed her eyes, drawing strength from the earth by pulling the energy up through her body, stirring and cleansing her chakras. She drew the energy up through the colours of the rainbow to the bright white of higher consciousness and the connection with the Universe. She raised her hands, sensing her connection with the planets and stars.

She didn't know how long she stayed there, but the light had shifted when she looked up again. Steve had cleared a bigger patch of weeds and was waiting for the wheelbarrow to be brought back. Elsie was reading her paper, but she'd want to get back. Lia inhaled again and slowly released her breath. This was her safe space. The community allotment was the closest to solace she had in the city. Even so, there was still a hole in her heart for the barren

GREEN *for* LOVE

beauty of Northumberland, and she wished she could go home. Shaking off her sentimentality, she wheeled the barrow back to Steve and without a word, swept up the weeds and piled them in.

"Sorry," he said. "I don't want you to be made an example of by the law, especially if the committee think it needs to focus on the cause, not on you. You've done so well. I wouldn't be your friend if I didn't tell you the truth."

She squeezed his forearm. "I know, thanks. But it's something that I have to do. My work isn't finished, and if it means we get more publicity because I'm some posh girl, then so be it. At least the issue is in the papers."

Jay teasing her about being a posh girl flooded back. Lia had never been good enough for her family because she didn't follow their values, and she would never be accepted for who she was by anyone else, anyone else that mattered anyway, because she was set apart. And Jay mattered, even though she probably shouldn't. Now the media loved to hate her, and she could use that to get attention for the cause. Why didn't Steve and the No More Oil committee see that?

"I'm sorry we argued. But can't you see we must go on? We're starting to gain momentum."

Steve nodded, picked up an armful of weeds, and threw them in the barrow. "Are we finishing now? I think Elsie is getting a bit chilly now the sun's gone in. I'll finish up here if you want to take her back."

"Thanks. You're a good friend, and I appreciate your concern." Lia grinned. "I'll text you when I need your videoing skills on the next action. Say hello to Hayley."

His smile looked a little sad. "Sure. Have a good evening."

"I will." Lia hurried towards where Elsie was sitting. "Sorry I was so long," she said as she approached. "You must be getting cold."

"Well, I could do with a cup of tea and a wee." Elsie tucked her paper away and clambered into the wheelchair.

Although she could walk a couple of hundred yards, she found it hard going up the hills, so after a few battles, she allowed Lia to bring her and take her back this way.

Thankfully, the lift in her tower block was working, and that always made it easier. Helping Elsie to get up the stairs with a basket of produce and a wheelchair wasn't easy. Lia wheeled her into the lift, and they were at her flat in no time.

"Cup of tea?" Elsie asked as she unlocked her door.

"Please." Lia tucked the wheelchair out of the way by the door.

"Would you like some supper from today's pickings?" Elsie asked.

She was such a generous soul, no wonder she had no money.

"No, you keep that for yourself. I picked up some veg yesterday that I need to cook at home. Let's watch the rest of your programme, and then I'll be on my way." Lia squeezed her hand.

Elsie smiled at her and picked up the remote. "Thank you. I don't know what I'd do without you."

Lia went into the kitchen to put the kettle on. They had the routine like clockwork. Elsie set up the channel, and Lia made the tea. "I don't know what *I'd* do without *you*. I need you to keep my sanity. Besides, you're busy every day playing cards with friends or watching TV," Lia said.

"But I love to spend the day outside with you. It's wonderful to be in nature."

Not for the first time, Lia wished she could get Elsie a cottage in the country. She seemed so out of place in this urban environment. She loved the simple life. She shouldn't be worrying about the music from the neighbours below and the shouting from next door. Lia often felt closer to Elsie than her own mother. She envied Jay being able to afford a place for her mum. In reality, Lia could probably afford to do something similar for Elsie if she didn't support the environmental charities.

She wondered if Jay would approve or not. How strange that her thoughts always circled back to Jay. Their night together had been special, but clearly Jay didn't share the sentiment. She

GREEN *for* LOVE

had never implied she did anything otherwise, so Lia shouldn't complain. And yet, Lia wanted to be special, to be someone to her. It was bad enough she had never been number one with her parents, but it hurt more to be just another woman to someone like Jay.

Just once, she wanted to be someone's number one.

Chapter Nineteen

THE FOLLOWING MORNING LIA'S phone pinged with a text message. *Hey there, are you in London? If so, would you like to go dancing with me? J*

A thrill coursed through Lia but just as quickly merged with confusion. After the way they'd left things, she wasn't certain she'd ever see Jay again, except on opposite sides of a protest. Her fingers hovered over the keys. Go? Don't go?

She sighed. *Yes, I'm in London once a week. It will be nice to dance, but as I'm taller, shouldn't I lead?* Lia grinned and pressed send.

A few seconds later a reply pinged. *Ha, you just want to be top. If you want to lead, that's fine with me. Does this Thursday work for you? J*

She would so like to be on top, but it seemed Jay wanted no more than friendship. Dancing could be fun and would be a change from the rather intense No More Oil meetings. And she wasn't in the mood for casual hook-ups. Jay had spoiled her for that, damn the woman. If only she could let go of the belief, or delusion, that Jay was supposed to be her soulmate.

That Thursday, Lia pulled Jay towards her as they were shown the steps for the waltz and then they arched their backs away from each other. This dancing was surprisingly good for her core, and it was a nice alternative to yoga. Plus, she wasn't going to complain at holding a gorgeous woman in her arms. She was surrounded by Jay's spicy cologne, and she inhaled deeply, committing it to memory. It reminded her of an English wood in autumn when the leaves turned yellow and red.

"Head up," Jay whispered and straightened Lia's posture with firm hands.

Even in the following position, Jay was trying to lead. Lia tried not to notice the buzz of energy radiating through to her core from where their hips touched. "This is surprisingly erotic," Lia whispered back.

Jay's eyes widened as though such a thought had never occurred to her. "We don't have to touch at the hip if you're uncomfortable. Most people aren't touching."

She pulled away, leaving a cool space between them. Lia pulled Jay's hips towards her own, and Jay turned pink. "Is this okay?" Lia took the opportunity to grind her hip against Jay's. The exhalation from Jay's lips was very satisfactory.

"More than okay. But I'm not sure I can concentrate on the dance."

Lia dared a glance back to see Jay was struggling to keep a neutral expression. Her eyes gave her away though. "Just as well it's quite straightforward then." Lia counted them in, and they joined the other dancers.

As they glided across the wooden floor of the community centre, Jay moved with ease and was light on her feet, and Lia loosened her grip, so she could be subtly guided in a wave of backward and forward, up and down, and around. It was smooth and flowing, and she loved being at one with her body, like a soul-centred yoga session. No wonder Jay lost herself in this.

Jay's face glowed with serene concentration as they floated round. Parts of Lia's body pulsed, and it wasn't in the slow one two three either. God, she was so taken with Jay. She wanted to kiss her now as they spun on the dancefloor then take her home to bed. She'd never thought of ballroom dancing as sexy before, but this was like tortuous foreplay.

Lia stepped forward instead of back and trod on Jay's toe, breaking the spell. "Sorry, I wasn't concentrating." *I was thinking how I'd like to take you to bed and have sex with you until dawn.*

GREEN *for* LOVE

Jay's smile seemed more like a grimace, so it must have hurt. Lia went back to counting and focusing on the task, delighting in watching same-sex couples dancing together. It was such a thrill to be surrounded by others like her, being able to be themselves. When the track finished, everybody clapped and thanked their partners.

"We'll have a five-minute break," the dance tutor said.

Jay relaxed but continued to hold Lia's hand.

"Thanks." Jay breathed out and looked at their clasped hands. "You're a really good dancer. When you follow instructions," she said and grinned.

Her grin was adorable, like that of a mischievous child. Lia could imagine Jay as a young girl: determined, hard-working, and always the person others gravitated to, given her open nature. "Thanks. I have a good teacher. I'd love to do that again."

They were so close, Lia could feel Jay's heart beating fast in her neck, from exertion or desire Lia didn't know, but it matched her own. She leaned forward but was interrupted as two men approached and tapped Jay on her shoulder.

"Not wishing to barge in on your necking session—much—but I wanted to meet this goddess you've coerced into dancing with you."

Jay thumped the intruder on his arm. "Hey, Adam, I'd say it's good to see you, but I never lie. Hello, Ben. He forced you to come again then? Let me introduce you to Lia. It's her first time, so be nice."

Adam, the thinner and taller of the two men, took Lia's hand from Jay's and bent over it like a Regency gentleman. She could almost imagine him as one of the haut ton.

"Charmed, I'm sure, and I'm delighted that Jay hasn't been abandoned in her hour of need. I'm Adam, and this gorgeous hulk of a man is my better half, Ben."

Adam removed his hand from Lia's and patted Ben on his very solid pecs that seemed to be bursting through his tight shirt. Ben smiled with the infatuation of someone in love. "Lovely to meet you both. Jay has spoken a lot about you, Adam."

"All wonderful, I'm sure. Now what did you think of the waltz? Did I see you leading?"

Lia laughed. "More like being pushed around into the right position."

Adam touched her arm. "Tell me about it. She's so bossy, that one, but I'm sure you have her covered."

Jay rolled her eyes. "Are you sure you don't need some water to cool yourself down, Adam?"

He dramatically mopped his brow in mock offense. "Ooh, I know when I'm not wanted. Come along, honeybun. Lovely to meet you, Lia. Look after her; she's a good egg." He blew air kisses before dragging Ben away.

Jay shrugged. "Sorry about Adam. He's not normally so over the top. He's still trying to impress Ben."

"He's lovely and obviously very fond of you."

Jay's expression softened. "Yes, I'm fond of him too, and he's lovely with Mum."

Lia tamped down a twinge of jealousy. She wasn't sure Susan approved of her. But she had no claims on Jay. They were clearly never going to be any more than friends and maybe dance partners. Yet it was great to be given access to such an important part of Jay's life. And Adam was right; Jay was a good egg, and she seemed to have scrambled Lia's brain.

When the class finished and people packed up their bags, Adam and Ben came over to join them.

"Anyone coming to the pub?" Adam asked.

Jay groaned. "He only wants to go so he can ogle the bartender and his huge biceps."

Adam put his hand over his heart. "All those pints he pulls. I feel sorry for him, that's all."

Jay mock-glared at him, and Lia hid her smirk at their antics.

"I thought—I hoped—that now Adam is with Ben, that would

GREEN *for* LOVE

stop, but no. They both sit there and stare and give him marks out of ten. Honestly, it's like watching *Britain's Got Talent*."

They all laughed. "How would you know? You've never willingly watched any entertainment. Your poor mum has to talk to little me about the goings on in TV land." Adam grabbed hold of Jay and stage-whispered to Lia, "She's such a snob. She doesn't like the pub because they don't sell her favourite whisky."

Jay's face turned crimson, and Lia chuckled. "I can imagine. Ardbeg is a bit of a connoisseur's drink." She squeezed Jay's hand to show she was teasing. "I'm sure it's fine if you like drinking smoke."

"I know what I like, and I appreciate the finer things in life." Jay's face relaxed into a smile, and she winked at Lia. "It must be my sun in Taurus."

There was a twinkle in Jay's eye, as if to say, "*See, I was listening.*" Lia winked at her to acknowledge her, although she wanted to fling her arms around her and feather her with kisses.

"Ooh, are you into astrology? I'm a Leo," Adam said.

Lia nodded. "I can see that."

Jay shook her head and smiled. "Oh, no, are you two going to talk astrology all night? We'll have to talk football, Ben. Did you see the Bees won again on Saturday?"

Lia coughed. Would Jay keep on surprising her? "You like football?"

"No," Ben said before Jay could answer. "She's a masochist; she supports Brentford."

"Ha ha." Jay pretended to punch him on the arm. "Ignore him, he supports Chelsea. Do you follow the beautiful game?"

"I come from the North East; it's a religion up there. Everyone supports Newcastle."

"Why aye, man," Adam said in a terrible impression of the accent. "But you don't speak like a Geordie."

"No." And there it was, being different again.

Clearly seeing her discomfort, he gave her a big smile. "That's just as well. I'd never understand you. Me, I only watch football so I can admire their legs. Are we on? Please say yes."

He hadn't been excluding or judgemental. That was so refreshing. She needed to learn to trust that not everyone was like her family or peer group. They all seemed genuine, and she was enjoying their banter. It was lovely to take a peep into Jay's personal life. Lia glanced at Jay, who shrugged noncommittally.

"Sure, why not."

The pub was old-fashioned and quite dark inside, with stained glass windows and a pervading smell of stale beer. It was relatively quiet now, with a few tables free, although there was debris from previous occupants. Presumably it was an after-work pub, and people had gone home to the suburbs.

Jay ordered the drinks at the bar, and the boys sat on the mock-leather banquette.

Lia took one of the wooden chairs opposite them. They really did watch the bar man and discuss how his biceps flexed. She couldn't help but steal a glance at him.

"Maybe I'll go and help Jay carry the drinks," she said, not wanting to witness their objectification, even if it was for fun. She deliberately stood so their view would be restricted, to audible groans from behind. "Need a hand?"

Jay pushed the pints across to Lia. "Thanks. Don't mind the boys. They're only joking." She bit her lip. "Sorry if they're a bit much. Adam likes to hold forth because he has to hide himself during the day. He works for one of the smaller merchant banks, and it's such a macho culture that he can't be who he is there."

Another one wedded to an unsuitable job. "Why does he stay?"

Jay's expression dropped. "He doesn't talk about it much, but he has massive debts from when he first came to London, and he's trying to clear them. He wanted to get into the theatre, but there are hundreds of people for every role, so he took a well-paid job as admin assistant in a bank. He's bored out of his brain."

"I can imagine. I'd feel trapped doing something like that."

"Can you take their pints? I'll bring our drinks in a second."

GREEN *for* LOVE

"Of course." Lia picked up the glasses and carefully carried them over to the table.

As Adam chatted and entertained them, Lia snuck a glance at Jay. All her wariness had gone, and her face seemed softer as she smiled and bantered. Her aura glowed with clarity. And she'd made it clear that she was off limits. Watching from the sidelines was all Lia could do.

Chapter Twenty

"IF THERE'S NO OTHER business, I'll bring this meeting to a close. Thank you, everyone, for all your input. I think the final report and presentation we've produced for the board is so much more diverse, thought through, and challenging than would have been the case if it had only been us here at Magenta. Don't forget we have the celebratory dinner next week. Please confirm with Marta before the close of play today whether you'll be able to come." Jay scanned the room and tried not to linger too long on Lia, who had the audacity to wink.

Jay had spent the whole of the meeting trying not to stare at her, thinking about their night together and their fun evening dancing. She was seriously questioning her rule of no do-overs. Lia had looked so beautiful as she lay on the bed, and it had taken everything Jay had to walk away. Jay hadn't missed the sadness in her eyes as she did. And they hadn't spoken about that night since.

She rose to shake hands with the committee members. She was sad to see this conclude. The meetings had been lively and informative, and she had begun to think of everyone as colleagues. Now she just needed to convince the board to implement the recommendations in full. She already had Oliver's blessing on the report, so that would help. In the periphery of her vision, she noticed Lia hang back, and she smiled to herself. Maybe they could go out for a celebratory lunch. Not everything had to be about sex, right? "May I see you afterward?" Jay whispered to Lia, who nodded.

She had almost succeeded in getting rid of everyone when Ian said, "Lia, can I give you a lift?"

So much for having time together.

Lia shrugged as if she were nonchalant to staying or going. "Sure, thanks. I just need a quick word with Jay. I'll see you at the car park in two ticks."

It was infuriating but also for the best, given that they'd found solid ground for once.

"Thanks again, Ian," Jay said, and they shook hands.

"Remember what I said about the wider context." He gave her an intense stare as if willing her to change the presentation they had just poured over for hours. Then he swung around and exited the room.

Jay struggled to find the words she wanted to say, and there was an awkward silence as Lia packed her bag and settled it on her shoulder.

"I'd better go. Don't want to keep Ian waiting." Without waiting for a reply, Lia strode to the door and opened it.

"I'll see you to the lift," Jay said, cursing her cowardice. How could she admit what she wanted? She closed the door behind them and followed Lia down the corridor towards the elevators. As she trailed Lia's seductive walk and mesmerising perfume, probably some handmade essential oil-based concoction, Jay searched for an excuse to take what they had to another level. "Will you be able to come dancing this week? Or meet again?" *Damn*. She sounded too desperate.

For the first time, Jay had an echo of what the women in the club must feel when she gave them no more than sex, like she was hollow and unimportant. She had always been very clear about having no expectations. Expectations lead to disappointment, and Jay didn't need that. A shiver of discomfort and lack of control gave her pause. It was like her whole body resonated with excitement when she saw Lia, and when she was with her, it felt like a gift, not only physical, or even emotional, but somehow spiritual as well. She was sounding as woo woo as Lia. Her nonsense was rubbing off on her, but the fact that she couldn't say for certain it was nonsense anymore was more disconcerting.

Lia turned at the elevator doors and placed her index finger on Jay's chest. "Can you come to Northumberland with me this weekend? I'm going up today to see my brother and niece, but maybe you could join me up there on Friday. If you don't need to look after your mum, of course."

"I'd love to, but I promised Mum I'd take her to see her old card buddies this weekend." Never had she felt such a disappointment at having to do something for her mum. Ordinarily it was a task she did willingly, with love.

"You're a good soul." Lia stroked Jay's cheek, her expression changing from the feisty eco-warrior to a wonderful, considerate person. "I assume there are security cameras?" Lia grinned.

"Correct." Jay returned her grin. Red flags waved wildly in her subconscious, but she pretended not to see them. This blurring of friendship lines was going to be messy.

"Well, let's give them something to think about." Lia pulled Jay into a passionate kiss.

There was no doubt this was a kiss between lovers, but Jay didn't care. She relaxed into its warmth, and it seemed to promise so much more than just a goodbye. It signalled hope, reciprocation, and a desire to take it further. Things that had once made Jay panic and flee now sounded interesting, appealing, and like something she very much wanted. The elevator dinged, causing them to break away from each other. They jumped apart as the doors opened, but fortunately no one was there.

"I'll call you." Lia squeezed Jay's arm and then spun into the elevator, and the doors closed.

Jay leaned against the wall to compose herself. Lia was like a drug she couldn't get enough of, and she wanted to bang on the doors and ask her to come back. She inhaled sharply and marched back to her office.

Within a minute, Marta came in with a latte and a plate of Jammie Dodgers, Jay's favourite biscuits.

"I thought you'd need a pick-me-up. It sounded as though things were getting a bit heated in there."

"You're a lifesaver." Jay received the cup as if it were a precious gift. She took a sip and took the time to recalibrate and concentrate on work. "Ian and Lia don't think we've gone far enough. They think the presentation needs to be placed in more context. That doesn't fit how we normally do reports, but I'm wondering if I should include something broader, something that includes us getting involved with outside organizations. But I'm worried the whole report will be thrown out if the board think it's absurd."

"Oliver will support you whatever you decide to do," Marta said then took a bite of her biscuit.

Jay smiled as Marta brushed a couple of crumbs from her top. "I know. I think I'll put in a few paragraphs about the wider context and softer options such as insulating homes. Alistair might decide to take them out before the board meeting, but at least I've tried to be fair and reflect the wishes of the committee."

"That sounds like a plan. Would you like to give me your notes, and I'll type them up while you go and brief Oliver?"

"You're a star. Thank you."

"Isn't it dancing tonight? Don't you want to leave on time?"

"It is. We're doing the rumba now."

"Ooh, get those hips working." Marta pinched another biscuit and Jay's notes and turned to the door, wiggling her hips with an exaggerated movement as though she was imitating a rumba.

It looked funny and more faux seizure than anything else. Jay smiled and gathered her thoughts before going to speak to Oliver. Lia would be pleased her points and ideas had been included, and Jay was thrilled she could demonstrate she was being more open and not only seeking a technical answer. Who was she kidding? She was seeking Lia's good opinion. She was definitely more flexible now. As if being kissed in her own offices wasn't example enough. She touched her still swollen lips and smiled. How long would it take for the CCTV footage to be spread around? She hoped Richard wouldn't get a copy, but too bad if he did. She would live.

Chapter Twenty-One

LIA LIFTED GRAMP'S OLD binoculars and focused on an individual bird amongst all those honking and twittering like arguing children at school. But this was survival in the winter feeding grounds: no playing here. She couldn't bear to think that this could be lost and wouldn't be there for the next generation. Lia glanced across at Abigail, her nine-year-old niece, with an expression set in a frown as she stared through her own binoculars Tim had bought her.

"Auntie Lia, can you see the one with the damaged wing?" Abby whispered.

"Yes." They were silent for a few minutes as they watched the birds. Lia looked over at Abby, who seemed enamoured of nature as she was. "I'm so glad this place is here. It's worth sacrificing a little profit for the sake of contributing to nature as a whole." She wanted Abby to learn what was important, to try and influence her away from Tim and his constant drive for money. "We're the custodians of the earth, and it's our responsibility to ensure it continues for future generations." She could hear her gramps saying almost exactly the same words to her when she was Abby's age. She couldn't think of anything better than to spend some time with her.

After placing the binoculars up to her eyes again, she noticed the lack of her trademark bangles. She never wore them when she was bird watching as she didn't want to disturb the birds. But she felt naked without them, and wearing more appropriate country attire—moleskin trousers and a Barbour jacket—seemed to be like slipping on her childhood. When she looked across, she half expected her gramps to be perched on the stool, completely absorbed in watching nature.

Abby caught her staring and asked, "Auntie Lia, do you have a girlfriend?"

Lia blinked. Where had that come from? As far as Lia knew, Abby wasn't even aware of her sexuality. But she was a bright girl and watched and listened. It wouldn't surprise Lia if she'd overheard her parents talking about her. She knew they disapproved of her sexuality just as much as her activism. Tim made it clear he thought Lia should grow up, take responsibility, and get married to one of his wealthy landowner pals. "Um. I've been seeing someone, but I don't know if you can call her that." She had agreed to call Jay later so they could discuss when they could meet again. A smile ghosted across her lips at the thought of Jay seeing her in her landed gentry uniform. It was such a shame she was busy this weekend. It would have been exciting to show her around.

A skein of geese flew overhead in their tell-tale V formation, precise and efficient, adjusting their positions for wind and navigating to the same fields they visited previously. It reminded her of the precision in the array of vertical turbines Jay had been so proud of. "See those birds? How do you know they're not Brent geese?" she asked, admiring their flight through the binoculars.

"I don't know, because they're not landing on our land?" Abby said softly, as if she was scared to answer incorrectly.

"Good guess, but that's not the answer I was looking for. Brent geese fly in family flocks, not in a large v formation. But you're right that they're not settling on our land. Your great grandfather used to tell me we never owned our land; we just tended it for a while, and we should always leave it in a better condition than how we found it." She took a sharp intake of breath and looked up to avoid the tears in her eyes. How could Tim sell off any land, their inheritance, and their responsibility for the sake of a new combine and new roof? There must be other ways. She would speak to him when he returned from visiting his mates in Edinburgh. It was very suspicious that he was suddenly called away at the weekend when she announced she was coming up.

GREEN *for* LOVE

"Do you know which land your dad is thinking of selling off?" She tried to make it sound casual, but it still sounded too direct. She hadn't learned to be diplomatic. There was never much point. If she asked a direct question, she was more likely to get a direct answer, avoid misunderstandings, and not waste all the time.

"No." Abby looked up and shook her head before peering again through the lens. "Oh look, look, Auntie. They're settling."

A small family group fluttered and honked as they landed and started to devour the gleanings of grass and seeds in a flurry of activity. This was what made life worth living. Spending time with her niece, with her feet in the soil that her family had farmed for hundreds of years, caring for the environment and the wildlife. It was worth fighting for. If only she had a woman to share it with. She had a feeling in her bones that Jay was the one, her soulmate—if it wasn't for the damn company she worked for.

In the end, Jay would either be with her or against her. She thought about her constantly, and every time a text came in, she hoped it would be from her. Their initial raw energy had stirred over time and become more charged, until the air seemed to crackle between them when they were in each other's orbit. But it wasn't just about sex. Jay was funny in her serious scientific way, she clearly cared about her mother, and she related well to people. One day though, Lia would have to choose. She couldn't hold onto someone who didn't want her and still hope to find someone who did.

"I'm getting cold, Auntie Lia. Can we go back?"

Lia realised she'd been watching without seeing and hadn't noticed Abby was shivering.

"Of course, Abby. Let's go and get a hot chocolate." When Lia checked her phone, her heart did a little skip at the text from Jay.

Call me when you're free. J xo

Lia waited until Abby grabbed her drink and went through to sit by the fire. Lia loved the aliveness of the flames, the crackling and the shifting of logs as they released their energy to the atmosphere.

She picked up her phone, noticing a tremor as she called. "Hey. Is now good?"

"Of course. Let me shut my door."

Lia heard the sound of heels on a marble floor in Jay's swanky office in London. Clearly she'd gone into work at the weekend. Was she really looking after her mum? Doubt trickled down Lia's spine. "It's wonderful to hear your voice," Lia said, surprised she said it aloud. She picked up her bangles and slipped them on her arm.

"I wondered when we could meet. When are you back in London?"

"I thought I might come for the celebratory dinner."

"Great. Can you stay over? Oliver has offered me the use of the company flat where the dinner will be held. It has two guest bedrooms."

She licked her lips at the thought of spending time in bed with Jay. A throbbing between her thighs informed her that her body approved. But there were *two* bedrooms, meaning Jay had no intention of sharing one with her. She was reminded of her thought that she'd have to choose at some point. Apparently, she wasn't there yet.

Chapter Twenty-Two

LIA LOOKED AROUND THE private dining room. The ornateness put the private members' club to shame. She had never seen such an intricate crystal chandelier, even in some of the grand homes she had been in when she was a little girl. Obviously Magenta Oil had more money than sense.

She sighed. She had to stop her constant carping. It wasn't fair to Jay, who had been open and welcoming and had skilfully navigated the tightrope of very different opinions to conclude the report for the board with a consensus. Some of the committee members had made the most of the free champagne and were already worse for wear, and they hadn't even got to speeches and dessert yet.

Jay rose and tapped her knife against the glass. It gave a satisfying ring that echoed around the oak-panelled walls. "I want to thank you again for all your hard work and input into the report. I'll be taking it to the board next month and from conversations I've had with Oliver, we've determined that we'll be able to implement some of the pilot projects in the next three months." Jay scanned the crowd like a seasoned public speaker, engaging her audience. "I'll be honest, there are times I thought we would never agree on a solution."

She grinned at Ian who raised his glass, then winked at Lia. *Cheeky madam, she was enjoying this.* And she deserved every minute of it. Lia's heart expanded and glowed with the warmth. There was no denying it; she was rapidly falling for Jay, though it wasn't so much falling as being enveloped in a constancy of kindness and passion. She had never experienced such a strong bond with anyone before. It would be thrilling to spend another night with Jay, even if they were in separate bedrooms. At least she could enjoy the proximity.

Above the private dining room was their company flat and Lia's overnight bag remained in the living room, as though there was an option as to where she might spend the night. A shiver went down her spine.

Lia leaned back in her chair and sipped at her champagne. She was no longer an expert, but this was definitely not cheap prosecco. The bubbles in her drink reflected the bubbles of excitement she was trying to contain. As the various speeches rambled on, Lia's mind drifted back to the conversation she'd had with Steve and when she would take up her activism again. She had resolved not to embarrass Jay by being the face of No More Oil while she was on the committee, but she fully intended to take it up again if they didn't start on the implementation as they had promised in three months' time. She knew Jay would hate it, but she had to do the right thing.

Coffee was taken in the lounge and library, which seemed to consist of years of various petroleum trade magazines and books about the oil industry and business tycoons over the ages. It probably impressed most of Magenta's visitors, but Lia would just as easily set a match to the lot. Or maybe she would have them all pulped down and used as insulation for more houses and flats in Bristol. Over the mantelpiece hung a painting of Oliver, the CEO, by Carolyn Trent-Parker. It was one of her satirical paintings. Oliver was all smiles but in the shadow was the rear of a toad splattering in oil instead of mud. Lia grinned. She agreed with the artist—she wasn't entirely sure she trusted Magenta, despite the fact that she now trusted Jay.

She caught Jay's eye and smiled, hoping that the desire she felt, and wished was reciprocated, was clear in her expression. Jay's smile faltered a little, and she turned back to irksome Andrea.

Andrea was clearly trying to squeeze the last drop of value

GREEN *for* LOVE

from her time on the committee. Given how she had gawped at the surroundings earlier, Lia suspected she would be dining out on this experience for years to come and would insert into every conversation, *"When I was on the committee at Magenta..."* and bore her dinner companions like she had bored them all during the committee meetings.

Lia scanned the room of what had probably been a Georgian home at one point and was now nestled amongst the embassies and oligarchs' homes close to Regent's Park. She wished they would all go home now so she and Jay could slip upstairs. If only they'd be doing more than sipping a nightcap, but she needed to stop her flights of fancy. Jay didn't believe in soulmates or even dating.

She sighed, took another sip of champagne and stopped ogling Jay for a moment. Ian was watching her. He frowned then nodded slightly at one of the waiters, or maybe footman was a better description dressed as he was in a starched uniform. The footman stiffened and looked straight ahead, but the tail end of the movement indicated he had been watching her too. She shrugged. Who cared? What could they do? She wouldn't come here again or to Magenta, except maybe to accompany Jay to a company event, if only as a friend. Lia smiled to herself. That would put the cat among the pigeons. Lia would love to see the look on the executives' faces if they realised she was the thorn in their side.

It was past midnight by the time the last guests had gone. Jay thanked the staff profusely and held Lia's hand as they wandered up the wide carpeted staircase. Jay held the key to the flat in her other hand like a talisman. She had some difficulty getting the key in the latch, and they giggled until they finally fell through the door.

Jay shut it behind them and pushed Lia against the ancient woodwork, and they lost themselves in a passionate kiss, all lips, and tongues, and desperation.

"I've wanted to do this all night," Jay said, pulling Lia towards her, hands on her butt cheeks over Lia's thin sheath dress. "You're so hot in this, but I want to rip it off you."

Lia unzipped it at the side and shimmied out of it, letting it puddle on the floor, before she unbuttoned Jay's trousers. It looked like Jay was reassessing her no action replays rule. That was a great sign. The attention Lia had given to her outfit was definitely worth compromising her usual style to fit in with expectations. Maybe she could sacrifice a little of her radical stance if she was rewarded like this.

She was about to pull Jay's trousers down when there was a quiet knock on the door. They shared a startled glance. Jay put her finger to her lips and rebuttoned her trousers. After a couple of seconds, she opened the door. Lia heard the sound of the caretaker, Alfie, who had let them in earlier and taken their bags in.

"Ms Tanner, I'm sorry to disturb you, but I thought you and your companion might need to see the early editions of the newspapers. Pages five and seven respectively. If you need anything, please let me know."

"Thank you," Jay said. She fumbled to fasten the chain on the door and turned to Lia. "Did you hear that?"

"Yes." She snatched one of the papers from Jay and followed her through to the kitchen, spreading them out on the table.

When she saw the headline, she almost regurgitated her five-course dinner. *It's One Rule for the Rich.* Below the headline there were two photos side by side, one of her glued to the road outside Magenta's refinery, with the reflected blue light of the ambulance highlighting her face. The other was a photo taken several years ago in typical country gentlewoman pose complete with binoculars, wax jacket, and expensive boots. How had they got that picture? It was kept up in the house in Northumberland as a reminder of who she used to be and everything she rebelled against. She scanned the words that seemed to jumble and blur in front of her.

Cordelia Armstrong-Forde is a member of the landed gentry who profits from the land. She is also a hypocrite, because she is the face of the extremist anti-fossil fuel activist group, No More

GREEN *for* LOVE

Oil. Who can forget her screaming at a TV reporter, completely uncaring that an ambulance could not get through? The Daily Herald *has been informed that the extremist is also a beneficiary of a trust that will make a large profit if a secret land sale is made to Magenta Oil.*

The purpose of the land sale has not been disclosed, but Magenta was linked to the ill-fated fracking site in Cumbria in the late 2000s. Timothy Armstrong-Forde said he could confirm they were in talks for an undisclosed sum but did not know what Magenta proposed to do with the land. It is also suggested that Cordelia Armstrong-Forde has been seen in the company of a Magenta executive. So maybe the No More Oil slogan should be changed to No More Oil Unless It Is Profitable. No one at Magenta Oil was available for comment.

Lia's legs threatened to give out, and she held onto the table as her world began to spin.

"Shit." Jay swapped the papers to see if there was anything different in Lia's. "How did they find out about this? Did your brother leak details of a confidential negotiation? I need to call Oliver. Can you call your brother and find out? This is a serious breach of information, as well as being unprofessional."

Without waiting for Lia to reply, Jay sped back into the main bedroom. Lia slumped on one of the kitchen chairs to call Tim. Her insides churned as the information warred with her emotions, causing a rift in her psyche. It was typical that Jay was more interested in the impact on Magenta than Lia. It showed where she was in Jay's priorities. She felt humiliated and sick to her stomach and prayed that Tim wouldn't pick up. She wasn't ready to confront him about selling their land to an oil company. It went through to voicemail. She reread the articles, which said basically the same thing, but they hadn't changed on second reading. She was denounced as a hypocrite in bed with the enemy.

She slammed her fist on the table, which was probably heavy oak because it hurt more than she thought it would. She rubbed it with her other hand.

Jay bustled back into the kitchen with her briefcase in hand. "Sorry, Lia, but I've got to meet Oliver at work to go through this. Please stay here tonight. Most of the Tube lines will have closed by now, and there are no trains back to Bristol until tomorrow. Alfie will bring you breakfast in the morning and will see you out. I'm so sorry this has happened, but I could strangle your brother if he was the leak. We need to downplay the story. Don't wait up, I suspect we may be there all night." She kissed Lia on the forehead and stuffed the newspapers into her briefcase.

"Is it true the last big land purchase was bought for fracking?" Lia frowned, searching Jay's expression. "And did you know that my brother was selling my land to Magenta?"

Jay looked uncomfortable. "The fracking thing must have been twelve years ago or so. And it didn't go ahead."

"But it *was* for fracking? And did you know?"

"Oliver stopped it before it got any footing. And no, I didn't know about the purchase of your land, I swear. I'm sorry, I have to go." With a squeeze of Lia's shoulder, Jay departed, and the clicking in the lock echoed behind her.

So much for support. She would find out what time the earliest train was back to Bristol in the morning. She rubbed her fist again. The bruise began to blossom in a purple blue hue, but that was nothing compared to the bruise in her heart. She felt betrayed by her brother and neglected by Jay, not to mention humiliated by the media commentary. She put her head in her hands. There was no way she was going to sleep tonight. She might as well help herself to the glass of Ardbeg Jay had promised her.

As she sipped, she considered the night. There had been promise, but how much of that had been in her own head? Jay hadn't offered anything more than friendship. Lia had been doing the pursuing, hoping for another hot night in bed. Jay's position hadn't changed.

And now, oil fields stretched between them, and there was no way back.

Chapter Twenty-Three

JAY YAWNED AS MARTA sent off the press releases while Oliver spoke to his contacts at the serious papers. She checked her Longines watch and rolled her shoulders. They'd determined that their best bet was to swamp the media with the narrative of their new sustainable energy report. Bloomberg TV Europe invited her to go in and speak about it that afternoon. She let Marta know she needed a couple of hours sleep on the couch in her office, and Marta promised to keep things quiet.

Jay slipped out of her shoes and undid the top button of the new blouse she'd kept in the office. In future, she would wash them before she left them here. It was stiff, scratchy, and uncomfortable, but it shouldn't stop her from sleeping. She sank into the sofa with a sigh and drifted off.

She was awoken with a start when the door banged open, and Richard barged in and sat down, waving a paper in her face.

"What's this?" Spittle flew from his lips.

She supposed this was what they meant about people foaming at the mouth. "Just some journos with too much time on their hands delving into your deal, I imagine. Didn't you get Armstrong-Forde to sign a non-disclosure agreement?"

He paused in his red-faced fury, and his mouth dropped open, revealing his expensive gold fillings. "What are you talking about? I mean this." He waved the first edition of the evening paper in her face. "You've released a statement about some green bullshit we're supposedly implementing before the board has even had the time to review it. Dad and I are so pissed off about this."

"If you check with your father, Oliver has already cleared it with him and the rest of the board, and do I need to remind you, you're not a director?" Riling him up probably wasn't sensible, but she was desperately trying to keep her eyes open and her brain alert. She rubbed at her eyes. "It was only released to flood the media and swamp the earlier story that mentioned *your* Northumberland shenanigans." She frowned. "Which, incidentally, I don't remember any of in my inbox."

"What do you mean?"

Jay moved to her desk and picked up one copy of the morning's paper with the story of Lia's brother's deal with Magenta.

"Fuck. I need this." Without asking, he took the paper and stormed out.

Who knew who he was going to vent at next. Jay stretched and rubbed her eyes again, then looked down at the second paper she had open on her desk. Seeing Lia in her country lady outfit made her pause. How was she? Given how she'd tried to distance herself from her family history and that Magenta might be taking some of her land, she probably wasn't okay. An uneasy feeling in her stomach warned her that she'd abandoned Lia last night, and that she had been solely focused on the impact for Magenta. What did that say about how she felt about Lia? She would probably be furious, *if* she even spoke to her again.

Jay clicked open a new tab on her computer and searched for an ethical florist in Bristol. She was surprised by how many options there were, but she chose a locally grown flowering plant in the end that was delivered by electric vehicle and boasted having no plastic in any of its processes, and the flowers wouldn't die in a fortnight. It certainly wasn't the cheapest, but she hoped Lia would appreciate the thought.

She glanced at her watch again. She had an hour before she needed to leave for Bloomberg studios. Fortunately, they were in the city so one of the company cars could drive her there, and she hoped Neil would be on today because she enjoyed talking to him. She did her best to put Lia out of her mind and focused on

GREEN *for* LOVE

what she'd say on camera.

***

"This is Melanie Dobson for Bloomberg TV. Today I have with me Jay Tanner, Head of Science and Technology, at Magenta Oil. Welcome."

Jay's mouth was like a desert as the camera turned to her, the flashing red-light showing it was live. She managed a weak smile and tried to remember the script she'd agreed on with Oliver. For once her memory seemed to fail her. Lia would tell her to breathe and centre herself. The thought caused her to smile for real.

"I know you're here to talk about the new renewables investment and report that Magenta have released today, but before we do that, I'd like to ask you about a newspaper article that appeared this morning. Is it true that Magenta are seeking to buy land for fracking in Northumberland?"

A trickle of perspiration made its way down the back of her neck. Jay swallowed, trying to get some moisture in her mouth. She pictured Richard's red face as he'd stormed from her office. Did she really know what that shmuck was up to? "Magenta doesn't comment on speculation in the press about any investment opportunities. But I can tell you that we have stated categorically in the last ten annual general meetings that Magenta does *not* do fracking and is exploring environmentally sustainable options to make the company net-zero by 2040." Relieved she managed to sidestep the question, she proceeded to explain their investments in alternative technologies, hoping she could run down the clock to avoid any follow up questions. When she was in her stride, the facts and figures flowed off her tongue.

She was just relaxing when Melanie smiled through her caked makeup and raised her hand. Up close, she was much older than she looked on camera and was clearly as sly as an old fox.

"That's very interesting, but is it true that your name has been linked with the activist Cordelia Armstrong-Forde, who is also a beneficiary of the trust that's selling the land?"

Jay's fingers tightened around the water glass, and she hoped it wouldn't break with the force. "I'm surprised that a serious business programme would perpetuate such nonsense. I've been leading the committee that has drawn up the report with the assistance and input of various shareholders and stakeholders. Part of that exploratory work required visits to different projects, including the energy and insulation charity of which Ms Armstrong-Forde is one of the managers. So yes, I have been visiting a number of projects around the country in her company." She flashed a false smile, hoping she'd got away with it.

"But as a senior executive, you need to be above reproach and not have a conflict of interest. You haven't answered my question. Are you having an affair with the activist who regularly protests outside Magenta, even though she could also benefit personally from a massive land sale to that same company?"

"No," she said, hoping her fixed stare would convince the listeners. It wasn't a lie, not really. They'd decided to stick with friendship, regardless of last night's thwarted passion. "I'm dedicated to my work and wouldn't have anything get in the way of that. I believe in transparency." She smiled.

"So, there you have it from the horse's mouth. The meetings were for business, and Magenta is investing in environmental technologies, not fracking. Thank you so much for coming in, Jay Tanner."

Why did that feel like a trap had just been sprung? Jay smiled, hoping it didn't look like a rictus. In a scurry of activity and empty pleasantries, she made it back into the sanctuary of the company car, wondering what she could have said differently. Should she have defended Lia and her activism? Should she have said something about them being friends?

Neil glanced at her in his rear-view mirror. "How did your TV appearance go?"

GREEN *for* LOVE

"Okay, I guess. Although it was pretty scary." Relieved it was over and hoping few people had seen it, she sagged back into her seat, exhaustion draining her of thought. "Take me home, please." She slid the privacy screen closed and pressed the call button on her phone. "Hi. I'm sorry about last night, that I dashed off and didn't even ask how you were about it all," Jay said quickly before Lia could talk. She wanted to get an apology out before Lia hung up.

"I was hurt. It made me realise where I stand in the pecking order."

Jay tapped her finger on the armrest. "I'm sorry, but I thought the best way to deal with it was for Magenta to put out its own press release to swamp the story."

"Exactly. Your first thought was Magenta, not the woman who you had pressed against the door. As I said, you showed me where I stand."

Jay winced, but she didn't have a rebuke. It was true. Had Lia seen the live interview? Someone might tell her about it, even if she missed it. She sighed. "I had to deny we're having an affair. On TV." It felt like a full confession at church, but she wasn't expecting absolution. Fearing what the answer might be, she cleared her throat. "Can we see each other this weekend so I can make it up to you?"

There was a long moment of silence. "No. I'm going up to Northumberland. I need to have a very stern conversation with my brother, and I can't do that over the phone. I also said I'd take my niece to the bird hide. I'm afraid I don't have time for non-affairs where you might get pulled away to make Magenta look good."

"Oh. Right." Disappointment splashed cold water over her ardour. What had she expected? That they could reconvene where they had left off before they were rudely interrupted? "That's understandable, but I thought it would be nice to get together again soon." Despite the risks to her career, she couldn't just let Lia walk away.

There was another silence for a second before Lia said, "You made it clear what your priorities are. Mine are to sort out what my brother's up to and to spend time with my niece. When I've calmed down a bit, I'll be able to speak to you rationally, but I don't want to say anything I might regret. Oh, hang on, someone's at the door."

Lia must have placed the phone on a table judging by the clatter, and Jay could hear she was having a conversation with someone. Lia exclaimed, and Jay half smiled as she imagined her flowers must have arrived. She hoped they would be enough to bring her back into Lia's good books.

A few seconds later, she heard footsteps and the phone being picked up.

"Hey, thanks for the flowers. They're lovely. And thank you for getting eco-friendly ones. That's considerate." Lia sighed softly. "But flowers don't change things, Jay. I can't be someone's second thought, not anymore, and there's simply too much wasteland between us now. Take care of yourself."

Lia ended the call, and Jay closed her eyes trying to stop her head from spinning. Everything seemed to be crumbling around her. Her cherished career felt off balance, and her love life, not that she'd ever wanted one of significance, was infiltrating every part of her world.

She was never needy. She didn't enjoy the volatility of emotions. She lived life in the narrow spectrum of routine and precision, but now she was being thrown from one peak of the oscilloscope to the trough. She placed her hand on her chest to calm herself, to keep the roiling emotions down and back in their place. Lia and all these alien feelings had to be packed into a little box at the back of her mind so she could concentrate on the ordered world she'd created. There was no other way.

Two hours later, Jay carried the last of the shopping bags into her mum's kitchen and gave her a peck on the cheek. "Hello, Mum. No russets today, so I got you some braeburns as normal." Russets

GREEN *for* LOVE

were her mum's favourite apples, but Jay had given up explaining that they weren't available at this time of year and had become more of a speciality apple. And she wasn't going to order some from New Zealand since Lia would give her a hard time about the food miles. She inhaled sharply. *Stop thinking about Lia and put her in the forgetting box.*

"That's okay, dear. How are you today? Would you like tea?"

There wasn't enough room for two of them in the tiny kitchen, but her mum always wanted to feel useful. She looked tired today.

"I'll make it, Mum. Go read the paper I've bought. I'll put it in the lounge and sort out your cup of tea when I've put all the shopping away."

"You're such a good girl, Jay. What would I do without you?" Her mum gave her a world-weary smile and hobbled her way into the lounge.

A few minutes later when Jay took through the tea, her mum had the paper open, a frown on her face.

"You want to see this. Your girlfriend is in trouble again."

"She's not my girlfriend." Jay ignored the twinge of irritation.

Her mum accepted the cup. "That's what the paper says, and I know I shouldn't believe everything in the paper, but I saw your face light up when she was here, and how you talk about her all the time. Call it a mother's intuition."

Despite wanting to stop this conversation in its tracks, as it might open a wound she didn't want to examine, Jay leaned on the back of her mum's chair. "What does it say?" She peered over her mum's shoulder at the photograph staring back at her. It was basically just a reprint of the article she'd read the night before. Her pulse quickened at the sight of Lia in her country clothing. It was a look that definitely suited her. There were no signs of the bangles or bohemian skirts. Lia was beautiful whatever she wore, and the throbbing of Jay's body agreed. She gave her mum's shoulder a squeeze. "Typical paper, making a mountain out of a molehill. Don't forget your tea; you don't want to drink it when it's cold." Jay sat on the chair opposite with her own drink. "How's your day been?" She leaned back in her chair while her mum related the minutiae of the day, which was the same as every other day, but her mum needed to talk, to have that connection.

Jay nodded, not commenting that her mum had told her the story of the bins being knocked over by a delivery driver a few minutes earlier. Her thoughts drifted to how fascinating it would be to see Lia in her home turf of the Northumberland estate, although she seemed so determined to stay away from it because of her family issues. There was no way Jay would be welcome there now. She sipped her tea to calm her nerves as the realisation slipped over her. She shouldn't have to choose between Lia and her job. Her whole career, her whole life had been working up to this next promotion and eventually to take over as CEO. Being with Lia would compromise that. The logical action was to accept that was an end to it, but her heart didn't want to. The thought of not seeing Lia again filled her with frustration. But logic was the only way to move forward. No matter how much that hurt.

Chapter Twenty-Four

TIM STOOD ON THE platform at Berwick-upon-Tweed station with his hand outstretched. Just as he was in striking distance, he snatched her case. "Finally. Come on, I've got to get back for a meeting with the Magenta people."

A cold shiver ran down Lia's spine. "Magenta? So it's true you're dealing with them?" She had to hurry to match his stride back to the Range Rover. He threw her bag in the back seat and settled himself in the driver's seat before she'd even opened the passenger door.

"I told you, we're going to sell off the parcel of marsh land that Gramps held onto for sentimental reasons. It takes too long to get the tractors between the sites. Six miles there and six miles back is a waste of time. If we sell it off, we can redirect the funds to getting the new combine—"

"Stop." Lia had to force the air back in her lungs and hold onto the grab handle to ground herself. "You don't mean the geese fields? You can't. That's where the Canadian geese overwinter and feed. It's an important habitat for them. Don't you get money for retaining that?" She glared at him. In all their conversations, he'd never said he was *actually* going to sell that particular piece of land.

"We did under the European Union. But there are different criteria now, so that will probably go. I want to get ahead of it."

"You can't do that. Even if you don't get money for it, you can't let those fields go. Can't you sub-let them for the summer if it's a question of efficiency?" She looked up at the sky hoping to see the geese come flying in, noisy honking flocks squabbling and establishing their temporary territory. It was nature at its most simple and spectacular. How she missed her gramps and all his wisdom. "We have a responsibility to nature," she said.

"You're a fine one to talk about responsibility. Why do you think I've been entrusted with looking after the estate? I've never been arrested for holding up an ambulance. Do you know how embarrassing it is to see your sister yelling at reporters and being dragged away by police?"

A tidal wave of rage surged through her. "If we don't stop big oil, we'll have no world left to inhabit. Climate change is already happening. Look around you. Why do you think we're growing crops that used to be only grown in the south of the country? It's getting drier during the year, and storms coming in from the North Sea are more virulent and more frequent. So why is Magenta sniffing around? Is it more onshore wind farms they're looking at? I know they're looking for suitable land for renewable sources."

Tim flicked a glance at her as he pulled onto the A1. He was silent, his jaw clenching.

"What?" she demanded, her voice rising.

Tim cleared his throat and stared ahead.

"What aren't you telling me?" She gripped the grab handle over the door so hard her fingers ached. "Tim?"

"They're looking at hydraulic fracturing of shale gas that might be present in the sandstone hills," he said slowly as if speaking to a child.

Trembling started from her hands and spread through her body. *No.* She stared at him, but he was focused on the road. Lia swallowed to keep down the nausea rising in her throat. "You're not serious? You mean fracking? It's illegal. That area is also where Berwick and the surrounding area get their water. You could end up poisoning people or draining the water supply and causing a drought."

Betrayal surrounded her. Tim had promised long ago that he'd talk to her before making major decisions to do with the land. And then there was Magenta. The lies, the reassurance. She knew she

GREEN *for* LOVE

couldn't trust them. There was no way she could trust Jay after all this. She'd specifically said they weren't looking into fracking. How stupid had she been to be duped like that? Tears welled in her eyes, making the landscape blur.

"The engineers have checked whether it's feasible. That's why they've been carrying out studies, but from what they've said, it seems possible. This will make a huge difference to the viability of the whole estate. We can get the barns done up as holiday homes, get a new roof on Hiburn Hall, and get an upgraded, efficient combine."

"Who will want to holiday here if there's fracking onsite? And why did they stop drilling in Cumbria, Tim? Because of earthquakes and other environmental issues." Lia could hardly speak for the rage choking her.

"Don't get all eco diva on me. This will make a huge difference to us as a family."

"So you can get a new toy tractor? No. Think of the geese, the birds, the water supply for Berwick. What would Gramps say?"

Tim slammed his hand on the steering wheel. "He isn't here. The birds will find another site. They'll adapt. We need to keep making money to keep the land, Cordelia. All your high flying, save the world nonsense won't pay the bills or fix the roof."

"No, no, no. This is wrong on so many levels." *Jay betrayed me.* That was the sharpest wound. How could she? She trusted her fine words and false assurances. As Lia stared out at the landscape she loved, she didn't bother trying to hold back the tears of anger and frustration.

There was no point arguing with Tim. She would speak to her parents to see if they could talk sense into him, but mostly she needed to speak to Jay. Maybe she could convince her to put a stop to this. But she had to calm down enough to be coherent. If she saw Jay now, she would probably smash something.

Half an hour later, Tim dropped her at the house and shot off to his office, insisting she wasn't allowed to disrupt the meeting. She was so rattled and upset that she didn't even argue.

Still shaking, Lia called Jay and was relieved when it didn't go to voicemail.

"Hey, good to—"

"You lied to me. You betrayed me. Now it's personal." Lia could hardly speak. Never had she felt such rage.

"What're you talking about? Lia, calm down. Tell me what's going on."

"You traitorous, lying bitch. I should never have trusted you. All this bullshit about Magenta being different. Did you befriend me just to find out about my family estates so your engineers could come and take it? That land has been in my family for generations." She hiccupped as she began to cry in earnest.

"Lia, until I saw that article in the paper, I had no idea Richard was looking into your land. I knew we were looking at Northumberland for our wind turbines, but I swear, I didn't know about your connection to it."

Lia barely kept from throwing the phone across the room. "Stop lying to me! Magenta is looking at the fields for fracking! You told me Magenta was looking to the future and renewables. We talked about the fracking issue."

"I'm sure you misunderstood. We're not doing that."

The gall of the woman, pretending not to know anything about it. How could a future CEO *not* know? *What bullshit.* Of course she knew what was going on. "Don't patronise me. My brother told me Magenta are looking to buy the site for fracking less than an hour ago. He's in a meeting with them right now."

"Let me talk to Oliver, and I'll get back to you. I'm sure there's a rational explanation."

"I trusted you. Corporate greed takes precedence over saving the world again. Was I a mug to believe you and your report? Will you even take it to the board? You must think I'm stupid. It was all for show, wasn't it?"

"No. I don't think that at all, and you have to believe me, I know

GREEN *for* LOVE

177

nothing about this. I'll call you back."

"Don't bother unless you have good news. If not, I'll fight you in court." She ended the call, her fingers trembling, and stormed over the yard to the estate office. She swung the door open and strode inside.

Tim jumped up, knocking a paper off the untidy desk. "Cordelia, I told you not to interfere."

A man in his mid-thirties in a tailored suit and expensive leather shoes that shouldn't be seen within ten miles of a farm, rose too, his expression one of disdain.

"Ah. This is your sister. The one causing lots of disruption and cost to our business. I'd like to say it's a pleasure to make your acquaintance, but you've cost me a lot of money and hassle. To be honest, I'm not convinced we want to deal with your family."

"Then I'm doing my job. Feel free to sod off." Lia crossed her arms and stared him down.

"No," Tim said, his eyes wild. "This is important. I'm in charge here. Responsibility for the trust has been given to me, not my sister. Cordelia, please leave before I ask George to escort you out."

"This is my home too. You can't throw me out—"

He snatched up the paper that had fallen on the floor and crumpled it in his fingers. "But I can tell you not to butt into a private business meeting."

"Which affects our family home and lands." At his scowl she raised her hands. "Okay, I'll leave, but tell me, Mr Magenta Oil—"

"My name is Richard Worthington, soon to be chief operating officer."

She tilted her head and glared at him. "I thought that was Jay Tanner?"

He laughed, every inch the caricature of a suited villain. "Given the questions asked in the interview, I'm not surprised you think that. But my father will be the next CEO, and I will be the COO. Then we'll go back to doing what we should be doing: looking after the shareholders."

"What about looking after the planet?"

"You were on the committee meant to delve into this, weren't you? These things take time." His smug smile suggested that time might never come.

"I don't want to hear your bullshit. Tell me whether you plan to use this land for a new kind of wind turbine or for fracking?" She glanced at her brother, who looked an odd combination of worried and angry.

"Have you been talking to Ms Tanner? That's one of her pet projects and is classified information. I'm sure our current CEO will be delighted to find she's been talking to the enemy and selling our commercial secrets."

Lia had to be careful. This snot-spouting slimeball was clearly a cunning fox. "She hasn't told me anything that isn't in the public domain."

He rolled his eyes. "Whatever." He looked at Tim, clearly dismissing Lia. "She's a sucker for supposed scientific evidence and won't sign off on anything unless it's proven in double blind tests and peer-reviewed by twenty nerds." He turned his cold gaze back to Lia. "Fracking is proven to be viable on this site, and there's nothing you can do about it because your brother has just signed the memorandum of understanding. I've got everything I need now. Tim, I'll be in touch, and we can arrange that squash game when you're in London."

He went to the door, which Tim hurriedly opened for him, and they left Lia behind without so much as a glance. She slumped in a chair, her head in her hands. Not only had he betrayed her, but Jay had too. She was right not to trust them. Not to trust anyone. Maybe her mother was right, and she was a huge failure. Everything she loved and fought for, she'd lost.

She let the tears fall and wished there was someone to lean on. But as usual, she was on her own.

Chapter Twenty-Five

Jay strode into Oliver's office, brushing past his assistant. He was on a phone call but took one look at Jay and said, "Max, I need to go. I'll call you in a few days' time."

He put his phone down on the desk and indicated for Jay to sit down. But she paced the room. "What's this about Richard cutting a deal to buy some land to begin fracking in Northumberland?"

"Sit down, you're making me dizzy. Have a butterscotch toffee and tell me what's going on." He offered her a cellophane wrapped sweet, but she flicked her hand to decline.

"We don't do fracking. Aside from it being illegal, we've told everyone we're investing in a long-term greener future. What happened to transparency?"

He shrugged and carefully unwrapped the sweet with an irritating squeak and popped it in his mouth.

"You said we're only exploring options. How come we're pouring a bucket load of money to buy land for fracking?"

"We're hedging our bets. The land can be used for fracking or wind turbines. If you're going to pace, shut the door, please."

Jay frowned but did what she was told, taking the time to arrange her thoughts and respond in a calm, logical way. "We've said we're looking at renewables. Are we lying?"

Oliver moved away from behind his desk and sat in the comfy chairs. Whenever he sat there, he mentored her, as a way of indicating a different conversation, so she knew this was important. And however much she wanted to have a resolution to her issue, she would let him impart his words of wisdom.

"Some of the shareholders aren't happy that we're going down the green route. I have my suspicions that they're being agitated by Richard and John, who will take any opportunity they can to oust me. They're doing it not only for the money but also for their own power grab. So far, the majority of shareholders and the board are on my side, but I'm not sure how long I can fend them off unless I make some concessions. One of those concessions is looking at all options that are brought to me. So yes, the particular land in the hills in Northumberland does seem to be viable for fracking, and we've given the go-ahead to buy that land should fracking become legal in the future."

Jay rubbed her temple and sighed. "That land happens to belong to the family of Lia Armstrong-Forde, the eco warrior who caused us problems and who you co-opted onto my committee."

He sucked on his sweet harder and tapped the arm of the chair with his well-manicured nails. "Ah. That's unfortunate."

"Unfortunate doesn't cover it. She's going ballistic, and rightfully so. I promised her that we were *not* doing fracking, and that if there were any land purchases then it would be for the vertical blade windmill project. She's just called to accuse me of lying to her and betraying her trust. Which appears to be true, even though I didn't know it."

He tilted his head slightly, his expression wary. "Jay, is it true what the newspapers intimated? Do I detect more than a professional interest here? I know Wendy and I want you to find someone, but are you sure she's not too hot to handle? A relationship with her could create a number of conflicts of interest. Like this issue around her land, for instance."

Too hot was right. Jay blinked back her image of Lia, her eyes closed in ecstasy, beautiful, ethereal like a Gaelic princess. Her stomach churned at the thought that she may never see Lia again. "That's irrelevant now because she obviously won't trust me again, and who can blame her? I wouldn't be surprised if she's planning another attack right now."

"I'm sorry if you're hurt by that. Don't you see it could never

GREEN *for* LOVE

go anywhere? Eventually in a few years' time, when you've been a board member for a couple of years as COO and you can show that you can run the company, you'll slip into my shoes as CEO. There's no way the shareholders, or the board, would accept their CEO being in a relationship with an environmental activist. It's a huge conflict of interest. I'm sorry, Jay, but it won't do. Optics matter, as you well know." He must have seen the look on her face as he continued, "But that's a long way down the line. We're talking years away. Who knows, maybe you can win her round to our way of thinking. Help her see that there's a middle road to be taken."

Jay snatched up a sweet from the bowl on the table between them. "There's no way she'd believe me ever again. *I* don't believe me. I feel like I've been left in the dark and blindsided, Oliver. I don't like it."

"I'm sorry you feel that way. You're right, I should have made certain you knew what was happening." He sucked on his toffee. "The land isn't going to be used for fracking, although it appears it could be used for both the new wind turbines *as well* as fracking should that possibility come to pass. Making it multi-purpose means it will be cheaper and easier to get permission for wind farms and therefore earlier to market and earning income sooner."

"Can I have that in writing?"

He stopped chewing and raised an eyebrow. "Don't trust me?"

"Not me." That wasn't totally true; he'd known she didn't have all the information the others had, and that made her uneasy.

"Ah. I see." He nodded, then stood to press the intercom by his desk. "Marta, can you make an extract of the executive summary of the board paper recommending the Northumberland land is used for the new wind turbine trial and email it to Jay? Thanks."

Jay breathed a sigh of relief. She hoped it would be sufficient to placate Lia. She still wouldn't be happy that Magenta were doing anything at all on her land, and she'd never believe that Jay hadn't known about it all along, but at least this was something. A middle road, like Oliver suggested. And with fracking still illegal, wind turbines were the renewable energy Jay had promised they were working toward. She shook her head. None of that would matter, not to Lia.

Oliver snatched another toffee as he made his way back to the comfy chairs and settled himself down, making a ritual of unwrapping the toffee. Jay always wondered what his dentist made of his addiction.

Oliver leaned against the chair and raised his arm against the back. "Now that we've got that out of the way. I had an interesting conversation with Max Van Hoeland before you came in about a project they're exploring in the Netherlands using mini turbines on motorways to generate power for street lighting. It's simple and reduces energy consumption. He's going to send over the spec. You'll need to assess the data to see if it's effective for us here."

Jay let the butterscotch flavour ooze sweetness on her tastebuds to soothe and calm. She stared at Oliver as he talked about other projects that had come across his desk, and for the first time, she wasn't entirely in tune with what he was saying. He made it sound like the best way to get the turbines up was to include the possibility of fracking. But if that wasn't going to happen, why was Richard in Northumberland talking about fracking to Lia's brother?

Something didn't taste right, and it wasn't the toffee. She didn't trust Richard as far as she could throw him. Jay twisted the sweet wrapper around in her fingers. She would investigate this issue further on her own and in her own time. She wasn't a liar, and she had thought that compromise and time would create something climate-friendly. Lia had helped her see so many new options and ways of thinking, and she'd thought she could get Magenta on board. Had she been naïve?

Ten minutes later, she went back to her office and checked her email. Oliver was telling the truth. He *had* recommended the use of wind turbines on the slopes, with fracking as a way to get the permissions in place and acceptance from the locals—the lesser of two evils. She exhaled loudly. Lia wouldn't be pleased about that

GREEN *for* LOVE

because of the potential for bird strikes, but she would know that Jay wasn't a liar. She forwarded it to Lia, showing Oliver's email. Normally she wouldn't send internal mails out into the world, but Oliver knew how important it was, regardless of what he'd said about them romantically. Lia was a virulent protester, and Jay needed her to know she hadn't bamboozled her in some way.

She'd known better than to get involved, to let her heart lead. Emotions weren't science. Her job and loyalty were here. Yet that felt so wrong now. With hands trembling, she called Lia on speed dial. "Have you seen the email from Oliver?" she asked when Lia picked up.

"Okay, I understand you didn't intentionally lie to me, although I still don't understand how you didn't know it was my land they were putting wind turbines on, or that they were putting fracking into play as an eventual option. You must be pretty out of the loop. While Oliver is in power with you supporting him, that's fine, but that toss pot, Richard, was adamant he would be the next COO with his father as CEO. And that puts my home in jeopardy, Jay."

Why was Richard so certain he was next in line? "All the more reason for me to fight to stay where I am and to keep Oliver in as long as possible." Jay let out a slow breath. It wasn't perfect, but it was something.

"Fine." There was a shuffling at the end of the line. "I'm sorry I jumped to conclusions."

Jay's shoulders relaxed a millimetre. "Does that mean you trust me again?"

There was a moment of hesitation. "I don't know, but I definitely don't trust Richard. His energy is like sandpaper, and his aura is a mask of sludge."

"We're agreed about that. I mean, not the energy stuff, which I don't get, but I don't trust him."

"Okay. I need to go." Lia finished the call.

Jay turned back to her laptop, but her vision was too blurry to focus on her outstanding emails. A sense of foreboding crept over her that she and Oliver may not be able to hold back John and Richard forever. If that happened, she would need to make a decision. So, she needed all the ammunition she could get, and to get that, she would need to do an investigation into the Northumberland land purchase. It might earn her some bonus points with Lia too, and maybe help to rebuild that trust she had fought so hard to win. She sent an email to Marta asking for the documents. It would give her something to think about in the long evenings alone again. Her breath hitched. She didn't want to acknowledge the pain in her chest, the overall hollowness of loss and abandonment. This was why she never got entangled with anyone; it only led to heartache and pain. She would do what she always did and bury herself in work. With a heavy lump in her stomach, she opened the next urgent email.

Chapter Twenty-Six

THREE LONG MONTHS LATER, the Russians invaded Ukraine and shocked the world and the energy markets. Jay stood at Marta's desk going through the final changes to the board paper for the emergency board meeting convened to determine how to respond to the crisis. She'd worked most of the night finalising the strategy for bringing the projects online earlier. The conference door banged open. Oliver rushed past without acknowledging them and slammed his office door.

"Have you ever seen him like that before?" Marta asked

"No. Never."

Marta chewed at her bottom lip, seeming uncharacteristically unsettled. "Should I go in and see if he's all right?"

"How about you make him a coffee? I'll see what's going on." Jay had rarely felt nervous knocking on Oliver's door. He was such an affable mentor that she had never been scared of him or what he might say. Normally, he was unruffled whatever seemed to come over his desk. "Oliver, it's Jay. Are you okay?" Stupid question. He was clearly not okay. Winner of the dumb question of the year award.

"Come in."

She entered to see him taking down his pictures and placing them on his sofa. Dread seeped into her bones and settled in her stomach in a hard ball.

"Can you ask Marta to get me a box from the post room?"

"What's going on?"

"You've seen the reports of the war?"

"Yes, of course. But you're not leading the invasion." Perhaps it wasn't the most sensible thing to be facetious as he glowered at her. Not a look she'd seen before and didn't want to see again. "Sorry. What's going on?"

"A coup in the board. I've just lost my job."

Her stomach churned, threatening to eject her breakfast. "What? Why? How?"

"Some of the institutional shareholders have complained to Alistair. They're saying they need a more ruthless leader to capitalise on the situation and look at all different alternatives, including lobbying for the laws on fracking to be changed, and to increase the capacity of our current oil production. It appears they think I'm too weak and that I should have anticipated this."

"You couldn't be expected to know what Putin was going to do. This is Richard and John's doing."

"Of course it is, but I didn't know they'd succeeded in turning so many of the full board. If it hadn't been the war, it would have been something else. We knew they were coming for us, but I placed my trust in people seeing through them. I was given an ultimatum, so I resigned."

The bile and nausea rose in her throat. "I'm sorry, Oliver. Though I'm sure you could get a job anywhere."

"I might retire. I'm fed up with the constant in-fighting and intrigue. Wendy will be pleased, although she'll want me out of her hair and on the golf course regularly."

He smiled for the first time since Jay had entered the office. He seemed lighter about the shoulders. As he became lighter, she became heavier and darker.

"Sorry, Jay, that means—"

"Yeah, I know. There's no way they'll have me on the board, never mind make me COO or CEO. I'll probably lose my job, or they'll give me the shittiest projects to deal with."

Oliver consolidated his bowls of toffees and proffered one to Jay, but she shook her head. He took one for himself. "That would be constructive dismissal."

GREEN *for* LOVE

She grasped the back of the visitor's chair as if it were a ship's wheel and could stop her from drowning in a stormy sea. "Would they care? Where would I get another job like this?"

He paused, laid down the last of his certificates and came across to hug her. He had never been physical before, so it was a surprise as well as a comfort. She was too rigid to relax into the embrace, much as she would have liked to be held, protected, and nurtured.

"You're a brilliant scientist with many additional skills. I'll write you a reference any time. If there's anything I can do, let me know."

Tears pricked the backs of her eyes. She had to get out before they overflowed. "Thanks, Oliver. Keep in touch." She returned to her own office and slumped on the chair, her head heavy in her hands. This was the end of an era. They'd lost.

She had no doubt they would scrap all her projects, except any required for the purposes of optics. What would she do? She needed to talk to a friend. She couldn't call Oliver while he was dealing with his sudden change of situation. Marta was too involved and it might put her in an awkward position. Her mum wouldn't understand, and Adam was only interested in dancing and pop culture. At forty-three, she had no other friends to turn to. A wave of loneliness engulfed her.

Without thinking, she called Lia. They hadn't spoken since Jay had forwarded Oliver's report months ago. But she'd thought of her every day, and many of her decisions were made with more thought for the environment. Lia needed to know that the worst had happened: Richard and his father were now in charge. "Sorry. I need to talk, and I didn't know who else to call."

"What's happened?"

Jay sighed with relief at the concern in Lia's voice, glad that she could talk this through. "Oliver has been forced to resign because he didn't anticipate Russia invading the Ukraine and the subsequent disruption to the fuel supply. John will take over as CEO and Richard as COO."

Silence stretched into a few awkward seconds. Maybe Lia wasn't the best person to call; she was too invested in the situation on too many levels.

"You have to get out of there," Lia said.

Despair flared into a white-hot rage. She counted to calm herself and deliberately uncurled her fingers before picking up her pen. She let the fear and frustration flow. "I can't, I have responsibilities, not only to myself but to Mum. She relies on me entirely now they've reduced her benefits. Where could I get another such well-paid job? It would have to be in another oil company, which would be stuffed with Richard clones, and I wouldn't have the influence to change them from inside."

"From what you've said about Richard and John, they won't be open to persuasion anyway, so you'll be wasting your time. What will they do, send you to Timbuktu?"

Jay gripped her pen hard. "Staying here means I can still look after Mum, and at least I have a hope of influencing strategy. I can't believe they would be so stupid to stop all of the projects already in progress."

"You know Richard will do whatever he can to get the fracking through, and that's not just theoretical, it's fact, and I'm taking it personally. We both knew what would happen if you and Oliver lost control. This needs further action. They need to change their minds," Lia said calmly.

Jay snapped her pen in two. Saying it was Lia's brother selling the land didn't seem wise when faced with a lioness on the hunt. "Does that mean you're going to retarget Magenta?"

"That's for me to know. If you're not for us, you're against us and everything we're trying to achieve." She sighed. "You know who I am, Jay, and what I stand for. I'm sorry you're dealing with difficult work issues, but it isn't surprising in the cutthroat world of lies you live in."

The pieces of pen clattered with a metallic clang as she tossed them into the waste bin, fractured and useless like whatever Jay

GREEN *for* LOVE

had had with Lia. She shouldn't have called. She'd been fine without someone to talk to before. "I don't have a trust fund to fall back on. I'm not from the landed gentry and can't fall back on the money from the estates." Jay regretted it the moment it left her lips.

"Thank you for letting me know about the change in leadership," Lia said. "I've been wondering how you are, hoping you might call. But it's business as usual. I'm well, thank you for asking. Just trying to save the planet, as usual." There was a moment of silence, as though she was waiting for Jay to say something, to explain why she'd called. "Anyway. Take care."

The phone went dead. Jay slumped her head on the desk and held back the tears. This day could not get any worse. There was a knock on the door, and she sat up straight. "Come in." She ran her fingers through her hair to smooth it into some semblance of order.

Marta popped her head through the door, her expression harried and her eyes pink from crying. "Jay, the board would like to see you now. Oh, are you okay? It's really upsetting about Oliver, isn't it? I'm not sure I can work for John."

"You can always work with me, Marta, but that will be a step down. I expect I may find myself banished to the Scottish refinery anyway. I'm not sure you'd want to follow me there."

Marta gave her a wan smile. "Thanks, I appreciate it. I guess we'll see what happens. Good luck, and you may wish to..." She indicated her own eyes.

Damn. Her mascara must have run, so much for not crying at work. She rarely wore makeup but had wanted to make an impression today. Turning up with smudged eyes would make an impression but not a good one. "Thanks, Marta."

Jay went into the bathroom to reapply her makeup before dragging her feet to the boardroom with a deepening feeling of dread. She inhaled sharply and knocked on the door.

"Come in, Jay," Bryn, the company secretary, said.

Clutching her files to her chest like a breastplate, she entered the arena, knowing like a gladiator that the odds were stacked

190   E.V. BANCROFT

against her.

John and Richard had a gleam in their eyes, and Richard looked particularly smug.

Alistair, the chair of the board, whom Jay had always liked until now, smiled at Jay but didn't meet her eyes. *Coward.*

"Jay, come in. Sit down. You probably know already that Oliver has resigned. We've asked John to take over as CEO and Richard to act as Chief Operating Officer for now, because we need to steady the ship. As the world is more tumultuous with this Ukraine business, we need to focus on securing immediate supply. That includes maximising output from the oilfields and exploring all options, including the less palatable ones."

"You mean fracking, I suppose. It's currently illegal in the UK."

Alistair nodded as if he was considering her words. "True, but John has very good connections within government and is sure he can persuade them to loosen the regulations in this time of crisis."

Knowing the fallibility of the government, Jay could believe they would force it through. "Given the public opposition, we would be locked in public inquiries for years, especially as the same land is used to supply water to the Berwick area. That would have a huge impact on our reputation." Jay grew in strength, despite feeling sick to her stomach. But she was fighting for Oliver's legacy, for her years of work and for her belief in herself. "Fracking has nothing to do with the immediate short-term supply. It would be much quicker to get the wind farm approvals through, certainly offshore. We could be supplying electricity to the grid in months, not years. Even the hydrogen would be quicker, and if we were to add in a hydrogen pump in each of our gas stations, we would have nationwide coverage in a couple of years."

"Too disruptive of my operations," Richard said, hardly disguising his glee at squashing her ideas. "Fracking would be an add-on, stand-alone project. In fact, we've set up the ownership through a subsidiary held through the Cayman Islands, so it's less traceable to Magenta and gives us plausible deniability. And if

GREEN *for* LOVE

you're planning to tell your eco friend about it, if they come after Magenta, that's on your head."

She smarted at the reference to Lia, but Jay needed to focus on the big issue here and unpack the personal later. "Magenta has always been about being transparent. You're ripping up our values in one ill-conceived move."

"Desperate times call for desperate solutions."

Her temper frayed in the face of his nonchalant lying. "You've wanted to do fracking for years, but I don't understand why you're so eager for it. The land would also be an ideal real-world commercial trial—"

Alistair held up his hand. "Thank you, Jay. I know how strongly you feel about such issues, but that's not a discussion for now. Clearly, we don't need your presentation on hydrogen now, because we won't be able to proceed while all of this is happening. Please stay behind after the meeting so we can have a conversation."

Alistair wound up the meeting, and with each minute that passed, Jay's anxiety rose. She even started to jiggle her foot, and she never did that. What was he going to say? Was she going to be fired or sent somewhere out of their way? Would she be able to bring her mum?

Finally, the rest of the board members left, with Richard extending an open invitation to celebrate his promotion. There was no way she was going to watch him gloat over securing the position she had worked towards for most of her life. He couldn't do the job as well as she could. He didn't have the same attention to detail, always saying he needed to deal with the bigger picture. That bigger picture didn't extend to considering the PR disaster the changes would be.

Her chest felt so tight she could hardly breathe, so when Alistair closed the door, cutting off the chattering, she thought she wouldn't be able to speak.

"Jay, thank you for staying behind. Normally, this would be a conversation that the CEO would have, but I wanted to discuss it with you, given your change in mentorship. Don't look so worried. I know how highly Oliver rated you, and I'm sure you're disappointed you didn't get the COO role, but we would like to give you a promotion in recognition of all the work that you've done. We're creating a new board-level role: Director of Technology and External Relations."

Jay's mouth dropped open, not quite believing what she was hearing.

"I can see you're surprised. Oliver always covered the external relations part, but John is such an accountant, he doesn't know how to explain things in words of one syllable. It's not his strong suit. Richard... Well, Richard can sometimes come across as a little more brash than we need. You believe in the work that's being done for the long term, the eco-friendly investments, and you know the projects intimately, so you would be ideal for the role. Congratulations on your promotion. It's well deserved—"

She couldn't take all this pompous posturing. Alistair had always been the voice of reason and logic. Surely he could see this was nothing but vindictiveness on Richard's behalf. Steeling herself to potentially be sacked, she said, "It's a poison chalice, you mean. I have to justify what Magenta is doing to the press, even though I'll have no say on policy. And I have to pretend like they're listening to my ideas as head of technology when we both know full well that I'll be forced to create technologies that only make more money and have nothing to do with environmental concerns. Does that sound right? Where's the integrity in that? I'm a scientist, not a word spinner."

"When you work in this industry, Jay, you have to learn to be circumspect. Being able to change and bend with new situations is crucial. Your integrity shows in how you choose to see the new situations and how you then express those ideas. We believe you'd be perfect at that."

And that would bring me in direct conflict with Lia. She had to swallow her tears. What a twist. It couldn't have worked out worse.

GREEN *for* LOVE

"When the activists hear about the fracking and the use of paper companies, they'll come at us from every direction."

Alistair stroked his thin moustache. "All the more reason they must never find out."

"They already know."

"How do you know that?" He really looked at her for the first time, and she refused to blink despite her eyes stinging and filling. "Is Richard correct that you're sleeping with one of their main agitators?"

Not anymore. "I know because the proposed fracking will occur on the land of one of the agitators, who also happened to be part of the committee on environmental impact we led. Richard told her himself."

Alistair nodded. "So, you need to find a plausible rationale. Is Richard correct about your relationship? Because that could affect your credibility and the ability to do the job."

"No, I'm not sleeping with one of the agitators. Not that it's any of his business. It wouldn't affect my ability to do my job." That didn't feel true, and she wanted to scream that her relationship with Lia was worth more than this. "Can I think about the promotion? I need to discuss it with my mum. It will probably entail me spending more time at the office rather than working from home, and that will impact on her and her care."

"Of course. I need to know by tomorrow so that we can issue a press release with all the changes. I do hope I'll be able to welcome you to the board. Oh, and before you ask, we can't split the role. It's all or nothing, and I'm sure you wouldn't appreciate a new Director of Technology being appointed above you."

So, the trap was sprung. She was given Hobson's choice. She couldn't take the technology position and leave the media crap out. She was scuppered, and they damn well knew it. She swept up her presentation papers on the hydrogen project and fed them into the shredder, along with her happiness.

Chapter Twenty-Seven

LIA SLAMMED DOWN THE phone on her brother.

"They've already got the draft agreement with Magenta to sell off the geese pastures. Tim won't budge."

She glared at her boss, although it wasn't his fault. Christian picked up his ringing phone and shrugged. He frowned as he listened and then stood to take the call in the hall, their accepted place to take personal calls. She hoped all was well with his wife and two young children.

Grateful for a few minutes on her own, she sent a quick text to Steve. They needed to up the ante on the Magenta campaign.

Steve, Magenta have the draft agreement to start fracking. We need to act this week. Their plant again, Friday? Lx

Sure. Same time, same meeting place? Sx

Lia placed her phone back on her desk, and a sliver of guilt shone on the block of her anger. It would upset and embarrass Jay, but she wasn't her concern anymore. Still, the raw aching in her heart said otherwise. Jay had made her choice clear. The last several months without her presence had been awful. Lia woke in the night, reaching out for her. She wanted to pick up the phone, chat, flirt, make plans. But the chasm between them had grown too wide. So she'd thrown herself into her charity work, and after a while, the comments about her spending time with an oil exec had dwindled so she could do her job properly. She'd also spent more time in Northumberland, getting under Tim's feet and seeing how the farm was working, which wasn't as bad as she expected, though she wouldn't tell him so.

Jay had said it was better to fight from within, but that was like turkeys voting for Christmas. It was just an excuse to keep living her lavish lifestyle and enjoying the importance of being a director, even if it was for a money-grabbing oil company. Bloody sun in Taurus, always needing status.

None of that stopped Lia missing her with an ache that was almost painful. She couldn't describe the longing she felt, how she missed her touch, her smell, her laughter, the clash of their interesting discussions, and her raw vulnerability when she spoke about her mum and her upbringing. However she cut it, Lia had real feelings for her, regardless of *everything* else.

She had to stop moping and going around in circles in her head. Her bangles rattled when she woke her computer and scanned through her emails to prioritise her workload. A few minutes later, Christian returned with two glasses of filtered tap water, which he placed on the table between them in their cramped office. He sighed as if he had the weight of the world on his shoulders. He flicked back his ponytail, a sure sign he meant business.

"Lia, I need to talk to you."

She frowned. What was it now? She couldn't deal with any more hassle today. She was already simmering, her chest tight. She didn't need anything else.

"What is it? Are the council being slow in making their contributions to the insulation project again? Do you want me to go and charm them to open their wallets and put it higher in their priority list?"

"No, this is about the trustees. They were unhappy about the article about you and your ambulance incident. They said it gives us a bad name. A couple of major donors have pulled out because they don't subscribe to the actions of the charity, your actions. I argued that you've raised more funds from other donors than the two who have pulled out, but they don't want their name in the papers in a less than favourable way again."

"That was months ago. Why are they bringing it up again?"

He grimaced. "It's the land agreement with Magenta tied to

GREEN *for* LOVE

your family; there are questions about legitimacy. It seems like you and your family are in the news all the time now."

The comments were like gas that ignited her rage. "Thanks for saying I've brought in more than we've lost. You know as well as I do, there would be no charity without the work I've done, the funds I've brought in from tapping up family contacts, and the grants I secured for projects that make a tangible difference to the lives of Bristol's poor. The charity wouldn't survive without me—"

He raised his hand. "Don't go along this tack. They've asked me to tell you any further headlines, and they will terminate your contract."

"They wouldn't dare."

Christian leaned forward and put his hand on hers. She gripped the water glass so tightly, it felt like it could fracture at any second. Like her mind.

"Please don't go there, Lia. I can't save your ass again. They basically said that if I can't control you, my job will be on the line, and I can't afford to lose my job."

"I never thought you'd sell your principles for—"

He sat back with a snap. "I won't have this conversation with you. This charity was going before you came, and it will continue after you leave. Lia, I like you, I really do. But not everything is your way or no way."

"So now isn't a good time to say I want Friday off?"

He slammed his palm on the desk, making the pens rattle in a broken mug. "Have you not listened to a word I said? Please don't do what I think you might be doing. You court trouble, and the authorities have picked you out as a ringleader."

"But Friday is okay? I'm going up to Northumberland at the weekend."

What was a little white lie? She was planning to go up on the Friday sleeper to Berwick-Upon-Tweed but would be visiting the Magenta terminal beforehand. She knew where the weaknesses were in their security, thanks to the tour arranged by Jay. *Jay*. She must stop thinking about her. She wasn't her soulmate, not the *one*, whatever their charts and the psychic seemed to indicate. She blinked. That didn't bear thinking about.

He looked relieved and smiled for the first time. "Ah, that's great. Yes, that's fine. Are the birds still feeding?"

"Yes, although they'll leave very soon. It will be good to catch them, while my niece, Abby, is still interested in them. She's off to boarding school soon."

Christian's shoulders dropped with relief. "Good luck with that. Now, did you see the email about the new vertical wind turbines? They actually look good at producing electricity without being such a danger to birds."

Yes, Jay showed me their trial and was so enthusiastic to roll them out commercially. Lia's heart sank as she thought about the discussions they had about the pros and cons, and how they'd ended up making out on the sofa, neither accepting defeat but knowing that at the core, they were in agreement.

Not that Magenta would ever trial them. It was such bullshit. From what Jay had said and what Lia had seen of Richard, there was no way Magenta would go along that path. He would do whatever he could to push through fracking, because that was more cost effective. But they never accounted for the environmental cost.

Magenta had to be stopped, and if that meant Lia crossed swords with Jay, so be it.

***

The air crackled with tension in the pre-dawn light. Steve looked around nervously.

"It seems deadly quiet," he whispered and handed her the wire cutters.

She nodded, not wishing to speak, and pulled down her balaclava with a mask of the new CEO of Magenta on it. She curled the perimeter wire back carefully and clambered inside.

GREEN *for* LOVE

Twelve other activists followed, and others entered through different holes down the fence line. Despite the chill in the air, her hands were clammy in her thin gloves. They kept to the shadows and away from the security lights. She had a desperate urge to cough, probably from the smell of petroleum fumes. How could they not see this was destroying peoples' lungs as well as killing the planet?

Avoiding the obvious security cameras, they sprayed the walls and storage units with slogans such as "No More Oil" and "Fracking Liars" using pre-prepared stencils. The smell of the spray paint clung to her nostrils, causing Lia to cough, but no guards appeared. She exhaled then rushed to the road near the entrance and shuffled into place.

Steve locked her onto Dave, her fellow conspirator, and then went down the row cuffing them all together in a line. She rolled her shoulders, ready for the onslaught. They were all in position when the area was flooded in light, and then there were people all over the place, running and shouting.

A large man yelled in her face. "Police. Stop what you are doing. Under the emergency powers granted to us, you are under arrest for trespass and damage to property. You do not have to say anything. But it may harm your defence if you do not mention when questioned, something which you later rely on in court. Anything you do say may be given in evidence."

"No more oil. No fracking. No lying or greenwashing. Save the planet," Lia said loudly, hoping Steve was catching it all on camera.

Hands pulled at her, rough and harsh, pulling at her arms where they were locked together.

"Ow," she yelled.

"Stupid bitch," the policeman muttered as he uncuffed her.

He dragged her towards a waiting police van and pushed her into the van. She fell on her knees, but fortunately, she was wearing thick pads. Still, a bruise would inevitably bloom.

This group of police were much rougher than any she'd

encountered before, probably because they now had more power to intervene, and they seemed to delight in using that power. Or they didn't like to have to make arrests this early in the morning. Lia didn't know and didn't care. They'd made their point. It took them another forty minutes to uncuff the rest of the protesters, and by that time, the press had arrived and were filming the whole thing. Lia watched in satisfaction.

She was taken to a police station, crammed into the van with the other protestors in a mass of tangled bodies and squashed flesh.

One young man she didn't know kept farting. "Sorry, I'm shit scared. My dad'll kill me."

Lia rested her head against the cold metal of the van and shut her eyes, trying to centre herself. At least this time she hadn't had to look Jay in the eye as she'd been driven away.

"I need a wee," Lia said, after several hours in a holding cell.

The man pointed at the lidless, seatless toilet bowl in the corner. *Great, no privacy.* No toilet roll, either. Or handle, presumably so people couldn't flush any evidence.

There was nothing to do but wait, boil in her anger, and rub where her body hurt from the rough handling. Eventually, she was taken into a small interview room with two wooden chairs and a table. The odour of sweat and a faint hint of cheap aftershave wafted in the air.

A female police officer started recording and asked her a couple of questions which Lia refused to answer until she saw a solicitor. The police officer huffed out an exasperated breath and left Lia alone again.

A few minutes later, a duty solicitor looking tired and harried was escorted in. "I need time with my client," the solicitor said, and with a scowl, the police officer left.

"Can you phone my parents to bail me out, please?" Lia asked. She wondered how long it would be before she could be released. This place was hostile, and she desperately needed a shower and

GREEN *for* LOVE

to apply arnica on her bruised knees and arms.

The middle-aged woman yawned and rubbed her eyes. "Let me do all the talking. You ought to prepare yourself for not getting home tonight. They've arranged a special magistrates' session to deal with the protestors. In total, about twenty of you have been arrested. It will take some time to process you all, and they're not in the best of moods. I strongly recommend you plead guilty. You were caught red-handed, and it's all on video. If you plead guilty, they have to look at reducing your sentence."

Lia went cold all over. "Sentence? Won't it just be a fine?"

The solicitor raised her eyebrow. "Almost certainly not. This isn't your first offence, and you're being charged with criminal mischief. That can carry a sentence of up to ten years, not that I think you'll get that. If you're lucky, it will be dealt with today by the magistrates and won't go to the Crown Court."

The world became very grey and narrow, and Lia wondered if she was going to faint.

After her solicitor left, she was led in handcuffs to a different holding cell with a toilet and a wooden pallet bed, and it smelled of disinfectant. Small window bricks that couldn't be smashed let light in, but she had no view. She was told she had to wait for the special magistrates' court.

All this waiting. Christian would be livid if she didn't get out. So would her parents. They'd forgive her eventually; they always did. Lia attempted to centre herself to be calm and strong.

Sometime later a woman PC came in and handcuffed her again. She had never felt so humiliated in her life.

The magistrate looked down his nose at her. "Cordelia Armstrong-Forde, you come from one of the oldest families in England. You are a shame and disgrace to your name. I see you have offended previously, so you will not be able to buy your way out this time. The sentence for you can range from zero days to ten years in prison. However, given the nature of crime, which was a protest based on environmental issues and not one of criminal intent involving the harm of other people, I'm sentencing you to thirty days."

Lia fought to keep the nausea down. She hadn't been allowed to say a word. Nor had her solicitor, who still looked like she needed a nap. She wasn't escaping today. She trembled and sweated, and her legs felt wobbly. This was real. She was handcuffed again and escorted her back to the holding cell.

"There's overcrowding at the women's prison, so they may keep you in this cell for the rest of your sentence," the constable said. "Get comfortable and be grateful that Holloway Prison's closed."

The door clanged shut, and the sound echoed against the barren, stained walls.

This couldn't be happening. She should be going home to talk to Tim, to persuade him not to sign the final agreement with Magenta. Now Tim would be furious, and how would she explain to Abby why she was in prison? Jay would never speak to her again. And why should she? Jay had tried so hard and been clear what she had been fighting for. It wasn't her fault her boss had been forced to resign. Christian was a great boss, but he'd been adamant about her toning down her activities. Surely he wouldn't fire her.

Lia paced the cell, cringing inside, thinking about what her parents would say and what Christian would do. She had never wanted to go outside as much as she did now, to feel the sand between her toes and watch the birds take flight. She heard banging and someone else wailing. It sounded like a wounded bird, not a human, and went on for hours. Overhead, a meshed neon light flickered in an irritating pattern.

She slumped onto the bed and began to shiver, so she slipped under the coarse material of the sheet. However often she turned on the lumpy mattress and pulled up the thin blanket, she couldn't get comfortable, or escape the noise of sneakers squeaking on the tiled floor, or block out the harsh lights. Doors clanged open and shut as people were alternatively incarcerated or released, and the vibration reverberated throughout her body. Toxic negative

GREEN *for* LOVE

energy screamed in her head. She rubbed her temples but that did nothing to eradicate the vibrational torture. For once, she hated being so receptive to energies. Her usual reflective dome wasn't protecting her from the unsettling sources that were clawing at her. How was she going to survive thirty days of this?

The police officer had said she had no legal right to a phone call, and because this was a holding cell, there were no visitation rights either. Lia tamped down the panic that fluttered in her chest and got up to pace her cage again. There was nothing she could do but wait and feel out of control, no choice but to eat the slop they called food. The lights remained on even though it must be night-time. She couldn't sleep anyway; her body was too jittery.

The wailing and clanging of doors continued until she lost sense of time, till she was sick and disorientated and didn't know which way was up. *They're only walls and a door.* But it didn't matter how many times she said it, negative energy permeated through the stonework walls and tormented her. Years of anger, anguish, and fear seeped from the stones and threatened to strangle her. No matter how much she tried to protect her energies with meditation, horror screeched and whistled through her brain. Thirty days. She threw up the bit of food she'd managed to choke down. How was she supposed to survive this?

***

By day five, she seriously thought she might lose her mind. But there was no question, the enforced solitude was forcing her to reflect on her behaviour. She had always been so sure before. But she'd thrown away everything, for what? A principle, a belief that she was right, and that hers was the only way to make change. She'd been so stubborn, so bull-headed about the ways things had to be. Instead of working *with* people, she'd demanded they work her way or no way at all. Jay understood that it took a team, that things had to be done a certain way. She worked with people to create understanding in a gentle way that didn't mean she ended up in a cell.

No doubt Jay would find out that she'd used the knowledge of her trip to the refinery to work out the weakness in their security. Jay wouldn't want anything more to do with her. And it served Lia right. She shuffled around to make herself more comfortable on the ledge-bed thin mattress.

This wasn't what she wanted for her life; it wasn't who she was. She turned over in her not-sleep, and the smell of urine and disinfectant seeping into her nose made her want to gag, even though she laid her face on her arm to filter the stench and shade the light.

"Oh, Cordelia, what have you become?"

She shot up. *Gramps?* But when she peered to where the voice had come from, there was only the same four walls. She wiped her eyes with the back of her sleeve. Gramps would be so ashamed of her. She had always wanted him to be proud of her, to see what she had achieved. When she'd left for Bristol University, he'd shaken his head and said economics wasn't for her, but she'd been adamant. Her parents said she couldn't be trusted with the stewardship of the estate, but she'd show them she could manage money. When her gramps had died, and she'd dropped out, she'd been searching to find herself ever since. The ashram wasn't it, and now the No More Oil activities didn't seem right either. Perhaps it was time to acknowledge that this wasn't her path after all.

She should be home in Northumberland trying to dissuade Tim and Magenta from proceeding with the fracking, not stewing in a cesspit that no amount of sage burning would ever clear of the toxic energies. Her family were right. She wasn't to be trusted with the responsibility of the estate, and she certainly hadn't demonstrated that she was worthy. When she got out, she would make amends and ask forgiveness from her mother for causing them so much anxiety.

She wiped her tears away before they could blend with the dirt in the blanket to create sludge. All she'd wanted was to feel good enough. Good enough to run the estate. Good enough to make a difference in the world. Good enough for the people around her to be proud of her. Instead, she'd proven that she wasn't good enough after all.

All the opportunities she'd missed because she was too stubborn and thought she'd known best. Her life had become so narrow and focused on her anger at the world, at changing the world. She'd blown it all.

When she got out of here, she would do what she could from behind the scenes but not actually take part in any more extreme activities. She couldn't. She'd go mad if she was ever forced to come here again. Somehow, she had to create a life that she was not only proud of, but also one that meant she stopped pushing people away. It was the only way forward.

Chapter Twenty-Eight

JAY STRETCHED AND RUBBED her eyes. She was getting nowhere with this; there were no loopholes in any of the agreements and documents. That was the disadvantage of having excellent lawyers. The only path she had left was to go back to the original land titles and any restrictive covenants, which meant requesting information from the UK Registry Office. A cup of coffee was in order.

As she rose, her door banged open, and Richard walked in. Her heart sank, but she put on a false smile. She didn't know how long she could work for this jerk, especially while he was still gloating he'd taken the job that was rightfully hers.

Richard stood toe-to-toe with her, trying to intimidate her with his extra height and bulk. She gripped her coffee mug like it was a talisman to ward off evil spirits, but it didn't work. He remained in front of her.

"It appears your girlfriend used your little personal tour around the refinery to suss out the security gaps. How else would she know to attack the wire at the back of the refinery research lab?"

"What do you mean?" Jay had a horrible feeling he might be right. How could she have been so naive? Had Lia just used her to stake out the place? Richard gloating was one thing but being betrayed by Lia was something entirely different. She leaned back on the edge of her desk for support, but she couldn't let him see the news had affected her.

Seemingly not noticing her reaction, Richard continued, "What's it like having a jailbird for a lover? Does it add a bit of spice?"

God, he was so smug, she wanted to slap him. Even after a short time with this new regime, she was being eaten away, every minute here like sipping poison one drop at a time. "Was there any purpose to your visit apart from to gloat?"

Richard smirked with the vainglorious delight of the victor. "I thought I'd let you know that there will be a security investigation into your relationship to determine whether you colluded with the ringleader to jeopardise Magenta's position."

She gripped her desk, desperately trying to cover her shock. This was a step too far, even for him. "You're kidding me. I've given my whole career to Magenta; you know I'd do nothing to jeopardise our position." She'd been pulled into this maelstrom because of her emotions, because she'd fallen for an enemy of her company. How stupid could she be?

She inhaled, trying to centre herself as Lia had shown her. The thought of Lia made her breath catch. So much for calming herself down. She shook her head to clear it.

"That's for the investigation to discover. I've recommended to the chair that your access to sensitive information should be restricted while the investigation is ongoing."

How could she do her job if she didn't have access to what she needed? She would be exposed when talking to the press. "What happened to being innocent until proven guilty?"

"I would say there's some pretty damning evidence."

He slapped a manila envelope on the desk. "Open it."

Dread gripped her chest hard as she slid some photographs from the envelope. The first couple were security camera stills of the tour that Jay had taken Lia on and showed them near the back of the labs. It looked as though Jay was pointing directly to the wire. The next few were of her and Lia kissing outside the elevator. There was another of Lia leaving the company flat after the disastrous dinner.

"In addition to facilitating a deliberate attack against the company, there'll also be an investigation into misuse of company assets. It's very clear that woman stayed in the flat all night. If you

GREEN *for* LOVE

look at the timestamp on the photos, you'll see she entered in the evening of one night, and this photo shows her leaving the following morning, several hours after you did. Staff in the flat have confirmed that only one bed was slept in."

He'd been digging for months, mounting evidence against her by searching out every video or camera that may have caught them unawares. Simply being with Lia had given him what he needed to go after Jay's job. "That's all circumstantial evidence. Nothing shows that I had any prior warning or knew anything about it."

Richard positively gleamed. "If that's the case, you're just a gullible sap and hardly director material."

He didn't wait for a reply but strode out and banged the door as he left. It was so typical of him, all drama and attention-seeking. She didn't know she could detest someone so much. She needed a plan. She sat and thought for a moment, and then the seed of something started to grow.

She walked out to Marta, who now seemed to be her only ally in the business, and as a PA, her power was limited. "Hey, Marta, I need a copy of the title deeds and restrictive covenants on the Northumberland fields."

Marta shifted in her seat. "Jay, I'm sorry. I'm not allowed to help you anymore. I've been reassigned to Richard, but since you asked me to do that half an hour ago, I'm sure I'll find the work I've already done somewhere on my desk."

Jay managed a weak smile. "Thank you. And sorry you got caught in the crossfire. It was never going to be pretty."

"I talked to Oliver yesterday. He would love you to call him." Marta winked.

"Is that so? Thanks." Did he have news of a post somewhere else? She returned to her office. So much for being indispensable. They seemed to have dispensed of her like a shot. She needed to get out. It may be too late to do anything about her relationship with Lia, but she could regain her integrity and stop feeling so resentful.

Maybe she and her mum could move to somewhere with cheaper mortgages. Maybe she could get a job with a renewable energy company, or maybe Oliver had something up his sleeve. It was time to get proactive.

Chapter Twenty-Nine

THE POLICE STATION DOOR shut behind her. Silence wrapped around her like a cool towel on a hot day. *Bliss.* She was able to inhale deeply for the first time in thirty days. No stench of disinfectant and urine. No rage and fear tearing at her psyche. For a few precious, beautiful seconds, she breathed in freedom.

"There you are," Steve said.

And just like that, her bubble of joy popped. Now she had to face the consequences. He led her back to the car without response, and she slipped into the passenger seat, wanting him to break the tension.

Before he inserted the key in the ignition, Steve turned to her. "You're not going to like this, but both Christian and your parents want to speak to you."

She groaned and put her head in her hands before pulling back quickly. She still smelled of the cells. "Can I borrow your phone?"

He handed it over. "Help yourself."

Her fingers trembled as she called Christian. "Hey, it's Lia."

"You lied to me. You said you were going to Northumberland."

She flinched. "I did, I'm sorry. I had planned to go up on the Friday night."

"You deliberately went against my orders not to do more insane activism. I had to inform the trustees that you've been in *prison*, and they've terminated your employment with effect from last month. You're not permitted to return to work. Obviously, you need to relinquish the company flat."

If she hadn't already been sitting down, she would have collapsed when her legs started shaking. She felt sick, and the heavy feeling in her chest grew tighter so she couldn't breathe. It wasn't surprising, of course. She'd been warned and ignored them. It was all her fault. "I understand, and I'm truly sorry. How long do I have?"

"I persuaded them to let you move out this weekend, instead of throwing your things in boxes like they wanted to while you were in prison. Christ, Lia you are so bloody-minded sometimes."

Lia shuddered and felt so, so small. "I'm not sure how I can move all my stuff, or where I can move it to."

"That's not my problem. The locks will be changed on Monday morning, so you need to have everything out by then. Goodbye, Lia. I'm sorry it's come to this."

The phone went dead, and Lia stared back at the police station. Maybe it was easier inside where she didn't have other things to worry about. She'd worked with Christian for eight years, and it ended with one brusque phone call. Her life was slamming shut as hard and fast as the cell door.

"Did you hear that?" she asked Steve, and he nodded. "Can I come and stay with you in London until I find somewhere else?"

He shuffled in his seat and didn't quite meet her eye. "I've only got a bedsit. You could sleep on the sofa, but I can't have you in there for long. Hayley's coming up at the weekend."

This was going from bad to worse. She didn't want to think anything else could happen, but she ought to speak to her parents and Tim. She had more apologies to make before she could make any decisions about the future. "Okay, thanks. I'd better call the family now. Is that all right?"

He drove the car out of the car park. "Can you wait until we get back to my bedsit, so you can call France on the Wi-Fi rather than use my mobile data?"

"Sure." She gave a wan smile, grateful for small mercies. Steve was giving her a bit of time.

She'd never been to his tiny studio apartment before. A bed and small sofa, TV, shower room, and kitchenette was crammed

GREEN *for* LOVE

into one room. No wonder he'd been reluctant to let her stay. What did it say about her friendship that she'd never been here before? That she didn't know where he lived or how he lived. Was it really a friendship at all or had she just used him? Yet another sad realization thanks to her incarceration.

She phoned France using WhatsApp. "Hello, Mother, how are you?"

"Cordelia, how could you? After we asked you not to continue, you went against our wishes. And now you have a criminal record. I'm so disappointed in you. What would your gramps have said? I'll never be able to show my face in Northumberland again for the shame."

She bit her bottom lip, needing a hug, but her mother's vehemence jarred her, although it wasn't without merit. She cringed at the thought of disappointing Gramps. "I'm sorry."

"It's too late, Cordelia. You've been warned enough times, and now you have to live with the consequences. You made your point, but you went too far this time. Before you ask, we're not going to help you out financially anymore, and your income from the family trust is frozen. We've been subsidising your criminal activity. No more. It's time you took responsibility for your actions and settled down properly."

Lia swallowed her pride. "But I need to move my stuff, find a new flat and a new job. I hoped you might give me a loan from the trust fund until I get on my feet."

"No. You need to face the consequences of your actions. Call me when you're ready to face up to your responsibilities."

Another door clanged shut. Her heartbeat increased, and her hands felt sweaty as she called Tim. Maybe she could live with him for a while.

"Lia, how can I have you here?" he said. "You're a bad influence on Abby. She's still talking about how evil I am to be doing a deal with Magenta. It's none of her business what I do with the estate."

Lia rubbed her eyes with the heels of her hands. She was

filthy and needed to wash away the torment of the last month still clinging to her soul. Yet she had brought everything on herself, and she needed to make amends with Tim if she was ever going to see Abby again. "I'm sorry for embarrassing you and the family."

"Too late. You've turned Abby against me. No, you can't come and stay. I don't want you anywhere near my daughter. You're not welcome back in the family until you've accepted that you can't keep behaving this way."

Her hope dissipated as yet another door slammed shut. She had never felt so broken, so alone. "You've spoken to Mother?"

Tim cleared his throat. "Yes, we're both agreed it's for your own good."

"You make it sound as though I'm an alcoholic."

"You're addicted to causing trouble. It's just as bad, especially for the people around you."

She slumped back in the tiny sofa. "When can I see Abby again? I promised her I'd take her to the hide to see the birds migrating north."

"You should have thought of that before all your criminal activity. Think about your priorities, Lia."

She swallowed hard around the lump in her throat. "I am. I have."

There was a moment of hesitation. "Maybe we just all need some time, Lia. Get yourself together, okay?"

As she signed off, Steve looked across at her. "Do you want to take a shower and change into the clothes you asked me to hold on to? Then I'll take you back to Bristol."

"Thanks."

As she showered in the tiny cubicle, she let the tears flow along with the lukewarm water that felt like heaven. Everything was crumbling around her, as if she'd deliberately gone on a rampage, destroying everything she held dear. It was possible most of the relationships in her life were beyond repair, and she could only hope that one day, they'd forgive her.

And then there was her relationship with Jay. Why did it take

GREEN *for* LOVE

her losing her whole world for her to see it? But she couldn't exactly rock up at her place now and say, "Sorry, you were right." Jay would laugh her off the front steps.

Maybe, just maybe, she would reply to a text. She dressed quickly and picked up her now-charged phone. *Sorry, I was wrong. I hope you're okay. Lia xo*

She didn't expect a reply but that didn't stop her from hoping for one. But now she needed to call the only person who might be able to help her on a practical level.

"Hi, Gavin, it's Lia. Yeah, I'm in a bit of a pickle. I have to get out of my company flat. Could I keep my stuff in the storage unit at your place and maybe, do you have any job vacancies?"

"Hi, Lia. I heard from Christian. He's spitting feathers. He said I shouldn't help you, but you've been great at supporting us over the years. I could probably put some of your stuff in the container, yeah. But I don't have anywhere you could stay. We don't even have a spare room now that Jake is older. As for a job, it's not something I'd recommend. It's hard, physical labour in our warehouse on the night shift, unpacking and lugging around solar panels, preparing them for installation. And it's minimum wage."

"Gavin, you're a lifesaver. I'm not afraid of hard work, but can I get back to you on the job? Since I don't know where I'll be staying, I might be too far away. I'll let you know soon. Thanks again. I appreciate it." She ended the call, grateful that there was a chink of light in the darkness. She hired a van with the tiny bit of credit left on her card, but she didn't want to think how she would repay it. Her bank account was practically empty, thanks to all she'd spent on spray cans, black clothing, handcuffs, and the money that always came out for the various charities she gave to. *One thing at a time.*

She had to find somewhere to live that didn't need a large deposit. There was one person she could see. Elsie would probably put her up while she sorted herself out. What was it they said about being only two paycheques from homelessness? Staring at stark reality for the first time in her life, fear gnawed at her gut. All she could see was a hole in the bottom, and there was nothing to stop her from falling through.

***

Lia had thought she kept fit by running and working in the allotment garden but nothing prepared her for the sheer physicality of pushing around solar panels in the warehouse. The three blokes hadn't exactly made her welcome either, but she didn't care. She was simply grateful Gavin had given her a job.

Cycling home after working overnight meant her legs struggled to pedal with any zest. She slipped off her bike to lock it in the cage in the basement of Elsie's building, but her legs trembled so much she had to lean against the cold concrete until she felt stronger. *Please let the elevator work.* The relief when the battered metal doors opened had tears welling in her eyes. She slipped into Elsie's flat, hoping she could crash on the sofa before Elsie woke.

Unfortunately, teacups clattering and Elsie singing to Radio Two announced she was up and about. Without even showering, Lia dropped onto the sofa. If she could have just a few minutes, she might be able to face the world. She didn't have the luxury of keening with a broken heart, throwing anything to hand, or screaming and stomping to show her despair.

Instead, she would have to slip on her mask of resignation and move through life, numb like a robot, until she could get herself up and active again. Right now, she could do no more than take one day at a time when all she wanted to do was sleep.

Her eyes had already closed when Elsie came in. "Oh, good, you're awake. I thought you might like a cup of tea."

She smiled and accepted the tea in Elsie's best china cups, taking care to sip away from the crack.

"How was work, dear?" Elsie settled herself on the chair, obviously enjoying having company.

"Exhausting." She couldn't stay here, interfering with Elsie's day,

GREEN *for* LOVE

but she couldn't afford anywhere else to live. Her muscles burned, and her legs were purple from knee to ankle from knocking into the trolleys. After sleep, she wanted a long soak in a bath; what Elsie had was a tiny wet room with a shower that sprayed over the toilet roll unless she placed it on the high window shelf.

Elsie stared at Lia and maybe saw the drooping of her eyelids and shoulders. "I'll leave you to it, dear. I know you'll be tired."

"Thanks, Elsie. I'll get up before your programme this afternoon, and I'll try to find somewhere else. I can't put you out any longer. I'm very grateful you let me crash here." She couldn't believe they had laughed about the impossibility of Lia needing to stay with Elsie only a few months ago. Elsie hadn't asked her what had happened, but she must have seen it in the papers.

Elsie gave her a questioning look, then left the room. Lia turned over on the lumpy sofa, pulling up her legs so she could fit, and tried to ignore the sounds of next door's television and a child crying. She squeezed her eyes shut to stop the tears from falling.

She had always been able to rely on something or someone, and now she was squashed on a sofa, imposing on an elderly friend, doing a job that was exhausting and completely unfulfilling. As often as she'd talked about living like a regular person and how she didn't want to be seen as wealthy, she'd never really understood what it meant in reality.

She turned on the couch to stop the cramps in her calves, but a hard lump caught her under the ribs. She shuffled to get comfortable but the moment she moved, the lump got her again. After about three hours, she gave up and entered the small kitchen where Elsie was sitting, occasionally licking a pencil and doing the quick crossword. Good job pencils weren't lead anymore.

"Did you sleep? I thought you'd be out longer."

"In fits and starts. But I was awake, and I don't want to stop you from coming into your own living room. I've put you out enough."

"Help yourself to breakfast, and I'll pop to the Co-op for milk."

Without waiting for Lia to object, Elsie snatched up her bag and a walking stick and was out of the door. Lia stared out of the kitchen window across the city, towards the hills and the airport. A jet took off, carrying people off to holidays in the sun.

Lia couldn't believe how upset she felt. The anger that had fuelled her for years, that had kept her emphatic and uncompromising was spent, burnt out, and she was left as an empty shell. She should be campaigning, but now she didn't have the energy, the time, or the resources to spare for the cause. If only she'd been less adamant and self-righteous, she could have been making a real difference, not barely surviving.

Tears streamed down her face as she waited for the kettle to boil. She couldn't even go to her childhood sanctuary because it wouldn't be there anymore. They would pull down the hide and drain the marsh and grasslands, destroying the habitat for the overwintering birds. Where would they go? She wouldn't be able to look out across the plains and the sand dunes to the distant Lindisfarne Castle. If she closed her eyes, she could almost hear the distant calling of terns and oystercatchers, and close by, the crows in the tall trees squabbling over the highest branches.

She inhaled deeply and wiped her eyes with the back of her hand. Elsie wouldn't be long. She tried to centre herself and started on her gratitude mantra. She was grateful for what she had, all the privileges she'd had from birth and taken for granted. But they were gone, and she was an outcast. She couldn't get a similar job because she had a criminal record. She no longer had the support of the family, and she had blown her potential relationship with Jay. Everything was so much harder than she ever thought it would be.

She wriggled her shoulders to reset. "I am grateful for Elsie and the roof over my head, for Gavin with his storage and the job, and for both of them for helping me when no one else would." Having someone's love and trust was such a privilege and should be nourished and nurtured every day like an allotment.

Lia looked at the tags and squalor of the square outside. She didn't see any kids kicking a ball, just discarded fast food wrappers

GREEN *for* LOVE

and solid concrete. This was no place to bring up children or to dump the old or infirm. Lia couldn't change the world alone. Had anything she'd done made a difference?

Lia let the tears fall and felt an arm around her waist. She hadn't heard Elsie come in.

"You'll rise again," Elsie said.

Lia leaned into her and took comfort from the connection, grounding her, holding her tethered to the earth. Humans weren't supposed to live this high up in steel and plastic structures. They were meant to live with their feet on the ground.

Lia couldn't change the world, but she *had* made a difference to Elsie and the others, because their homes were now insulated. She turned and placed her arms around Elsie, who seemed uncomfortable at first but then relaxed into the hug. "Thank you, thank you so much for being the only person to welcome me into your home and for being there for me. I don't know if you know how much it means to me to know that you're my friend. I promise I'll get somewhere for you to live where you feel safe walking the streets, where you don't have to clamber up the stairs if the elevator is broken."

Elsie squeezed back. "Lia, you're such a kind soul, but you don't have to do anything for me. I have card nights with some of the women here. Now that you've got us cheaper electric and insulated our flats, we've all got a little extra cash to spend—enough for another packet of biscuits."

Guilt slithered down her spine like a snake. She had promised Elsie she would take her to meet Jay's mum so they could play cards. That wouldn't happen now. And she had to stop thinking about Jay, who hadn't replied to her text and probably never would.

She must have been squeezing Elsie too hard, because she grunted and wriggled out of her grasp.

"Would you like a cuppa? I'll make one and sit down and watch my programme. It's *A Place in the Sun* today. I imagine what it's like to go abroad. Would you sit and watch it with me?"

As they watched, Lia's eyes drifted closed, and she only woke when Elsie held out a cup of tea.

"If your job is that tiring, could you get another one?" she asked.

Lia blushed. Now she would probably have to have the conversation about prison with Elsie. If Elsie didn't know, would she throw her out? She took the saucer and waited until Elsie dropped onto her armchair. "I can't get another job because I would fail the DBS check. I went to prison for my environmental activism, for damaging property. They wanted to make an example of me."

Elsie nodded. "I saw the papers. But they must see you're a kind girl, a nice girl."

Lia turned around the cup in the saucer, the kindness causing a lump in her throat. When she regained her composure, she said, "The law doesn't care. Once it's on your record, it's there for good. And even though employers can risk assess me, it'll be difficult to get a job in the charity sector again."

Elsie took another sip of tea then cocked her head on one side. "What about that nice woman you brought round the other month, what was her name, Jay? Would she give you a job?"

Lia shook her head, misery seeping into her bones. "She won't want to speak to me again."

Elsie narrowed her eyes. "Oh. You liked her, didn't you? I could see there was a connection between you, all spark and crackling in your banter."

"That may be true, but I betrayed her trust."

"Oh?" Elsie sat back and settled in for a bit of gossip.

There seemed to be nothing she liked better. Another reason to get out of her hair and out of her flat—she wouldn't be subjected to a million different questions.

Nevertheless, she told Elsie the whole sordid tale, trying to keep her voice neutral. "So, I've lost my career and family. Worst of all, I betrayed Jay and any hope we had of having a relationship, even though that was always contentious."

Elsie sipped her tea. "That's a shame."

GREEN *for* LOVE

Which bit? Losing the family and love or the being in prison? Lia shuffled in her seat and waited for Elsie to elaborate.

"You need a bit of help now. She's a nice woman. She'd listen to you."

"She won't do that. She'll never forgive me, even if I apologise on my knees. Now I understand why she was so fixed on her job and security. I've been so arrogant."

"Are you sorry?" Elsie asked.

"For upsetting her, yes." Lia grimaced. "I still think being loud means you call attention to issues that need it. But I can see that I've gone too far. I never meant to hurt anyone."

"Would you do the same thing again?"

Lia paused and recalibrated herself. "No. I would do what I could with any other means possible, but I wouldn't deliberately break the law or do things that hurt the people around me."

And she knew with certainty that was true. It wasn't what everyone would choose. And she would do what she could to work behind the scenes to make the changes. In fact, the perfect person to work with would be Jay, with her logical scientific mind. What a shame they couldn't make a go of it, for so many reasons.

Chapter Thirty

"YOU'RE ALL SET," MARTA said as she attached the concealed transmitter in Jay's jacket. "Are you sure this is necessary?"

Jay nodded. "I don't trust them. I might need to go to Alistair and the full board, and it will be their word against mine." She stared at herself in the mirror of the ladies' bathroom, detesting herself for taking this post. Alistair had called off the investigation into her relationship with Lia, but it remained on her record like a black apple rotting the whole barrel of her exemplary service.

Her face looked more tired and lined than before, but it wasn't obvious from her expression that she was about to take one of the biggest risks of her career. Whatever happened in the next hour would change her future forever. She might not even have a chance to say her goodbyes if it came to that. She held Marta's gaze in the mirror. "Thank you for all your help with this. For your friendship, for everything."

"You're welcome, Jay. I've always been proud of Magenta, and if what you say is true, I'm ashamed. Oliver would be horrified."

"He would."

Jay wasn't going to tell Marta that she was also doing this for herself, to give Lia proof if she was prepared to listen. She'd had an apology by text but nothing since. If Lia had taken some action to show she meant it, maybe she would have relented, but right now, she needed to focus on work and clearing her name.

Yet, completely illogically, Jay still hoped that they might reconnect somehow. Despite Lia's betrayal, Jay couldn't deny that Lia's passion to save the planet was a beautiful thing. So much for never having more than one night. It toyed with her emotions, and she hated that. She hated caring about Lia, about her career, everything she had worked for. She felt like a flat battery that needed recharging.

"I'm not sure how this will go, and I'll probably have to leave. If so, I just want to thank you."

Marta smiled sadly. "I hope not. Thanks for being a great boss. I'll go and start the streaming now."

Jay inhaled sharply and checked in the mirror that she looked perfect. There were still two minutes left until she needed to go in, but she wanted to be prompt, so she exited the bathroom and made her way to John's office for the meeting with John and Richard that she'd pretty much demanded.

Straightening her shoulders, she clicked on the voice memo on her phone as her back up and knocked on the door with a confidence she didn't feel. *I can do this.*

"Come," John called, and she entered.

Richard was already there in the prime position at the small conference table with his father, looking out towards Finsbury Circus. It was a shock going into what had been Oliver's office. John had lined the walls with pictures of the oil refineries. She was almost surprised he didn't have a picture of a dollar bill.

"Sit down, Jay. What's all this about?"

Okay, straight to business then. She sat opposite Richard and John at the small conference table, being careful that her jacket didn't open to reveal the microphone.

"Thanks for seeing me. We can't purchase the fields in Northumberland. It would be illegal to proceed, because there's a restrictive covenant which disallows the sale for *any* purpose that will affect the wildlife, including the migrating birds, or anything that impacts badly on the environment. Fracking in the area would be actionable by law."

Richard turned scarlet to match his tie, but he didn't look surprised. He must've known and yet he still went ahead. *How stupid.*

GREEN *for* LOVE

John turn to Richard. "Is this true?"

"I...I'm not sure. I'm sure they wouldn't have put it up for sale if this supposed covenant was in force."

"That's why you do due diligence. You should've known this would come out eventually, or did you think you could get away with it? Did you really think no one would check to make sure the land was actually legally available?" Jay fought to keep her tone rational as she slid the relevant papers across the desk, with the covenant portions highlighted in yellow.

Richard's fingers tightened around the papers, but he didn't bother to look at them. "Surely that also stops you from doing your pet project as well?"

Jay leaned back in the comfortable leather chair. What came next? What could she do? A sliver of fear ran through her, but she slammed it down. She was in the right. "If they were conventional wind turbines, yes, you're right. However, I'm currently doing a trial at a different site for the vertical wind turbines which have a much smaller environmental impact." She gave a slight smile. "Regardless, that's not what we're talking about right now." Jay leaned forward and stared him down. "Do you really think the shareholders want to be lied to, or find out you have been proceeding illegally? Do you need me to go through the clauses, one by one, each one forbidding the disposal or use for any purpose that is detrimental to the wildlife or the environment? There are five clauses in total. We need to rescind the purchase immediately, or Magenta will pay for land that will have no use to the company. I'm sure the shareholders would love that." She glanced across at John. Amazingly, he was nodding.

Richard scowled. "No, that's not going to happen. We'll find another use for it, another way to make it profitable. If we can't do fracking there, we'll go somewhere else."

She squared her shoulders. This was her pitch, and she had to get it right. "With all the various technological advances that have happened under my watch, we could proceed to make a difference now. I'm going to request that we expand the various trials at the next board meeting." She slid another document in front of them. "This is a template of how we can get to net-zero within the next ten years, fifteen maximum. And just to reiterate, we cannot buy the Northumberland site for anything to do with Magenta. It's *illegal*."

Richard wiped sweat from his forehead. "We don't make as much money on green technologies and never will. That's what our shareholders are interested in, otherwise they would invest in other companies."

"And that's the crux of it, isn't it? The impact on the environment will have a much greater cost in the future. Many shareholders are getting savvy to that and are demanding green solutions, even if the financial prospects have to change."

Richard leaned back and steepled his fingers, but there was no question she'd rattled him. "That'll never happen. Shareholders are interested in their monetary return."

John was now nodding in agreement with Richard. He was so weak, he couldn't even make his own mind up. She could see this slipping away from her grasp. What would Lia do? She would be shouting and screaming at them by now, but that wasn't Jay's way. "But it could happen *now*. We have an opportunity to put in place a series of sustainable measures that will cost less than the purchase price of the land and the investment in the infrastructure." Jay slapped down the summary on the conference desk. "Here's the cost benefit analysis I've prepared with the help of the finance team. I want it taken to the board and discussed as an option."

John seemed to gather his confidence. "This will be a complete change of strategy, Jay. The board won't buy it."

Had he been in the company for the past fifteen years?

"Nonsense, that's what the board have been claiming all these years. This will deliver exactly what the board has promised it will deliver."

"The board has a different constitution now."

GREEN *for* LOVE

Jay's hope deflated like a wilting balloon. She'd known it was a longshot, but she'd had to try. "You can't continue with the purchase of the Northumberland site."

John smoothed down the paper Jay had handed to him. He hadn't even glanced at it. "I'll have the lawyers check it over, and if it's true, we'll pull out of the purchase."

"It's true," Jay said, certain of her facts.

Richard looked like a petulant teenager. "But we've already spent a fortune on engineering costs and surveys."

It felt like a playground argument rather than a business meeting. Jay swallowed hard and tried one last time. "I want this paper to be put onto the next board agenda and for them to decide."

Richard glared at her. "No, that will upset our plans. Dad, you can't let this happen."

John looked from Richard back to Jay. He'd always been a ditherer, affected by the last person who got to him. Richard had got to him; he would do whatever Richard said. That was never going to change.

She could see her future career in front of her as clear as if it was following GPS. Sitting here, proposing things that would be shot down, and she would become more and more resentful. That wouldn't work for her anymore.

She couldn't stay. Fear popped up in the form of her seven-year-old self coming home from school, ravenous and searching through the fridge, cutting off the mouldy crusts and scraping ketchup from the inside of a bottle with a knife to make a sandwich. Her forty-four-year-old self knew logically she would survive though. She might have to move in with her mum, or uproot them both to somewhere cheaper, but she could thrive. Her mental health and integrity were worth much more than the security of a job run by people she didn't respect.

She glanced up at John, who pulled at his tie as though it was too tight. "No," John said. "This won't go to the board."

Jay sighed. "In that case, I'll take the contents of this

conversation to Alistair and the rest of the board myself and tender my resignation. I can't work with people I don't respect, people who don't do the right thing or won't act beyond their own money-grubbing interests."

Richard laughed. "Look at you getting all noble. Is your girlfriend rubbing off on you, pun intended?"

"This is about good long-term business, but you're too greedy to see it."

"So what if we can't buy that parcel of land? Big deal. We'll find somewhere else, and we'll do the same."

"Under Oliver, Magenta always behaved with integrity and developed what he said we would." There was no point continuing this argument; they would never agree. "I believe I need to give you three-months' notice. John, you'll have my resignation letter on your desk by close of play today."

She rose, but John raised his hand to stop her.

"No. I can't have you meddling or stealing secrets for the next three months. I won't ask security to escort you, but you need to be out by the end of the day."

Jay snatched up her files and walked out of the room. She walked down the corridor and stopped the recording on her phone. What was she going to do now? She needed time to consider her options. She didn't want to transfer to another oil company stuffed with men like Richard, but oil was all she knew.

She stopped at Marta's desk. "Did you catch all that?"

Marta nodded, her eyes shiny. "I'm sorry you had to resign, Jay. I've enjoyed working with you. There are no good guys left now."

Jay blinked hard. "Can you make sure a copy of that recording goes to Alistair and the board? Thanks."

Marta came around the desk and gave Jay a hug. She tried hard to hold back the tears. She murmured thank you a few times before breaking off to go and clear her desk.

A few minutes later, Jay received an email from Marta informing her that she'd sent the file as requested.

GREEN *for* LOVE

She stared at the room that had been her domain, her life for the past twenty-odd years, wiped at a tear with her thumb, and started to clear the desk. Sometimes you needed to acknowledge that something had passed its time, whether that was a job or a relationship. And although it was frightening, she couldn't help but feel some relief too.

Carefully, she unhooked her graduation and professional certificates like she was taking down her persona and leaving a blank in its place. She wiped away a thin layer of dust with a tissue.

Her mum had been so proud when she had received them. "Look at you, a council house kid, a daughter of a cleaner getting a university degree."

That she had gone on to get a secondary degree and professional qualifications hadn't meant as much to her mum as that first degree, as she had never known anyone who'd been to university.

If she sold the Thameside property and lived with her mum, that would give her a bit of capital and time to work out what she wanted to do. A plan started to form in her head, and she would research it properly when she got home. First, she needed to deal with the loose ends here.

She sighed. She'd talk to Oliver after she'd decided on her plan, but first she needed to send a copy of the conversation to Lia. They may be over romantically, but Lia should know that Jay had principles and that she stuck to them. Sending Lia the audio file would have been a sackable offence, which was why she didn't ask Marta to send it to Lia on her behalf. How ironic she was doing her first illegal act as her last act in the company. It mattered that Lia realised Jay had been as good as her word, even if it was too late for anything between them now.

Chapter Thirty-One

LIA WAS TOO SHATTERED to open the strange email that came from an anonymous source with the subject heading, "You should know."

At least she could finally let Elsie have her flat back. Gavin had told her about another activist who was a member of the Green party and had a spare room in North Bristol. It made for a long bike commute to her new place of work, but she was hoping to get another job soon. She didn't like to admit that she wasn't strong enough to do the physical work. Her hands had started to harden up, and there was a sense of accomplishment in doing a job she'd never done before. But it was time to move on.

Her prison reputation didn't stand against her with her new roommate. Vivian was a much older woman who didn't talk much and smiled even less. One of her conditions was that Lia wasn't allowed to eat any meat or fish because Vivian didn't want it contaminating the fridge.

"That's no problem. I'm a veggie myself," Lia said, hoping to elicit a smile or even a common connection.

"I'm vegan. Switch the lights off when you leave the room."

As if she needed a lecture on the environment, but Lia simply smiled then followed Vivian up the steep stairs.

"Settle yourself in. Gavin has vouched for you, so you'd better pay up when you get your wage, or you'll disappoint him too."

Lia nodded and after Vivian left, she looked around. It was a glorified box room at the top of the house, probably the same size as her cell and also with bare floors. But it had a proper bed. Downstairs, there was old lino in the shared bathroom, but it had a toilet seat, something she'd come to appreciate immensely. After having nothing, even for such a short period, she now appreciated the little luxuries, and her ylang ylang and patchouli soap was a definite luxury in a shower she didn't have to share with anyone else. They were memories she wouldn't forget any time soon.

She would rebuild herself and her life, but she had changed internally. Even her passion was dimmed; where she had once argued with gusto determined to enforce every point, now she listened, taking in other people's viewpoints and really analysing them before she responded. She found solace with her hands in the soil, tending to her allotment, nurturing the vegetables, tugging at the weeds to stop them choking the vulnerable plants.

When she was alone, she shuffled on the squeaky bed, settled her core and cleansed her chakras to rebalance herself. When her email pinged with another reminder that she had not yet downloaded the file, she was reminded of the many emails she and Jay had sent one another.

Lia couldn't stop thinking about her, even after all their time apart. She missed the sparring, and the conversations, and Jay's kindness, though she couldn't expect to receive any more of that. Without Jay, everything was dull and lifeless like her unconditioned hair, faded and washed out. In her gut, she knew Jay was the one, her soulmate, and she had to try one more time.

She swallowed hard before placing the call. She crossed her fingers as she waited for the phone to ring, hoping and dreading in equal measure that Jay would answer.

"Hey, lovely to hear from you." Jay's tone was warm and welcoming, as though she was genuinely delighted to hear from her.

Lia couldn't stop her smile. "Hey, lovely to hear you too. How are you? No, before you answer that, I need to apologise." The floodgates opened ,and tears fell as the need to tell Jay everything overwhelmed her. "I didn't know how difficult it would be. I've lost my job, my flat, and my family wouldn't bail me out, so I spent a month in a jail cell, where I did a ton of self-reflection and thought

GREEN *for* LOVE

about you non-stop. I'm working on the night shift at Gavin's place in the warehouse, and until yesterday, I was sleeping on Elsie's sofa."

Jay took a sharp intake of breath. "Oh, Lia, I'm sorry to hear that."

Lia frowned and rattled her bangles. "You're not going to say I told you so?"

"No, I'm not. I'm sorry too. I should've heeded you. Did you listen to the file I sent through?"

The knot in Lia's stomach tightened. "The large audio file? No, not yet. What did it say?"

Jay blew out a long breath. "Just listen to it. You were right. I owe you an apology. Magenta isn't all it's cracked up to be. Richard and John are going to take it back to dirty fossil fuels. I've handed in my resignation."

Lia sat up on her bed. "But that job meant the world to you, and you've given your life, your whole career to it."

"I don't want to be part of a company that doesn't live by its principles. So I quit."

Lia felt nauseous and wished she could wrap her arms around Jay. It would shake her sense of self to change jobs. "I know it's not my place, but I'm proud of you for standing by your principles. What are you going to do now?"

"I'm not sure. It won't make an iota of difference to Magenta. In fact, it's probably saved them the cost of an expensive severance package." Jay sighed and then seemed to take a second to compose herself before she continued. "Believe it or not, I'm trying to get funding to roll out some of the trials that we did. I'm hoping that Oliver will invest. I assume your brother told you that Magenta have pulled out of the land sale?"

"He sent a text blaming me. He wasn't happy, but I love it." Lia shuffled down into the duvet.

"Did he say why it didn't go through?"

"Not really."

"There was a restrictive covenant put on by your grandfather forbidding sale for anything that would affect the wildlife or the environment. Clearly, he suspected something like this might happen."

Lia's heart expanded with love for her gramps and clogged her throat. "Thanks for telling me; that means a lot." She inhaled a cleansing breath, to give her courage to speak what she hadn't yet been able to. "I can't continue as I am. I'm broke, and I miss you. I know there's no reason that you would ever want to be associated with me again, but I'm trying to make amends and take on my responsibilities. I've asked to have a meeting with my family when I go to Northumberland this weekend, to have a real discussion."

"Really? Are you going to live up there?"

Lia started to fidget, not wanting to jinx her idea. "I'm not sure. I've got a plan, but I don't know if my family will agree. I don't want to talk about it in case it doesn't happen." Lia bit her lip and took the leap. "I'd love to talk it through with you when I've spoken to them. Could we arrange to meet up, maybe in London next week? I'd love to see you again."

"Sure. I'd love to see you too. Don't forget to listen to the recording. And thanks."

"For what?"

"For being open, for calling me."

Lia's hand shot to her chest. "It's me who needs to thank you. I'll be in contact when I've spoken to my brother."

"Let me know if you need a hand with that."

Lia laughed. "He's pretty pissed off right now. I don't think he wants any contact from any Magenta people, especially the one who's stopped the sale."

"As long as I get to keep in touch with you. That's all that matters."

Lia's heart began to flutter. "Now you're talking." She cradled the phone after they hung up. For the first time in months, she was inspired by possibility and the blossoming of hope.

Chapter Thirty-Two

IT WAS A FAMILY tradition to spend Easter at the estate, and Lia needed it now more than ever, to cleanse her soul from the torments of the last few months.

When she arrived, the first thing she did was ask Tim if Abby could go to the hide with her. "I'd like to see if there are any geese still here."

"No, Lia. I told you I don't want her associating with you. You're a bad influence."

Muttering under her breath, Lia stormed off. She knew she had no grounds to be angry, and Tim's attitude did little to improve her temper. Being estranged from Abby was yet another consequence she would have to deal with.

The wind was bitter as she tramped across moors and down to the feeding grounds. She opened the hide, hoping she wasn't too late to see the geese before they migrated north. She stared out at the grasslands and the small lake, but even though she raked the area with her binoculars, there were no geese. They'd all gone, and for the first time in many years, she hadn't been there to see them go. She felt bereft, as if she'd been left behind. She had no family and few friends and had blown her one chance at true love. Maybe when they met next week, she and Jay could become friends, although she knew she wanted so much more. Jay had seemed pleased to speak on the phone, and Lia had gone over and over their conversation. Her plan could work, and if they could overlap in business somehow, perhaps they could re-establish what they had.

She set the binoculars down as tears poured down her cheeks

in rushing rivulets, falling on her jacket and her hands. She cried for all the consequences of what she'd done. All her fears when she'd been lying in her cell had come to pass.

And yet, she wasn't broken. She would make amends, she would change, and she would have a genuine, honest discussion with her family. Here was a perfect place to have a rebirth.

Lia wiped her eyes and returned to the hall, enjoying having the wind behind her as she hiked up the stiff climb to the heather moors, teeming with bird call. In the distance, low over the hills was the unmistakable sky dance of a male hen harrier, swooping and somersaulting to attract the larger female. Lia lifted her binoculars to her eyes and followed the display, each turn and dive filling her heart with joy and gratitude that the gamekeepers hadn't managed to eradicate this couple, so beautiful, so rare that they were on the red list of endangered species.

Back in the house, she picked up a book and sat by the fire in blessed silence. She stayed out of the way and simply enjoyed the feeling of being home. After dinner, where the conversation had been somewhat stilted and only filled with Abby's excitement about her newest project, they sat in front of a crackling fire once again. Lia basked in the warmth and sipped an Ardbeg whisky that reminded her of Jay. She couldn't think of Jay now; she had a task to complete. Lia closed her eyes to centre herself, before she cleared her throat and focused on her mother sitting beside her. "I'm sorry for the trouble I've caused and for the shame I brought to you all. I know the cause is still necessary, but the methods I adopted were wrong. I'd like to make amends and to take on more responsibility. I have a proposal to make, so I hope you'll hear me out."

She took another sip and looked around the room to see their reaction. Her mother nodded for her to continue. "Gramps wanted the estate to prosper, not only monetarily, but also for the wildlife, for the environment, and for future generations. I don't agree with what you've been doing, Tim, and Gramps wouldn't either." She put up her hand to stop him from responding. "But I understand

GREEN *for* LOVE

that to keep the property, our home, going, then we have to keep money coming in. It was unfair of me to be on your back about the way you farm it when you're simply trying to keep the estate in good repair. I never took into consideration how hard you work and how much it takes to make things work. I understand better now, I think." She smiled at Tim's bewildered expression.

"My proposal is that the estate is split into two equal halves. I'll have the bird fields, the hilltops, the less productive land, and three of the farms. You'll have the more productive pasture lands that will make you lots of money, and you won't have to split the income in two. I'll convert the barns at Hiburn to make an eco-village for a small community and rent out cottages for eco-tourism, which means I'd be bringing in money to help take care of the estate as well. I'd like to have a solar farm and vertical wind turbines to produce electricity, and I also want the whole of the west side of the heather moors, to protect the bird corridors." She held her breath waiting to see how Tim would react.

He narrowed his gaze, looking thoughtful. "That's ridiculous. Where would you get the money from? You'd need to have a ton of cash to invest, cash you don't have since you've given it all away."

The look in his eyes though wasn't mirth. He was listening to her, and rather than jump down his throat, she needed to engage. She willed her fingers not to grip her glass too tightly. "I'll find eco investors. I have enough contacts to find viable funding, and I'll apply for government grants as well, which are available to people trying for sustainability."

"You can't have the moorlands; I need that for the shoot."

"Maybe, maybe not. We'll need to flesh out the details. The moors are also the perfect habitat for the birds of prey, a protected species which makes them part of the covenant on the land, which you and your gamekeepers seem to overlook."

Tim slammed down his glass and turned to their parents. "And what happens when she goes to jail again? What happens when her ideas cost more than they bring in, and we can't repair the roof again in five years?"

Lia looked over her whisky glass at him. He was rattled. "Tim, I understand why you're worried, and you have every right to be. I was wrong, and I've learned some things about myself that aren't all that pleasant. But I'm still part of this family, and I know my ideas are sound."

"Timothy, your gramps was right. We do need to work the land within the context of nature around and about. Lia has a good point," her father said slowly.

Lia startled at the novelty of him siding with her. She studied him as he struggled to speak. He was frailer now than he used to be, as though being ill and retiring had shifted his perspective.

"Yes, I was ashamed of her behaviour too," her mother said. "But Cordelia has apologised, and I can see the impact it's had on her. We're more ashamed that you tried to sell off the land to an oil company, of all things. Yes, Lia failed in her responsibility, but so have you." She shook her head when he began to protest. "I know you've done it because you have a certain way of doing things, and you believe what you're doing is for the best." She looked at Lia and gave her a small smile. "Lia was doing the same. I'm prepared to give you both another chance."

Lia sipped at her whisky to hide her smile. The alcohol warmed her insides but not as much as finally receiving the support and acknowledgement from her parents. This is what she had been seeking all her life, and it was too precious not to bask in it.

Her mother turned to Lia. "I'm sorry. I think you've been a lost soul ever since your gramps died. We should have been there for you. We've been doing a lot of talking since your stint in jail too." She huffed and rolled her eyes. "Not a sentence I thought I'd ever say. But we wanted you to be more like us, something you aren't. You've always been you, no matter what anyone else thought. That's impressive, even if it drove us crazy sometimes."

Lia had to close her mouth. She'd never heard her mother apologise. Any normal mother would have given her a hug, but

GREEN *for* LOVE

her mother only patted her leg.

"We'll go to the lawyers in Newcastle tomorrow and come up with a way that will split the estate fairly."

Lia wanted to hold this moment in her memory to treasure as the day her life changed trajectory. "Thank you," she said through the lump in her throat. She so wanted to call Jay and tell her the news, but it would have to wait until later. A knot tightened in her stomach. She'd love to be able to do the project with Jay, but most of all, she just wanted to see her. To be with her.

On the sofa opposite, Tim clasped Diana's arm so hard she winced. "Is there no option on this?"

His protests were cut short by a glare from their mother.

"Okay," he mumbled.

Diana whispered to him urgently, and Lia couldn't hear all of what she said but she caught, "Man up. Stand up for yourself, for me, for Abby."

Tim hissed something at her then turned to their father. "Surely you don't agree that we should give away five and a half thousand acres to a jailbird? What's she ever done to prove herself?"

Their father shook his head. "You heard what your mother said. You've done enough damage. We trusted you, and you broke that trust. We're not giving away half of the land. We're splitting the estate, as perhaps we should've done from the beginning. It's time for Cordelia to have her chance to make a go of it, and if she fails, well, you'll be able to say you're right."

Lia swallowed. Having set down the gauntlet, she now needed to find investors for her idea. It should be like trying to find funding for her charity, right? Now that her parents had agreed to her proposal, plans and thoughts swirled together in a beautiful rainbow of possibility.

Maybe Elsie could live up here if Lia made sure the cottages were warm and properly insulated, and she could sit and watch the work on communal allotments. Perhaps Jay could bring her mum up here. They always talked about getting her mum and Elsie together. They could play cards and entertain themselves in the evenings and live surrounded by nature. If only Jay would see that they were better together and take a chance on her too. If only she could convince her of that when they met up.

She paused, took a breath, not daring to believe the whisper of what could be, ephemeral, just a fingertip away.

Chapter Thirty-Three

A FINE DRIZZLE SETTLED on the leaves and Lia's hair as she walked through the park. With the rain, it would fall into tight curls, but she didn't care. She was free. Never again would she take for granted the ability to breathe in the polluted air of London or walk where she liked amongst the green shoots of spring. She needed to be outside and for the moment, this was the best she was going to get. Besides, she was too ashamed to meet in the club.

She needed to bare her soul and ask Jay's forgiveness properly, in person. Lia bit her lip and tried to centre herself. Walking normally grounded her, but her nerves jangled with each step she took.

The Darth Vader tune sounded on her phone, and she swiped to accept the call, glad for the distraction. "Hello, Ma, thanks for calling back. Thanks for doing the transfer of the land so quickly. It means I can get started. I'm seeing people today who I hope will invest." She ought to change the ring tone. Her mother had been more supportive and informative in the last few days than she ever thought possible. More Yoda than Darth Vader.

"That's great news. Where are you?"

"In London. Thanks for continuing to pay for the club subscription for me. It's the perfect base to put out feelers for my proposal." The reality was that she had slunk in and out of the club trying to avoid being seen by anybody who might accost her, but it was convenient.

"Good luck. I have faith in you, darling," her father said in the background.

"I must go, Pa needs me. Call me if you need anything."

"Thanks, I will. Love to you both." She ended the call and

continued to walk towards the park entrance by the Tube station, where Jay said she was arriving. Her heart expanded with the acknowledgement she was being treated with respect and affection, and she sent gratitude to the Universe.

In the middle of the park, the harsh blare of traffic was no more than a background hum, punctuated by the occasional ambulance siren or motorbike. Branches dripped large drops of water as they shook in the breeze, their spring leaves shiny and green. If she covered her ears, she could almost believe she was fully immersed in nature, and that helped her breathe and clear her head. She focused on the meeting with Jay. So much was riding on this and not only for the sake of her new business.

Her breakfast felt heavy in her stomach. Would Jay want anything to do with her now that she'd changed? The month inside combined with the intense warehouse work had done nothing to improve her looks; the mirror confirmed she had more lines and deep shadows in contrast to her even paler skin, and there were more white hairs among the blond. She must look a sight. The thrill of excitement she'd had earlier submerged under a tight ball of uncertainty.

Inside, she'd changed even more. The confidence that bordered on arrogance, bred from privilege, had seeped out like the rain. She hoped Jay liked the slightly more sedate, open version of her. She was beginning to like that version of herself more every day.

She wiped the hair from her face, and her heart picked up its pace as she recognised Jay coming towards her, sensibly carrying a large golfing umbrella.

She had a broad smile on her face. Maybe she really was pleased to see Lia, even if she was a mess. She walked faster, and they quickly covered the ground between them. Then she was in Jay's arms, which was a bit tricky, because Jay had rested the shaft of the umbrella against her shoulder, and Lia had to stoop to get below the cover. Their faces were so close she could feel Jay's warm breath, which was a contrast with the cool rain trickling

GREEN *for* LOVE

down her back.

Lia relaxed into a hug. She'd wanted exactly this for so long, and now she didn't want to let go.

"It's so good to see you, though you look half-drowned. Sorry I'm late, the Tube had some cancellations, so I had to change line," Jay said in a jubilant babble and squeezed tighter.

With every second she held on, Lia's doubt subsided, and the churning in her stomach settled. Maybe it would be all right.

"Are you okay?" Jay asked, her breath hot against Lia's cold ear.

Lia didn't know if they were tears or raindrops on her face, but she knew this was good, this was right, and it made her feel alive. "Sorry," she whispered and pulled back to look at Jay. "We need to talk." There was a slight tremor in her voice, and it wasn't only from the cold. She needed to get through this conversation before her courage failed her. Here she was, renowned for having the courage to face the vitriol of angry officials and members of the public, blanching at what Jay might say.

"I know." Jay sighed. "The rain's stopping. Shall we walk and talk?"

Lia needed to let all the pain and anguish come tumbling out. All the well thought through apologies she'd concocted while lying in prison vanished from her brain. "Sorry I betrayed your trust, and for attacking the refinery again. I knew it would upset you."

Jay stared at her as if searching for the truth, then she nodded. "I did feel hurt and betrayed, I'm not going to lie, and it gave me some difficulties at work."

They started walking again, and Jay explained she'd been on the brink of an investigation and been strait-jacketed in what she could do in her role. Guilt seeped into Lia's veins. She hadn't thought about the consequences for Jay and that her actions would jeopardize her job. The joy she had felt tracing through her nerves earlier dissipated, and she slowed her pace.

"Hey." Jay stopped strolling and caught hold of Lia, turning her to face her. "I've forgiven you. In fact, your comments helped prompt me to see what was going on and realise that just because Oliver had integrity and could set the tone and boundaries, he couldn't control what everyone else did. I had blinkers on, and you helped me take them off."

Lia was tempted to run her fingers up the back of Jay's undercut but squeezed Jay's hand instead, as if trying to impress upon her the sincerity of her apology. "I'm sorry it's been such a mess at work. I did a lot of thinking when I was inside."

"Meditating?"

Maybe if Lia had meditated before, she wouldn't be where she was now. "No, reassessing my life and what I stood for, looking at the errors I'd made, and how I was driven by anger and resentment and a general feeling of never being good enough for anyone." She shook her head, not wanting to travel down the martyr path. "I'd rather not talk about that right now, if that's okay. I had a lot of time to think about us, and how we are together. I always knew there was a soulmate for me out there, and even though the tarot indicated it might be you, our combined charts showed we needed to learn from each other, but I didn't believe it."

Lia raised her hand as Jay was about to speak. She had to get this out, or she may never be able to say it again. "I know you don't believe in romance or soulmates, and you aren't looking for love, but I also know you feel this too. More than just physical attraction, there's a pull to each other. Or maybe it's my wishful thinking, I don't know." She was reminded of her earlier arrogance and backed down.

She closed her eyes briefly to open her throat chakra to clear her self-expression. She envisaged being immersed in blue light and coughed. "You've taught me that there's more than one option, that there can be ethical people in an unethical business trying to facilitate change from within. I'm sorry you had to resign, but I admire your integrity. That's worth more than a riverside apartment."

"It doesn't pay the bills though," Jay said, a twinkle of amusement

GREEN *for* LOVE

in her eyes.

Lia stared at her. Wasn't Jay going to respond to anything else she'd said? But she knew Jay needed to mull things over logically, considering the options before she spoke. Lia had seen that when they worked on the committee together. While patience wasn't one of her virtues, she needed to respect the way Jay handled things.

Jay pulled Lia's hand to her lips, kissing her wet knuckles with soft lips and sending a shiver down Lia's body.

"Thank you for saying that. I think we've learned from each other. Your fire inspired me to challenge Richard and John directly. Your passion is infectious, and I want to lean into it. What are you smiling at?"

"That sounds a tad romantic for you. You'll be talking about your intuition next," Lia said.

They laughed and some of the awkwardness eased. They continued walking around Green Park, in a more companionable silence, close but not touching. The benches and trees glistened with the recent rain, and a distant hiss of tyres on tarmac surrounded them.

Lia waited for more. She'd wait as long as Jay needed. Eventually, though, the silence unnerved her. "I'm sorry. I know I was stubborn, thinking I was always right, but I'm trying to work on that, to be more open and listen to other points of view. I want to try and make amends."

Jay caught Lia's gaze and smiled. "It's okay. You don't have to keep apologising, but it's good you're being open. I need to apologise too, for being blind to what Richard and John were doing, for being naïve."

Lia caught and squeezed Jay's hand then let it drop. She was supposed to be letting Jay lead on this, but she wanted to touch her so much, to feel that connection on a visceral level, but she'd lost the right, if she had the right in the first place. She swept her arm to show their surroundings. "Isn't nature wonderful? When

I was inside, I tried to visualise trees after rain and walks on the moors, and windswept sand dunes. This is freedom. I don't think I'll ever take it for granted again."

Jay pulled her close for a side hug. "It must have been horrible for a sensitive soul like you."

Lia returned the hug, taking comfort from the warmth of the embrace, a warmth that spread to her toes. "I still have nightmares from all the negative energy. You're the first person who's recognised that it was hard for me. Thanks. And just in case you're wondering, I've renounced my membership to No More Oil. That doesn't mean I won't fight to save the planet by any legal means possible and do what I can to set up a small eco project that I hope will be replicated elsewhere, but my activism days are over."

Jay stopped and pulled her into a fierce, passionate kiss. She wanted to meld into the embrace, to express her gratitude and thanks and love for Jay without words. Because she did love Jay. Though she couldn't say it. Jay didn't believe in love. She didn't want anything more than casual sex. Yet, Jay had agreed to meet her after all she'd done to her, and she was kissing Lia back, so it must signify something. But Jay had to be the one to say something.

If all she could offer Lia was friendship, and maybe a business partnership, Lia would take it. So she held on and deepened the kiss.

"Get a room," someone shouted, and they laughed and broke apart.

"I guess we should go back," Lia said, and they turned towards the distant exit.

"What's happening with the plan you mentioned? Is that why you're in London?" Jay asked.

Lia so wanted this to go well. "That's one of the things I wanted to talk to you about. The estate in Northumberland is being split into two. I'm converting barns to set up an eco-village to have a like-minded community, plus a few holiday cottages, a restaurant, and eco-lodges by the sand dunes. Planning permission granted,

GREEN *for* LOVE

there will also be a wind farm away from the flight path of the geese, a solar farm with pollinator plants underneath so I can keep bees, and I'm going to have a second hide by the sand dunes for birdwatching for tourists. I'm seeking funding for the energy production. Well, for all of it, really."

Her heart hammered in her chest, and she stopped to face Jay to see her reaction. "I don't know if any of this appeals to you at all, but I thought—I hoped—maybe we could do it together? With your energy expertise—"

"Oh my God, that's perfect. That's exactly what I've been looking for. I've talked to Oliver, and he's agreed to invest in my new sustainable energy business. I've been looking for the right projects to invest in." Then as if her business brain suddenly caught up with her enthusiasm, she said, "I'd need to check all the business plans and cash flow forecasts, of course."

Lia couldn't breathe from the excitement of having Jay so quickly interested. And an investor, as well... "But you like the idea in principle?"

Jay swung around and an arc of spray flew from her umbrella, casting tiny rainbows as the newly revealed sun caught the droplets. "Of course. It's a wonderful suggestion."

Her face was such an expression of unfiltered joy, it reminded Lia of how Jay looked in her post-orgasmic bliss. Desire pumped through Lia's veins, amping up her need to get Jay out of here and into bed. Without making a conscious decision, she leaned forward. To hell with waiting for Jay to make the first move. She wanted to celebrate. "I want you, now, back at my room at the club." A flicker of self-doubt edged in. "If you still want me?"

Jay pulled her in to kiss her. "I thought you'd never ask. Come on."

When they arrived in the club, they ran up the stairs to Lia's room and shut the door behind them. They ripped off their coats and jumpers and dropped them in a sodden mess on the floor. Lia pushed Jay gently back onto the sofa and kissed her. "Are you sure about this?" Lia asked, rediscovering her lost confidence.

"Yes," Jay said huskily.

Lia unbuttoned Jay's shirt and kissed the fabric of Jay's white bra, while she slid her fingers behind Jay's back to undo the clasp. Jay shrugged off her shirt, and the bra straps slipped off her shoulders, followed by the cups, exposing Jay's glorious breasts. Her nipples, already taut, hardened under the brush of Lia's thumb.

Jay arched up to her touch. "Please," she said.

Lia had this moment, but Jay had never said she wanted more than casual sex. She bit her lip, desperate to know more, but she couldn't pressure her, and she should be grateful for whatever Jay would give her.

Jay pulled at Lia's blouse. "This needs to come off."

They removed their clothes in a frenzy, tossing them on the floor. Jay held Lia's smaller breasts, and they crushed together, nipples peaking at the skin-to-skin contact.

Lia replaced her fingers on Jay's breasts with her tongue. She gently bit and licked Jay's nipple, then slipped her hands slowly down over her belly to the triangle of coarse hairs. "You're so wet." Lia felt her own arousal flood her, echoing her statement, She would explode if she didn't get relief soon.

Jay groaned, pushed her hips up to Lia's touch, and pulled Lia's hand closer. Lia's fingers delved deep, Jay's pulsing inviting her inside, so she pushed gently at her entrance and was drawn in. What started slow and sensual soon became fast and frantic, and Jay bucked with the rhythm.

"Harder, yes, yes."

Lia's clit throbbed, and her heart pounded in unison to the speed of the stirrings of lust. Jay tensed and trembled, her muscles tightening around Lia's fingers, and she came with a shudder, a letting go and coming together. The final breeching of defences between them. Jay's eyes fluttered open into unfocused satiation. Her lips curled up into a glorious smile. Lia had never seen her so relaxed, so beautiful as this. She wiped away a strand of hair from

GREEN *for* LOVE

Jay's sweat-drenched forehead.

Emotions bubbled, and Lia struggled to keep from saying what was in her heart. Would Jay finally see and feel the rightness of this? Lia wanted so much more but didn't dare hope. In a flash, Jay flipped Lia over, nibbling at her breasts and tracing Lia's body with her hands, causing a trail of goosebumps in their wake.

"Fuck me," Lia pleaded, not too proud to beg for the release she knew Jay could give. As Jay slipped through the slick heat of her arousal, taking her fast, Lia surrendered herself completely, and her orgasm came hard and quickly, cracking open her soul to let the sunshine in.

Jay didn't remove her fingers and maintained a slow pulse as Lia regained her senses and met her rhythm. Arousal spiked again. The cleansing and awakening of her sacral chakra opened with the heat and vibration from red to bright orange, shifted into the yellow of the sun and finally swirled green in her heart chakra. *Green for love.* "*I know, I know,*" she wanted to cry out, but she had just enough mental acuity left not to declare it and let it reverberate around the club. With each thrust and gasp, the past trauma of the prison was excoriated until she reached the still white light and space of a second orgasm that spasmed through every nerve in her body.

She collapsed back and stared at Jay, wanting to absorb every detail of her face and commit it to memory. She knew with certainty she wanted to be with Jay for the rest of her life. They might not be able to change the whole world, but they could protect part of it and build something special together.

She lay back, exhausted but sparkling with happiness. "That's one way to have a business meeting," Lia said.

"Mm. I think that concludes our meeting for today, unless there is any other business," Jay said.

The glow of the second mind-altering orgasm was enough to give her the extra push she needed. "I'd love it if you came up to see what we're doing in Northumberland, to see the investment.

250   E.V. BANCROFT

If you like the set-up, maybe you could move up there? And your mum could come too. I've got a cottage that's being adapted for wheelchair users. Elsie has agreed to take over one of the other cottages when they're finished, and we did say we'd get them together..."

She stopped when she saw Jay's excitement drop and the sparkle in her eyes slip, even if her smile remained in place, false and heartbreaking to witness.

Jay blinked and canted her head to one side as if deciding whether Lia was serious or not. "Are you saying what I think you are? That you'd like me to live with you? Isn't that a bit U-Haul?"

Panic thudded a rhythm in her heart, fast and loud. She could see Jay withdrawing with every heartbeat. "There's a spare bedroom and an old dining room that could be made into an office for you—"

"Thanks. That's very generous of you and food for thought. I'd need to think about it, talk to Mum and see the business plan first."

Even as Jay spoke, back-pedalling in her formal politeness, Lia wanted to stretch out and pull her back into her arms. *Damn. Too hard, too fast.* It was so easy to revert to old behaviours, bulldozing her way forward instead of reading the room and moving more thoughtfully. The feeling of loss was compounded by Jay sitting back on her knees on the bed and putting an even bigger space between them, as if she needed the physical distance to give her perspective.

Lia swallowed hard. How stupid to think she could have it all. "Have a think about it. Work through it with your logical brain and let me know." Lia smiled but a knot of nerves balled in her stomach. Jay hadn't said they could be anything more than a business arrangement with off-the-scales sex thrown in occasionally. She'd take it, whatever Jay had to offer. "Can you stay the night?"

Jay arched her eyebrow. "As long as we can eat at some point. I've worked up quite an appetite."

Lia was glad she hadn't slipped and said the l word, even though it infused every interaction between them. Jay needed some more

GREEN *for* LOVE

time, and Lia would give her whatever she wanted. "Thanks for forgiving me and for giving me a second chance, despite my fiery temper and stubbornness. Even if this is all we have, I'll always be grateful to you. Thanks."

Jay curled a strand of Lia's hair in her fingers. "You're welcome, and you're still a romantic."

A frisson of fear crept over Lia. Was she being over-dramatic? Was this one-sided? Was Jay still thinking this was just a short-term fling? "I'm not pushing, and I respect you'll need time. But can I ask what your gut reaction to my proposal is?" She took a ragged breath. "I admit I've got my hopes up, and just a hint of what you're thinking would help..."

Jay paused then she locked eyes with Lia, fixing her with an intense gaze that made her heart patter. "I'd like to see you again. I'd like to run a business with you, to stay with you, and explore where we go on a more serious level, but I also need to talk to my mum."

Lia collapsed with relief and lay across Jay, determined to make the most of every moment they had together.

Chapter Thirty-Four

IT TOOK ANOTHER TWO weeks before Jay could make it north, and she was surprised how far it was from London. The journey seemed never-ending, and she couldn't believe her mum hadn't chased her up yet. As if on cue, her phone rang on the Bluetooth speaker in her car.

"Are you there yet?"

Jay checked the road around her and overtook a lorry. "No, I'm on the last leg."

"Blimey, you left hours ago. I was sure you'd be there by now."

"I stopped in Newcastle to recharge the battery. I wasn't sure it would get me all the way up there." Jay inhaled the smell of her new Mercedes electric car and pushed down the guilt at what Lia might say. It was a luxury and probably completely impractical for driving around on a farm, but she wanted to cling to something from her previous life, to remind herself she'd made it once and had been successful. Lia would say it was her sun in Taurus enjoying the good things in life. She shook her head and concentrated on the conversation.

"Are you all right, Mum? Is Adam checking in on you?"

"I'm fine, and you shouldn't ask him to do that. He's so busy."

"He loves it. Any excuse to talk about the soaps. No one else will indulge him."

"I'll miss him if we move up north."

Jay sighed. She needed to head off her mum before she ambled down the negative path she'd been on after Jay had mentioned a possible move. "So will I, Mum, but he can come and stay. Lia said Elsie's coming up to live in one of the cottages. She watches the same sort of programmes you do, and she plays cards. We'll get you together soon. I'm sure you'll get on really well."

Her mum sniffed, and Jay could almost imagine the pout on her face.

"It's such a long way away, and it gets so cold. I'm not sure I could live in such an isolated place."

This was a conversation she needed to concentrate on, so she pulled into a layby on the right close to sand dunes. She couldn't see the sea from here, but the sky seemed huge, such a contrast from the slivers of sky she saw in London. "Mum, you're even more isolated in suburbia. There'll be a proper little community up here. All the cottages will be insulated, and there will be a community allotment you can sit in when the weather's nice. Your cottage is being adapted for wheelchair use, and it'll be lovely and cosy."

"Have you decided if you're going to live with Lia yet? Or are you going to find a different place to rent nearby?"

"I still don't know."

"What does your heart say? Not that big brain of yours."

She inhaled sharply and settled her shoulders. "I love her."

"If you love her, why wouldn't you want to live with her?"

Her mum's gentle voice encouraged her to open up. Whatever reservations she had about Lia, her mum wanted her to be happy. "I'm scared." This conversation was heading into an area she didn't want to uncover, but she seemed powerless to stop it.

"What are you scared of?"

"What if I'm like my dad and I play the field then run at the first sign of trouble? I don't have the best track record. I'm so lonely and I really like her, but the set-up scares me—"

Her mum snorted. "You're nothing like your dad. He was self-absorbed, and you're not. He would have left anyway; we'd grown apart. I was desperate to have a child and he wasn't. We were so young when we got together, and he was only interested in his own selfish needs—we both were. You're nothing like that. And I wanted you, chose you. That's love. Love isn't some big gesture or

GREEN *for* LOVE

grand speech; it's the choice you make every day. Now it's time for you to choose, even if you are scared. You don't know if she'll hurt or abandon you, but she seems as smitten as you are, so I don't think that's a problem. Are you ready to choose her?"

Jay was more than smitten. She was enthralled and captivated by Lia's passion, her energy, her vision of a better world, and her kindness. She brightened her life, and Jay no longer wanted to imagine life without her.

"And it's not as if you can get her accidentally pregnant, is it?"

Jay laughed, and the tension slipped away.

"I don't say it much, but I appreciate what you do. It's about time you put yourself and your own needs first. Does Lia make you happy? Does she appreciate you?"

"Yes, of course." Tears welled up, and she brushed them away before they could fall. Now wasn't the time to get emotional. "Thanks for saying that, Mum."

"Then what are you waiting for? Go and tell her, Jay. If anyone deserves happiness, it's you."

"But I—"

"Go on, I'll be fine. I'm already looking forward to seeing the cottages."

Relieved her mum seemed to be coming around to the idea, Jay blew out a breath. "Thanks. I love you, Mum."

"I love you too. Now go. I hate to see you pining away for her. Don't forget to call me when you get there safely," her mum said and ended the call.

Had she been pining? There was no way Jay could face her until she'd sorted out her head and her twirling emotions. She needed to settle the jittery feeling in her stomach, so she got out of the car to stretch her legs.

Jay lost herself in the exertion of scrambling to the top of the dunes, sand collapsing with each step. She stretched at the top and looked out along the coast at the wide bay, admiring the necklace of castles built to keep out marauders. The wind flayed her with tiny stinging granules of sand, but she didn't care and breathed in deeply to inhale the fresh salty air like Lia had shown her.

What was holding her back? Was her mum right? Lia was keen to cement their relationship, and there was no doubt there was something special between them. And she wanted this. It was everything. It wasn't just the business and a place to call home, it was spending time in the special world that Lia created around her. This wasn't about logic and the cold balance sheet of pros and cons; this was being real about what she felt.

Jay placed her hand over her heart to stop it fluttering and forced herself to take deeper breaths. She felt she was spinning out of control like a gyroscope on a boat at sea. From the first seduction at the club to the recognition of who was throwing the paint, to the challenge at the AGM and the committee meetings, Lia had melted Jay's heart one broken rule at a time. She'd lived with those self-imposed rules all her life. No do-overs, no mixing work and pleasure, no letting anyone in, no falling in love. Jay gulped. She didn't know what love was, did she? She'd never felt this all-consuming desire before. She'd never been in love before, never even been open to love. It was all too much, and she was desperate not to lose herself and become completely absorbed by Lia.

And yet, like a thirsty woman being given one swig of water, a short fling wasn't enough. She wanted to drop to her knees and drink her fill of Lia the feisty, Lia the passionate.

A seagull squawked beside her as if mocking her thoughts. Her romantic thoughts. She'd never admit she'd been slipping into such mawkishness, but the reflection time had been what she needed. She knew what she wanted.

She shivered and turned to walk back to her car, her resolve set. She called Oliver to distract herself a little.

"Hi, Jay. The transfer has just gone through, and it should hit the project bank account within the hour."

Jay expelled a breath to release the tension that had settled in

GREEN *for* LOVE

her shoulders. Another piece set in place. "You're a star, thanks."

He laughed. "Honestly, it's the least I can do. I'm so angry at what happened, but I'm trying to let it go by knocking a golf ball around. My drive has improved no end now I imagine it's John's or Richard's head."

Jay laughed. It was good to speak to Oliver, and she missed his wisdom. "I hope you're still happy to be a non-executive director?"

"Of course. Someone has to make sure you don't spend all the cash on hot cars and hotter women."

She felt her cheeks burn. "I have bought myself a new car actually." She paused at Oliver's laughter. It wasn't that funny. "It's electric."

Oliver snorted again. "Of course. Is this because a certain hot woman you're into is a bit of an eco-warrior?"

She grinned. "Well, there won't be a conflict of interest anymore."

"About time too. You need a bit of fun and someone by your side. She'll be a challenge, but you know that already. I hope she's as smitten with you as you are with her."

"Smitten? Such an old-fashioned word." Funny how he echoed what her mum said, though she knew it was true, despite her protestations.

He cleared his throat. "Did I tell you how much I admire you for not bowing to financial pressure and going for a job with another oil company?"

"Thanks. This way I can put my money where my mouth is and implement new technical innovation. It's high risk but should be interesting, with potentially high reward." She heard a toffee paper being unwrapped. He hadn't kicked that habit then.

"I've faith in you. To the tune of five million, and more, if it proves successful."

Her heart squeezed with excitement, and she gripped the steering wheel, not quite believing it. That investment would make all the difference in getting the new business off the ground. "I know, and I'm grateful. I'll send you through the complete business cases for each of the projects along with the risk analysis and recommendations."

"No need. You're the CEO. I trust you. And thank you for taking on Marta."

"That was a no brainer. She's the perfect person to be the face of the business in London and schmooze with all the important investors. That's you, in case you hadn't gathered. And that means she'll keep you in line."

He laughed. "That's nothing new. It'll be lovely to work with both of you again. Let's have lunch when you're next in London. I have to go. I promised I'd be at the course in forty minutes."

"Thanks, Oliver," Jay said but the line was dead. The urgent side of him hadn't changed, but he seemed more relaxed than she'd heard him in years. She made a note on her phone to send a thank you gift to them both. Now she needed to think about the other issue.

She was "smitten," for lack of a better word. She wanted Lia to drop everything and for them to fall into bed and make love until dawn. Before they did that, though, they had to clarify what they wanted.

All her adult life, Jay had felt so superior, being ruled by laws and logic, and now she was a dribbling mess, yearning for a woman who broke all the rules, who believed in auras, and psychics, and the energies of stars. And she would gladly be subjected to it all. Even if she wasn't sure about soulmates, she did choose Lia, and she would choose her every single time. Jay was getting ahead of herself though. She needed to focus on the business at hand.

Finally, she drove over a level crossing to make her way up towards the hills with a distant view to the sea. The name Hiburn gave away that it was set uphill and among round top hills that would be ideal for wind generation and storage, as long as it wasn't in the direct route for the migrating birds.

She pulled up in front of an old stone farmhouse, one that had probably stood for a few hundred years after the acts of union

GREEN *for* LOVE

negating the border fighting between Scotland and England and allowing people to settle in large model farms. She switched off the engine and got out, shaking her legs to encourage the circulation.

There was no sign of Lia. There was no reply when she pulled the old metal doorbell, although she heard the distinct sound of ringing from inside. Jay gave up and wandered around the back of the house. She was surprised to see Lia helping a man lift a large water butt into place by another cottage.

When Lia saw her, her face lit up with delight. "Jay! Hang on two seconds."

"Can I help?"

"No, we've got it." They laid the water butt down on a brick plinth. "Sammy, this is my friend and hopefully, business partner, Jay."

Jay tried to keep the smile on her face, but her heart sank at being described as Lia's friend.

"Jay, this is Sammy, who's been helping me make some changes around here so that the whole complex is more sustainable."

The young man wiped his brow and shook Jay's hand. He grinned, and his handsome face lit up. "Great to meet you. I feel like I know you already, because she won't stop talking about you. I hope you're not as hard a task master as this one. She's so keen, she never stops for a break."

"Okay, I get the hint. Off you go. Have a break. I need to take Jay to see both sites anyway," Lia said.

"Right you are, boss." He winked at Jay, then turned back to Lia. "When I get back, I'll couple up all of the pipes."

"Thanks. You're a treasure."

"Not really. Just hoping that if one of the cottages comes up, you can let me have it at a reasonable rent." He grinned again and had a twinkle in his eye.

Jay had no doubt he had used that smile to charm all the women and all the gay men too. Adam and Ben would be drooling over him, for sure.

"I'll see what we can do." Lia returned his smile, then he turned and walked back towards his car.

Lia turned to Jay, and she seemed as shy as Jay felt, until she laid her hand on Jay's forearm as if she needed to check Jay was real. Her touch left a trail of goosebumps behind.

"I can't believe you're actually here. Are you warm enough? It's a bit chilly today. This will be part of our rainwater capture system. I must show you the fields by the sand dunes before it gets dark, and would you like to see the hide? And you must see what we've done with the cottages, but maybe I can show you later. Oh, sorry, you probably need to freshen up. Would you like a cuppa first?"

Jay laughed at the effervescent joy bubbling from Lia as she raved about the projects. She could envisage herself being swept along like the tide submerging the causeway to Lindisfarne each day. "Maybe just a pee, then you can show me everything."

Lia nibbled her bottom lip. "Were the business plans okay? Is there anything that you need further details on?"

Lia's uncertainty was adorable. She'd noticed that Lia's confidence had slipped since she'd been in prison, and she no longer took anything for granted. "I've already told you the business plans were great, and we can talk about the risks and sensitivity analysis later when it's dark. Can you show me the loo? Then we can get going. I'd like to see all these projects before it's dark."

"Yes, of course. Follow me. I can't believe you're actually here on my farm." Lia pulled Jay's hand.

Where once her passion fuelled rage, now it fizzed in every excited exclamation like an explosive display of fireworks, all lights, and stars, and different colours. Jay loved it. She loved Lia.

"I missed you," Lia said as she led her to the farmhouse.

The unexpected gravel in her voice was enough to get Jay pulsing with desire, clear and urgent. Lia held out her hands, and Jay sank into them. To feel her pressed against her, enveloped by her tall body, was too much. Jay's heart began a fast trot. "I missed you too." And all she wanted to do was taste Lia's lips again, to

GREEN *for* LOVE

spark the passion that simmered below the surface of her skin whenever they were together. Jay grabbed Lia's Barbour jacket and pulled her towards her, merging their lips, their tongues, and with a frenzy she didn't know she possessed, showed Lia how much she missed her. Lia kissed her back with increasing urgency, pressed Jay against the ancient wall and pushed a thigh between Jay's legs.

"I want you," she whispered as she cupped Jay's breasts.

In the distance, a car door closed, and Lia jumped back.

"Now is not the time for Sammy to be given his first view of lesbian porn."

"How do you know it's his first?" Jay felt the pang of loss and the cool air where Lia had been, but her arousal kicked up a gear at the thought of what Lia intended.

"Let me take you down to the other site before it gets dark. It's beautiful, looking across to Lindisfarne Castle on Holy Island in the distance. Normally I take the electric ATV or bike it, but it would be quicker in that." She indicated Jay's car.

Jay grinned. "I'm surprised you'll allow a vehicle onto the farm."

"Cheeky. The plan is to get an all-electric four-wheel drive vehicle eventually, and there'll be electric charging points outside each door."

Jay rolled her neck. Driving was the last thing she wanted to do, but the thought of riding on the back of an ATV even if it was road legal didn't appeal very much.

A few minutes after she'd freshened up, they climbed into her Mercedes. Jay glanced across at Lia as they took their seats. She wanted to capture and bottle the enthusiasm on Lia's face, so if it meant another twelve miles in the car, that was fine by her.

As they travelled down the hill towards the flat expanse of the bay, Lia chattered on about the projects. Her enthusiasm was palpable, and Jay couldn't help herself. "Are you sure you want to encourage people to drive their cars up here for holidays?" Jay kept her smile fixed as Lia scowled, pleased to see Lia's fire had returned.

"Hopefully they'll come by train and bike, and it'll mean they won't go by plane abroad." Lia nudged Jay in the ribs. "You're teasing me, aren't you?"

"Hey, don't attack the driver. I don't want to end up in a ditch." Jay concentrated on the single-track road. As a Londoner used to driving in slow traffic, she couldn't believe how fast tractors and locals drove down these narrow roads with infrequent passing places. Would she ever be able to live here? And just as importantly, how long would her brand-new car remain undented?

"Here we are," Lia said. "If you pull over."

They got out and clambered over the dunes looking out to the tide rushing in covering the sand. It was dramatic and breathtakingly beautiful. Lia caught hold of Jay's hands and intertwined their fingers. The warmth and excitement shot up and down Jay's body. "Do you feel settled up here now?" Jay asked.

"Well, I'm living in a caravan for the moment, because the farm roof hasn't been repaired yet. The first barn conversion is almost finished, and I'm glad to have somewhere to live over the winter. Lovely though it's been in the caravan, I don't want to face the north-easterly winds and winter storms in something that could be blown over."

"That wasn't what I was asking," Jay said. She moved closer to Lia, so their hips almost touched as they stared out over the fields leading down to the marsh and sand dunes. There was something haunting and evocative about the site. A curlew called the high-pitched trill of shoreline desolation. "Are you happy with the settlement with your brother and do you feel at home now?"

Lia's smile was soft and sweet. "More than I have in years. There are still things to work out, but my soul is happy in a way that I didn't think was possible."

Jay couldn't keep her eyes off Lia's lips. She was so painfully beautiful, and it took all of Jay's willpower not to lay her in the grass and make love to her then and there.

GREEN *for* LOVE

"Let's go back and when Sammy has gone, I'll show you around the barn conversions," Lia said.

The yard was deserted when they returned to the Hiburn farm. They stepped inside the almost finished barn, and Lia pulled Jay towards her. Jay blinked as Lia gave her a coquettish smile that set her heart beating at double time. Jay held Lia's gaze with an intensity any tango dancer would be proud of. The air was charged with sexual tension, anticipation, and desire, tugging them together. Jay held her breath as Lia captured her lips and kissed her hard, and Jay was falling and losing herself.

All her fears collapsed like cards as they found their way back to each other, reconnecting. Loneliness slipped away, and her heart filled with a joy that expanded her chest and caused her breath to catch. "I love you, posh girl," she whispered and kissed Lia's forehead. She meant it with every fibre of her being, every tingle of energy within her body.

Lia's eyes widened before she smiled widely. "I love you too."

Jay felt the warmth of the emotion through every cell in her body. As she followed Lia upstairs to a bedroom, she knew this was where she needed to be. Lia was her home.

Chapter Thirty-Five

THROUGHOUT THE SUMMER, THEY worked hard on the barn conversions and setting up the projects. At a tip-off from Oliver, Jay had secured the purchase of some trial sites that were now producing clean green electricity, and that had taken off some of the financial pressure. Today was the day her mum and Elsie were going to join them, and Jay stomped her feet as they waited for the train in an early autumn wind.

She almost expected to see a steam train chugging along the old Victorian line, but when the London to Edinburgh train pulled in, it was modern, and the doors opened with a satisfying hiss. The staff were efficient, affixing the ramps for her mum, and they were considerate as they wheeled her onto the platform to where she and Lia waited. Jay tipped the porter and removed her mum's large handbag from her knees to give her a big hug.

"Hello, Mum," Jay said. She stepped back, and Lia hugged her mum too.

"Hello, Susan. Lovely to see you again. Welcome to Northumberland."

Her mum grunted and returned the hug. Jay groaned inwardly, hoping that her mum wasn't going to be grumpy. They'd had plenty of conversations over the last few months, both in person and over the phone. Sometimes her mum had seemed fine, and other times she'd been reluctant.

"Mum, play nicely. Lia's gone out of her way to make things comfortable for you. I know it's a big step coming to see if you can live here, and if you don't want to that's fine, but I'm staying." Jay had hoped her mum would be excited rather than fractious, but that wasn't to be. She glanced between Lia and her mum, not sure how to resolve the issue, then caught sight of Elsie, struggling with a suitcase.

"Oh, there's Elsie. Let me help her with her bag."

Lia placed her hand on Jay's arm. "I'll go. You stay with your mum." She strode off to give Elsie a hug and pick up her bag.

"Behave, Mum," Jay hissed.

"Sorry, Jay. I don't want to make a scene, but I'm not sure about this."

"So why did you come up to see if you could live up here?"

"I wanted to be close to you."

Jay squeezed her mum's shoulder to comfort her. "Here's Elsie. You got on in London. Won't it be great to have her as a neighbour?" Jay stepped forward to give Elsie a hug. "It's lovely to see you again. I know it's a bit different from Bristol."

"All right, Jay. It's lush here. It was so beautiful seeing the countryside on the way up. I can't believe I'll be living in it. You can see so much from the train. I'd love to go to Edinburgh one day, too. I've never been to Scotland."

"Edinburgh is fabulous. You'll love it. You remember my mum, Susan? It will be lovely to have her as your new neighbour if she decides to stay."

"Haven't you decided yet? When Lia invited me to come and live near her and her new allotment, I jumped at the chance. There's nothing for me in Bristol. And I know what she'll do to make the house warm, although there's not much she can do about the outside." She shivered.

They shook hands briefly, and her mum gave a half-hearted smile.

"Let's get going," Lia said. "Get you out of the cold." She wheeled Elsie's case, while Jay pushed her mum in the wheelchair.

"It's a real adventure. I feel like we should be on *A Place in the Sun*," Elsie said. "Although maybe it would be a *Place in the Frozen North*."

GREEN *for* LOVE

"I watch that too," her mum said. Her frown softened and she smiled at Elsie. "Have you been up here before?"

"No, never, but nothing ventured, nothing gained, and I know they're both good souls."

Jay let Elsie follow Lia, and she brought up the rear as they walked out in single file from the platform to the car park.

"I couldn't ask for a better daughter. Jay's done so much for me. I know I shouldn't begrudge the change, but I find it very hard."

Elsie paused and waited until her mum was pushed level. "We'll work it out. I'm sure we can watch TV together. Do you still play cards?"

Her mum's face brightened. "Yes, I play rummy with my friends every fortnight. Or I did. I was hoping Jay might play with me, but she seems to be as busy as she was when she worked for a big company."

"Well, that's what we'll play then, and if the girls can join us, all well and good. I'm hoping I might be able to do something in the allotment that Lia promised me was already established."

Her mum shook her head. "I'm not sure I could do that."

"We've made some tall wooden planters out of old railway sleepers, so no one needs to bend down," Lia said as she unlocked Jay's car and placed the bags in the boot. "Susan, you sit in the front with Jay, and I'll sit in the back with Elsie."

Jay shot Lia a grateful look. It wasn't like her mum to be so negative. Maybe it wasn't such a good idea for her to move to the other end of the country. She needed to get her on her own at some point and talk it through.

As Jay drove south towards Hiburn, Lia pointed out Lindisfarne Castle on Holy Island and Bamburgh Castle in the distance, vertical monuments in a bay of sand dunes and low-lying land. This area was beautiful, with its huge skies, and even her mum seemed impressed. Jay let out a long breath and pulled off the side road that led up to the main farm on the hills. Lia explained about the solar park and the vertical wind turbines that were being set up, and Jay smiled to hear the enthusiasm back in her voice. It was wonderful to see Lia settle into herself. She still had nightmares of her time in prison, even though she knew she'd had it easy compared to some. But she didn't want doors to be locked so she couldn't get out. If they left the house or locked up at night, Lia wanted the key beside her at all times.

Lia chuckled when Elsie leaned forward between the seats and said, "You sound like *EastEnders*. I keep thinking you're going to talk about Albert Square."

"Nah, I'm from West London. Different accent. You sound like you ought to be a pirate." They all laughed.

"Well, that makes us even, I guess," Elsie said.

They pulled up at the cluster of outbuildings.

"Elsie, this is your bungalow," Lia said. "It's the old piggery, but it's been beautifully done out inside. Susan, you're in the slightly larger cow barn. We've adapted it for your wheelchair, although I hear you don't think you need it very often. That's great news." She turned and pointed. "Ours is the old farmhouse. We have a couple of outbuildings for holiday lets and three more barns that we'll convert for residential housing. We thought you might help us choose the decorations, and of course, we can all interview the potential residents, because we want this to be a proper little community where we all look after each other."

"Can we have some single or widowed men in them?" Elsie asked with a twinkle in her eye.

"Let's see who applies," Lia said when she'd stopped laughing. "I suspect it may be families. The local odd-job man, Sammy, is certainly interested."

"It might be nice to have children around," her mum said as Jay wheeled her back towards her own cottage.

She seemed to be relaxing a little and warming to Elsie again.

"We'll come around later. We put welcome boxes in your fridges, but we thought we might go out for a meal this evening if you're up for that? There's a lovely pub down the road that has very

GREEN *for* LOVE

good food. It's walkable and wheelchair-accessible, but if you want us to drive, we can take you down," Lia said.

Elsie waved goodbye and went to her door. She turned back to them before going inside. "Thank you so much for this. I can't tell you how much I love it with old and new friends." She smiled at Susan. "I'd love to go for a meal this evening and to see the local sights. Will you come?"

"Do you mean to the pub or looking for eligible men?" Susan asked, and they chuckled.

Okay, this could work. Jay exhaled a long cleansing breath like Lia had shown her.

"I'll help Elsie settle in," Lia said, following Elsie inside and casting a secretive smile at Jay.

Jay grinned and pushed the chair up the ramp to her mum's bungalow. "Welcome to your new home, if you want it to be." Jay parked the wheelchair, put the brakes on and helped her mum out of the chair. "We've even managed to get a recliner in. Did you see Lia has set up a bird feeder for you?"

Her mum staggered to the recliner and lowered herself down. Her hands worried at the armrest of her chair.

"What's wrong, Mum? Don't you want to be here?"

"I think it may take a bit of getting used to, but I'm worried they're all so posh."

"Oh, Mum, Elsie's not posh. She used to live in a council flat in a tower block in Bristol."

"Yes, Elsie seems nice. I know you're very fond of Lia. I can see how happy she makes you. But what if something went wrong between you, and we had to leave our homes again?"

"I know you hate being dependent on anyone, but we have proper legal agreements drawn up to protect everyone. You'll *never* be thrown out of your home." She held her mum's hand. "We're safe here, I promise." She knew with certainty that was absolutely true. This was where they belonged, all of them. The future was beautiful. It was green, and it was theirs.

Epilogue

Two years later

IT WAS STRANGE TO walk through Magenta's marbled reception area. Jay didn't recognise the receptionist. It appeared there had been a wholesale change in personnel since John and Richard had taken the helm. Alistair had been vague about what he wanted to talk about, and despite herself, Jay was curious. She had discussed whether she should attend the meeting or not, but Lia encouraged her, saying that knowledge was better than ignorance.

Alistair's personal assistant asked Jay to wait in the conference room. This had been the scene of many successes in the past, and it seemed poignant to no longer belong. Jay was brought back to the present when the door of the conference room opened and Alistair entered. Judging by his smiling face, she assumed it wasn't bad news.

"Jay, thank you so much for coming to see me."

"Sure. I admit I'm curious."

"Let's sit down. I hope you were asked if you wanted a drink?"

"I'm fine, thanks." She could have stayed in bed with Lia rather than being here, and she didn't want to stay longer than she had to. Each passing minute increased the chances of bumping into Richard or John. If she never saw their smug faces again, it would be too soon. And London now felt like a warren where the walls were closing in.

Alistair's PA came in with coffees and quickly left, closing the door behind her.

Alistair set down his coffee cup without taking a drink. "Okay. I

272   **E.V. BANCROFT**

don't know if you've been following Magenta's share price?"

Jay nodded. "It's plummeted like a stone. I suppose even shareholders don't take kindly to all the scandals and lies."

"Precisely. Which is why both Richard and John have taken a severance package, and the board has asked me if you'll take over as Chief Executive Officer."

This wasn't what she was expecting. She'd heard of Magenta's difficulties, but she only had a passing interest in what was going on. Lia followed the ins and outs more closely, only because she kept apprised of environmental issues and not because she had any further interest in Magenta itself. "Why? Why me, and why now?" she asked.

"When you sent that file through with the recording of your conversation with Richard and John, it was clear things were happening without the board's consent. It made us wonder how many other things were going on that even you weren't aware of. Richard's land grab was the tip of the iceberg, but we didn't want to let them go until we knew how much of the iceberg was underwater." His eyes were hard. "Turns out, there was enough to sink Magenta entirely. But it took time to find it all. Now they're gone, and we need someone with integrity and intelligence to take over. What do you think?"

Jay tapped her fingers on the desk. She could have what she'd worked so hard for, and it was being handed to her on a plate. How easy would it be to slip back into the corporate world with a generous pay packet and all the trappings? She smiled as she thought of the windswept north, of the way she could traipse through fields holding Lia's hand, and of the wonderful differences they were making to the planet, all on their own. "It's very flattering. But it's a no. You may not have seen, but our new business has been given the new eco business award."

Alistair looked uncomfortable and shuffled in his seat. "I know. Oliver told me."

Interesting Oliver was still in contact with Alistair. He hadn't

GREEN *for* LOVE

mentioned it at their quarterly lunch appointment. She still suspected Oliver had put Jay's name forward for the award. This did give her an opening though. "We might be interested in taking over some of the new technology projects that were trialled but have been left to fester over the last few years. Although I'm not sure how much they'll be worth as the technology is moving quickly. I could ask my accountants and lawyers to have a look. I'm not interested in anything else."

Alistair clasped his hands together so tightly his knuckles paled, showing off the dark hairs on his fingers. "Oliver said that you'd probably say no. Are you sure I can't persuade you if I throw in the company flat as part of the remuneration package?"

Jay laughed. She'd never actually got to sleep in the flat. "Thanks, but I live in a beautiful part of the country where the rush hour is a herd of sheep. I'm living in a community that includes my mum, who is very happy there and now virtually recovered, and I'm living with a wonderful woman. But thanks for the offer." She smiled. "I'm sure it can't have been easy to eat humble pie."

Alistair sighed. "No. You're right." He sat back and picked up his coffee cup. "Are you still looking for investors? If so, I may be interested personally."

Jay's smile broadened. It had been worth getting out of bed just for this. "Now that's something we can talk about. We're looking to expand into hydroelectric in Wales, so that's a definite possibility."

Alistair returned the smile. "I hoped you might say that, so I've invited a consortium of investors to have a chat later over dinner this evening. Do you have a brochure or prospectus? Can you make it?"

"That's a definite yes on both counts. Thanks, Alistair." She leaned back and took a sip of coffee. She couldn't wait to tell Lia. When she'd left this place two and a half years ago, she could never have dreamed this would be the outcome; that she would have everything she wanted, that she and Lia were making a difference with their company and changing the country one eco project at a time, and that the company that had shut her out would come grovelling back. She was even beginning to believe Lia when she said that sometimes the best things emerge from the darkest times.

Lia was definitely the best thing to happen to her.

After dinner later that evening, and after securing sufficient funds to set up a hydroelectric plant in Wales, Jay sat at the bar in the London club sipping an Ardbeg whisky. She savoured the burn that slipped down her throat and settled in her stomach.

She didn't look up from her paperwork when the door opened and closed with a whoosh. When the leather stool beside her depressed with a hiss of air, she looked around to meet the eyes of a tall woman with strawberry-blond hair falling to her shoulders. Her slightly bohemian attire was out of place in such an exclusive club.

"Are you actually engrossed in that, or are you avoiding talking to me?"

That voice, so cultured. Maybe Jay had fallen in love with Lia the moment she'd strolled up and oozed confidence. She sure as hell felt it now when she looked into her beautiful eyes.

It had taken Lia some time to regain her confidence after she'd left prison, but now she was strutting her stuff like she had when they first met, albeit with a little less carelessness. Seeing her this way again, so much like the first time, sent a shiver down her spine. Jay nodded to Alice. "Another for me and one for the stunning woman beside me."

Alice bustled off to prepare the drinks, and Lia leaned forward until her breath huffed onto Jay's cheek. "Do you come here often?"

"Only when I was lonely and wanted to take someone to bed with me, without strings and no complications. But I haven't done that in a long time and seem to have got myself involved in all sorts of strings and complications." She grinned and licked her lips.

"Glad to hear it. I too found what I was looking for. The Universe pushed my soulmate into my path, although I tried very hard to fight against it. It took me some time and some disastrous turns before

GREEN *for* LOVE

I could finally believe that her clear green aura, which resonated with her green chakra, really proved how much she loved me," Lia said, a mischievous twinkle in her eye.

Alice returned and gave her a crystal tumbler of whisky.

Jay returned Lia's grin and raised her glass. "If that's what you need to believe I love you, that's fine by me. Personally, I think it's time to celebrate the new eco business of the year with a nightcap."

"My thoughts exactly." Lia raised the tumbler to clink against Jay's. Then she placed her hand on Jay's forearm. "As I walked in, I thought, hmm, maybe that gorgeous woman plays for my team. I should talk to her and see where the evening takes us."

Jay bit her bottom lip and couldn't quite meet Lia's eyes. "There's something else I'd like to present you with, but I don't know how you'll feel about it. I know you fight passionately for what you believe is right, and you're a posh girl, and I'm only a poor girl who sees scientific rationale behind everything. We shouldn't mix, we shouldn't be together, but somehow we work. I love that we've received a major accolade for our joint venture, but I'd like to be more than business partners and lovers." She pulled the small box from her pocket and set it on the bar. "I considered a proposal in some romantic place, but you wouldn't like that, and it seemed more fitting to do it here, in the bar where we met." She opened the box, then turned and held Lia's hands in hers. "Cordelia Armstrong-Forde, will you marry me?" Jay held her breath and watched for Lia's response.

Lia put her hand over her mouth and didn't say anything. A tear trickled down her cheek, and Jay's heart beat faster as she waited for an answer. *The* answer.

Finally, after what seemed like a millennium, Lia gently touched the box. "Yes, I'd love to marry you." Lia's eyes misted up as Jay slid the simple gold band with its huge sapphire onto her finger. "It's beautiful."

"Will I need to ask your father's permission?" Jay smiled.

Lia fixed her with a serious look. "No. I'm in room seven. We should take this upstairs and continue our conversation up there. Without words."

Without hesitation, Jay picked up her glass and swigged down the contents. She already knew which room Lia was in because she'd had to crawl out of it this morning for her meeting at Magenta. "It's early. Do I need to tuck you up in bed with your cocoa?"

Lia drank the rest of her whisky and threw enough notes on the table to cover their drinks and a generous tip. "Come on, Dr Tanner. I need to get to know you better now that you aren't so caught up in big meetings."

They smiled at each other and linked hands. Jay had no idea if her heart chakra was glowing green and clear, but she knew it belonged to Lia and always would.

Author's Note

I really hope you enjoyed reading *Green For Love*. If you did, I'd be very grateful for an honest review. Reviews and recommendations are crucial for any author, particularly one early in her career. Just a line or two can make a huge difference.

Thank you.

Other Great Butterworth Books

Of Light and Love by E.V. Bancroft
The deepest shadows paint the brightest love.
Available from Amazon (ASIN B0B64KJ3NP)

Stolen Ambition by Robyn Nyx
Daughters of two worlds collide in a dangerous game of ambition and love.
Available on Amazon (ASIN B09QRSKBVP)

An Art to Love by Helena Harte
Second chances are an art form.
Available on Amazon (ASIN B0B1CD8Y42)

Where the Heart Leads by Ally McGuire
A writer. A celebrity. And a secret that could break their hearts.
Available on Amazon (ASIN B0BWFX5W9L)

Call of Love by Lee Haven
Separated by fear. Reunited by fate. Will they get a second chance at life and love?
Available from Amazon (ASIN B09CLK91N5)

Cabin Fever by Addison M Conley
She goes for the money, but will she stay for something deeper?
Available on Amazon (ASIN B0BQWY45GH)

Zamira Saliev: A Dept. 6 Operation by Valden Bush
They're both running from their pasts. Together, they might make a new future.
Available from Amazon (ASIN B0BHJKHK6S)

The Helion Band by AJ Mason
Rose's only crime was to show kindness to her royal mistress...
Available from Amazon (ASIN B09YM6TYFQ)

That Boy of Yours Wants Looking At by Simon Smalley
A gloriously colourful and heart-rending memoir.
Available from Amazon (ASIN B09HSN9NM8)

What's Your Story?

Global Wordsmiths, CIC, provides an all-encompassing service for all writers, ranging from basic proofreading and cover design to development editing, typesetting, and eBook services. A major part of our work is charity and community focused, delivering writing projects to under-served and under-represented groups across Nottinghamshire, giving voice to the voiceless and visibility to the unseen.

To learn more about what we offer, visit: www.globalwords.co.uk

A selection of books by Global Words Press:
Desire, Love, Identity: with the National Justice Museum
Aventuras en México: Farmilo Primary School
Times Past: with The Workhouse, National Trust
Young at Heart with AGE UK
In Different Shoes: Stories of Trans Lives

Self-published authors working with Global Wordsmiths:
E.V. Bancroft
Addison M. Conley
AJ Mason
Ally McGuire
Emma Nichols
Helena Harte
Iona Kane
Robyn Nyx
Simon Smalley
Valden Bush

Ingram Content Group UK Ltd.
Milton Keynes UK
UKHW020806020623
422771UK00015B/468